A PSYCHIC WITH CATITUDE

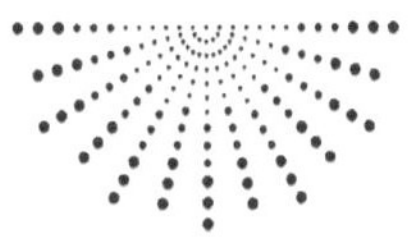

A PSYCHIC WITH CATITUDE

REG RAWLINS, PSYCHIC INVESTIGATOR #2

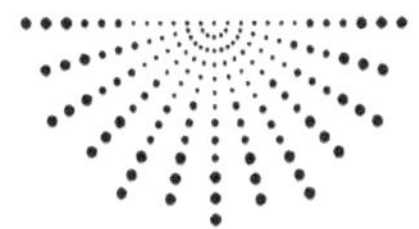

P.D. WORKMAN

ISBN: 9781989080641 (IS Hardcover)

ISBN: 9781989080634 (IS Paperback)

ISBN: 9781989080603 (KDP Paperback)

ISBN: 9781989080610 (Kindle)

ISBN: 9781989080627 (ePub)

pdworkman

Apple-achian Treasure

Vegan Baked Alaska

Muffins Masks Murder

Tai Chi and Chai Tea

Santa Shortbread

Cold as Ice Cream

Changing Fortune Cookies

Hot on the Trail Mix

Recipes from Auntie Clem's Bakery

Zachary Goldman Mysteries

She Wore Mourning

His Hands Were Quiet

She Was Dying Anyway

He Was Walking Alone

They Thought He was Safe

He Was Not There

Her Work Was Everything

She Told a Lie

He Never Forgot

She Was At Risk

Kenzie Kirsch Medical Thrillers

Unlawful Harvest

Doctored Death (Coming soon)

Dosed to Death (Coming soon)

Gentle Angel (Coming soon)

AND MORE AT PDWORKMAN.COM

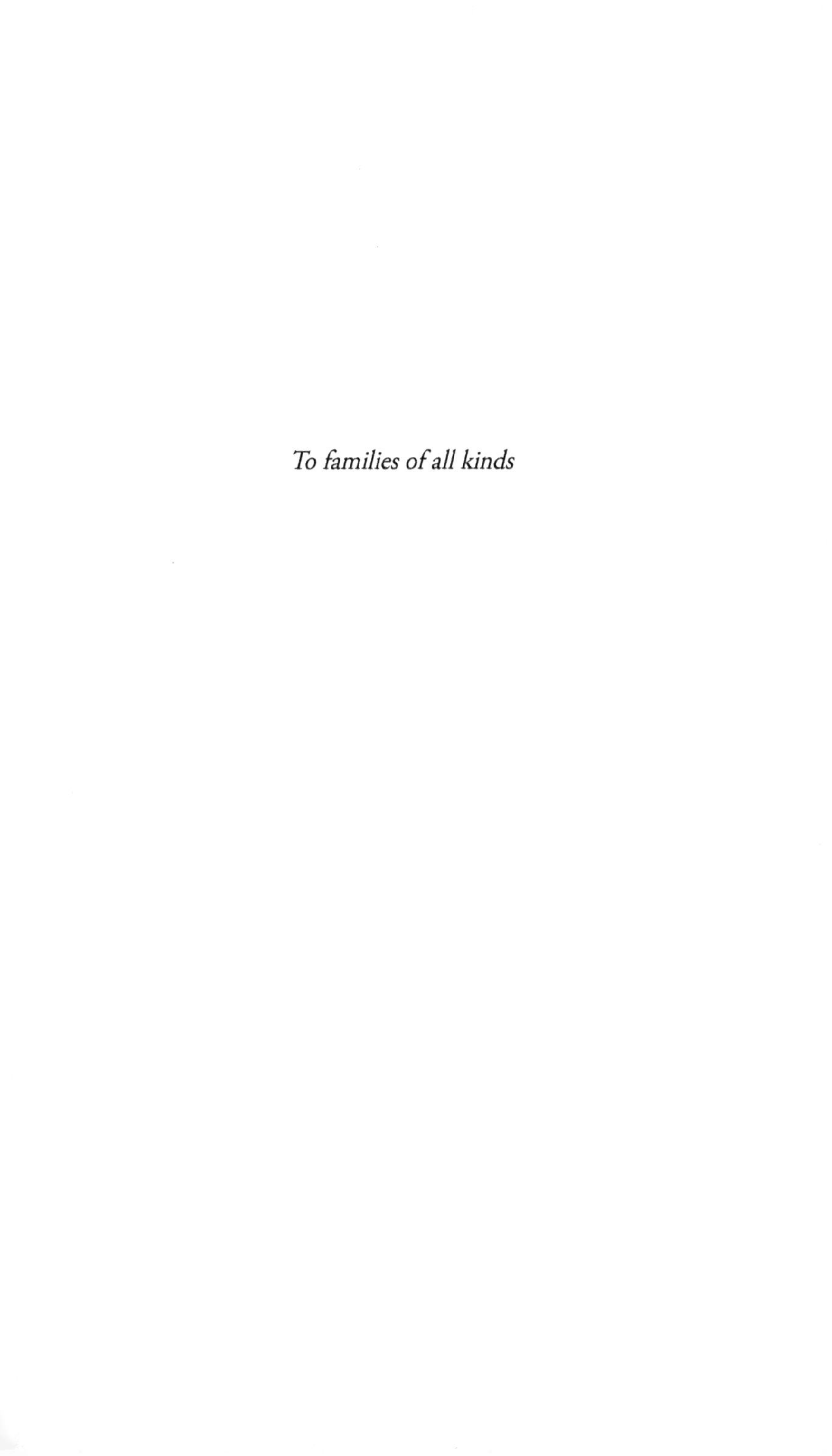

To families of all kinds

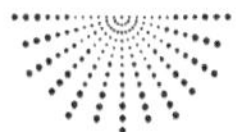

"How are you doing?" the dark, handsome warlock asked in a husky voice, touching the spot on Reg's hand where Hawthorne-Rose had cut her, sending goosebumps all the way up her arms and down her back.

She tried not to let him see her reaction, smiling with unconcern and inching away from his touch and the heady scent of roses that grew stronger whenever he turned on the charm.

Reg ran her hands through her red cornrow braids to gather them together and pushed them back over her shoulders.

"I'm fine," she said airily. "Looking forward to catching up on my sleep now that Warren is all taken care of and won't be disturbing my dreams. How about you? You look…" Reg searched for a word. He wasn't glowing quite as much as he had when he'd stolen her psychic powers, but he was definitely looking… well-fed. "Uh… you look relaxed."

Corvin nodded, leaning against her doorway, his movements languid. Hospitality would normally have dictated Reg invite him in, but she wasn't quite as naive as she had been. It was best to keep her cottage a safe sanctuary and not extend invitations to potentially predatory visitors.

"Marta—Detective Jessup did manage to… share… some of

Uriel Hawthorne's hoard with me." Corvin took a deep breath in and let it out again in a sigh. "You don't know how satisfying it is to fill a hunger that is so…" he looked deep into her eyes, stirring a different kind of need in Reg, "so profound and prolonged."

But Reg did have some idea of what he was talking about. He had allowed her to feel that hunger when she had reached out to him. Reg couldn't imagine living with that kind of hole needing to be filled day after day.

"You should probably be getting on your way," she told him.

"Is it getting to be too late?" he teased. "Is it past your bedtime?"

"Yes," Reg agreed, not letting herself be drawn in. "It's time to feed the cat and go to bed. We can talk tomorrow. You can *call*." She held up her phone to indicate it.

"I'd rather talk to you face to face."

"And I'd rather be able to breathe." Reg again shifted away from him, but the roses and his glamour followed her. She began to close the door. "Good night."

"Good night, Regina. Pleasant dreams." His words reached her as she shut the door on him. Reg shot the bolt and stood there for a few minutes, waiting for the racing of her heart to slow.

She switched off the light, and just as she was turning away from the door, a black shadow streaked across the floor, making her jump and let out a shriek.

It was Starlight, of course, her tuxedo cat. Darting around the room madly, as if tearing after some invisible mouse.

"Regina?" The direction and volume of Corvin's voice suggested he was still standing on the other side of the door. "Are you alright?"

"Yes. It's nothing. Just the cat."

He chuckled. "Goodnight, cat."

Starlight crouched in the shadows under one of the wicker chairs in the living room. Reg heard him hiss a kitty curse at Corvin.

"Now, was that very nice?" she asked him. "He was just wishing you a good night."

Reg went into the kitchen. As she expected, Starlight quickly left his hiding place to join her, letting out a couple of demanding meows and rubbing against the door of the fridge.

"There's food in your dish," Reg pointed out to him, determined that one day he would actually eat the cat food she bought him instead of demanding to be treated like a human being. She had hoped that once Warren's case was solved, he would stop be so demanding and settle in to being a normal cat.

But he was anything but normal.

"Other cats eat cat food," she went on.

He didn't even look at his dish, rubbing against the fridge and waiting for her to take the hint and get him his dinner. He must have thought her a particularly stupid human, that he had to keep repeating himself all the time and didn't have her properly trained yet. Sarah, when she had last stopped in for a visit and to make sure that Reg was okay now that all the excitement was over, had automatically walked to the fridge to have a look through the contents and provided Starlight with a couple of tasty morsels, without even asking Reg's permission.

"And Sarah doesn't even like cats," Reg said aloud.

Starlight glared at her, clearly trying to convey to Reg that if someone who didn't like cats could read him well enough to know what it was that he wanted, surely someone with a little bit of telepathy could figure it out.

"I know what you want. I just don't think I should satisfy your ever whim."

He continued to stare at her, his disparate blue and green eyes hypnotic.

Reg sighed. "Fine. But you'd better let me sleep tonight and not keep tearing around here like a Tasmanian devil. Or I'll start locking you in the bathroom at night."

Sarah had suggested earplugs. Reg didn't think she should have to wear them when the cat knew very well that she wanted him to be quiet at night. But she was close to breaking down and buying some.

Reg opened the fridge. She moved slowly as Starlight wound around and between her legs, intent on tripping her up so that he could have a chance at the entire can of tuna instead of just the portion she planned to give him.

She spooned a little on top of his dry kibble, telling herself that if she put it on top of his food, at least there was the chance that he'd eat some of the dry kibble along with the tuna by accident. Even though she knew very well that he was quite adept at eating around it.

"There. Now you've had your supper, so it's time for bed. I'll see you in the morning."

* * *

Reg awoke in the morning with cat breath on her face. She opened her eyes, knowing before she did that there was going to be a cat face a whisker away from her own.

"Go away."

Starlight stared back at her, unblinking.

Having had her powers stripped from her for a brief period of time, Reg knew that the feelings that emanated from him, the warmth and intelligence mixed with disappointment and disdain, were part of the psychic energy that Starlight put out. Normal people without any sense of the invisible forces that swirled around him, would just see a cute cat and not feel any of those emotions.

"I need more sleep. I'm still recovering."

She had plenty to recover from, with all that had happened over the previous couple of weeks. But there was no softening of Starlight's gaze. It was light outside. The birds had been singing for hours. Being a nocturnal creature, Starlight had burned off his energy and needed replenishment.

"Just a few more minutes," Reg insisted. She turned her face away from him and closed her eyes again.

Starlight climbed over her and around to her face again. He began to paw at her nose and mouth. Soft paws, no claws. Having felt those claws in the past, Reg was grateful for that, but was not happy with the cat doing his best to wake her up. She reached out and pushed him off the bed.

He went over backward and flopped unceremoniously onto the floor, without a chance to dig his claws into the bedsheets. Reg felt a little bit bad about that.

A little.

Starlight retreated from the bedroom and changed tactics, sitting himself in front of the fridge and yowling mournfully. Reg stuck her fingers in her ears and tried to ignore him, but even with the sound blocked out, she still knew he was complaining and she could feel him calling to her. She pushed herself up and climbed out of bed.

She made the mistake of not shutting the bathroom door tightly, and when she washed her hands and her face with cold water, Starlight pushed his way in through the door and jumped up on the counter to investigate the running water and dip a paw into the sink. Reg flicked her wet fingers at him, and Starlight went flying off of the counter and skittered out of the room. Served him right for waking her up.

She checked her various social networks and email addresses as she ate breakfast standing at the kitchen island. Starlight chowed down on leftovers from the night before. She knew that Chick-Fil-A was probably not the best choice to keep him healthy, but it at least kept him happy and he wasn't bugging her for anything else while he was at it.

She'd gotten messages from a few new contacts looking for her services as a psychic, some of them through her advertising and some by word of mouth. Her successes over the past few weeks were beginning to be spread around the community. Though she had gone to Florida with the plan of focusing on offering services as a medium, reaching out to the spirits of those who had left the mortal plane, most of the email and direct messages she had received were for other psychic services, and that was okay with Reg. She sipped at her incredibly fresh Florida orange juice while reviewing them. Acting as Warren's medium over the previous couple of weeks had worn her out and she was happy to do some lighter jobs, things that wouldn't suck all of the energy out of her.

"Finding lost objects and predicting the future sounds just fine to me," Reg said aloud to Starlight. "A little palm reading or laying down the tarot cards. That's so much less taxing than channeling spirits."

He looked up from his food for a minute, mouth slightly open as if she had caught him mid-bite. Then he gave his attention to his breakfast once more.

Reg's palm itched, and she scratched it automatically before remembering the cut from Hawthorne-Rose's knife. She yelped in pain. It wasn't deep—nothing that required stitches—but it burned whenever something brushed over it. Starlight looked up at her sharply.

Even though he wasn't yet finished his breakfast, he left it and rubbed up against Reg's legs, looking for reassurance that she was okay.

"It's fine. Just scratched myself."

He continued to rub against her. Reg leaned down and picked him up carefully. "Nothing to worry about. Just a little scratch."

He nosed at her face and sniffed the injured hand she held out to him. He lifted his whiskers into a sort of a cat grimace and sneezed. Reg put him back down on the floor. She did *not* need cat sneezes on her breakfast.

* * *

There was a light knock at the door. Sarah opened it and breezed in. Reg had slid back the bolt, as she did when she knew she had appointments, figuring that she was safe from intruders during the daylight hours. But she hadn't been expecting a visit from Sarah.

Of course, with the frequency of Sarah's drop-in visits, Reg hadn't *not* expected her, either. Her landlady didn't exactly give her the peace and privacy one would normally expect with a rental property. It didn't help that Reg's summer cottage was right on Sarah's property, in the back yard of the big house.

"You have company," Sarah announced. She was a slightly overweight, grandmotherly woman, who claimed to be both a witch and much older than she looked, which Reg would have put around her late fifties or early sixties. She was wearing a loose-fitting blouse patterned with pink flowers, and rose colored slacks.

Behind her was a young woman, probably just into her twenties, big-eyed and uncertain. She was diminutive, with short, curly brown hair.

"She came to the main house," Sarah said. "I thought I'd just bring her down for you and make sure you have everything you need."

Reg had been taking care of herself for years, but Sarah didn't seem to think she could manage on her own. It *was* nice to have someone who was willing to keep the fridge stocked and steer new customers toward Reg, but at the same time, it could be a little irritating to always have someone in her business.

"You could have just pointed her this way. And yes, I'm fine. I have everything I need."

"You shouldn't be doing so much. You should take a little break and give yourself some time to recover."

"Breaks don't pay the rent. I'm fine. This isn't difficult work." Reg looked toward the young woman, waiting for Sarah to take her cue and leave.

Sarah instead ushered the woman into Reg's living room as if she owned the place—which, technically, she did—and bent down to pet Starlight, who was curled on his back on one of the chairs. Sarah wisely patted his head rather than scratching his stomach, which Reg had discovered was a dangerous prospect. Starlight seemed to offer his cute tummy for scratches solely as a means of baiting unsuspecting dupes in order to claw and bite their hands.

"Thank you, Sarah."

Sarah finally got the hint. She smiled and said goodbye to both Reg and her guest, leaving them alone.

"Sorry about that," Reg said. "She means well."

"Oh, no, I am sorry." The young woman's cheeks were pink. "I know you said I should go around back, but I forgot. I should not have bothered her."

"She doesn't mind. Obviously. So…" Reg scooped Starlight up and sat down. Starlight wriggled and squirmed until Reg was forced to let him go, and then he stalked off to one of the bedrooms. Reg looked back at her visitor. "How can I help you today?"

"I hoped you could tell me my future… I have a sister I haven't seen for a long time and I want to find her."

Reg nodded. "Sure, of course. Did you want me to read your palm? Or the cards?" She had recently added a beautiful crystal ball to her props. She motioned to it. "Maybe gaze into the crystal?"

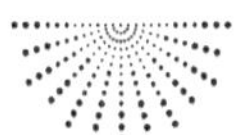

When the doorbell rang later on that afternoon, Reg knew it wouldn't be Sarah, but she hadn't been expecting any other company either. She looked through the peephole and frowned, trying to decide whether to open the door or not. She could pretend that she wasn't home, and hopefully Detective Jessup would go away and leave her alone.

But she would undoubtedly know by the fact that Reg's car was parked behind the cottage that she was home. She could be out for a walk, of course, or off running errands on foot, but…

Reg took a deep breath and opened the door. She forced a smile for Detective Jessup that hopefully looked perfectly relaxed and natural.

"Detective Jessup… how can I help you?"

Hopefully, Jessup wasn't there to say that they had received any complaints about Reg operating as a psychic. She'd done her best to encourage Reg to move away from Black Sands already. Reg had hoped that since she'd helped to save Detective Jessup's life, the police department would stop harassing her and let her operate in peace.

"I was… in the neighborhood," Jessup offered. Clearly a falsehood. "Do you mind if I come in?"

Reg hesitated. She had learned that inviting people in could cause problems, defeating the wards that Sarah had set to protect Reg and the cottage from harm. But as far as she knew, Detective Jessup didn't intend her any harm and didn't often use her powers, which seemed minimal.

Physically, Jessup was unassuming. A woman of around Reg's age, in her early thirties, small and slim, with Asian ancestry. Her body language was not threatening or authoritative as it had been when she'd confronted Reg before.

"What's this about?" Reg stalled, looking behind Jessup to see if she was with a partner. Obviously, Hawthorne-Rose was no longer in the picture, but there might be another burlier, more aggressive officer lurking nearby.

"You're not in any trouble," Jessup said, "but I'd rather not talk on the doorstep."

"Um… okay. I guess." Reg stepped back from the door but didn't explicitly tell Jessup to enter, watching to see if she were prevented from entering by the cottage. Reg really needed to learn more about the wards Sarah had set and how they worked. She couldn't rely on something she didn't understand.

Jessup entered without any apparent difficulty. Reg led her over to the living room to sit down. She heard Starlight jump down from where he had been sleeping in the bedroom to check things out. She watched him out of the corner of her eye to see if he sensed any danger from Detective Jessup. Reg wasn't sure whether she was just feeling anxiety because of what had happened with Hawthorne-Rose, or if she were sensing some new threat from Jessup. Reg hadn't had enough time honing her skills to be able to tell the difference. It was pretty sad that she had to rely on a cat for his opinion.

Starlight turned his head and looked at her as if reproaching her. Having four legs and fur didn't make him less reliable than a human being. What difference did species make to his psychic abilities?

Reg put her hand down near the floor and made kissy noises

to invite Starlight to come closer. He sat for a few minutes, looking at her without moving. Then as she turned back to Jessup, deciding Starlight wasn't going to help, he got up and walked over to her. What an attitude.

Jessup was waiting patiently to get Reg's attention back.

"Uh… sorry," Reg said. "I just wanted to make sure…" She trailed off, not sure how to explain it without giving offense. "Um, never mind."

Jessup raised her eyebrows, then shrugged. She looked around the cottage. Reg had the distinct feeling she was looking for something to comment on, to engage in a little small-talk before getting down to what she had really come for.

"Just tell me what it is. I don't need to be eased into it," Reg told her.

"Well… okay, then."

But Jessup still didn't seem to know where to start.

"I'm not in trouble?" Reg asked, repeating what Jessup had said at the door.

"No. Oh, no. This isn't about anything you've done. Well, I suppose it is, sort of… but it's more about… what you *could* do."

Reg narrowed her eyes, trying to sort that bit out. "I'm not going to do anything that will get me in trouble."

"It's nothing like that. I actually… wondered whether you would consult on a case."

"Oh!" Reg sat back, shocked. She hadn't seen that one coming.

"I know we barely know each other and you haven't established yourself as a professional police consultant or anything like that… but I'm stuck here… and it's not the kind of thing I can take my time on and hope to involve you sometime in the future. I need help now."

Reg nodded reassuringly. "What kind of case? Not… anything to do with Uriel Hawthorne or any of… those guys…?"

"No. Completely unrelated. It's a missing child. Adolescent."

Reg thought back to the times that Erin had run away. Or one of the other foster children she'd known. Or Reg herself. Erin had been the real runner. Even when she became an adult, she'd always bolted when things got too uncomfortable. Reg would get out when she knew there was *real* trouble ahead, but she wasn't like her foster sister, disappearing at the first sign.

"Well, at least that's something I have experience with."

Jessup's expression brightened. "Really? You've consulted on cases like this before?"

"No. But… I've been close to a lot of runaway cases."

"I hope that's what it is," Jessup sighed. "I mean, I know kids can still get hurt or in a lot of trouble when they run away. They don't have any idea the kind of trouble they could find themselves in. But…"

Reg turned it over in her mind. "You don't think she was a runaway? You think she was kidnapped?"

"She disappeared overnight from her bedroom. That kind of scenario, it's usually voluntary… running off to meet a boy or party, taking off and starting a new life… but I'm afraid it might not be that simple this time."

"Did this just happen today? Don't you… get the FBI involved or something? I thought this was the kind of thing where they'd have a task force and be blasting it all over TV… I don't know, bugging phones and chasing down all of the pedophiles in the area…"

"We're doing what we can. I'm not the only one on the case. But… if you could use your talents to find her… or tell me something about where she is…"

"I can give it a try," Reg agreed. "What's it going to hurt?'

"Exactly." Jessup nodded vigorously in agreement.

"Do you have something that belongs to her?"

Jessup looked awkward. "Well… no. I didn't think of that."

Exactly how did she think Reg was going to connect with the teen? There were probably runaway teens all over Florida. The warm weather would make it easy for them to live rough. Not like in New England where living on the street meant freezing to death at least half the year.

"Can't you do it just with her name?" Jessup suggested. "Or if I tell you what we know?"

"I can try. But… I don't know. That's a pretty tall order. Usually, I need to hold something that belonged to the person. At least the first time."

"Sorry. I didn't think of it. Her name is Calliopia Papillon."

Reg blinked. "Well, that's quite a mouthful! Were her parents royalty? Or movie stars?" She shook her head. "Calliopia Papillon." Reg stared into the crystal ball, focusing on the name. Where would Calliopia be? With a name like that, how could she blend in anywhere?

She felt Starlight's soft paws on her leg, then he jumped lightly into her lap. Reg gathered him into her arms and rested her face on top of his head, trying to access his psychic powers to augment her own.

Where is Calliopia?

She didn't know the local area very well, and that was a problem. Even if she saw Calliopia in her surroundings, she might not be able to guide the police to her. But at least she'd know what kind of shape the girl was in.

How is Calliopia? Is Calliopia okay? Calliopia Papillon…

She could see shapes moving in darkness. Not see them, exactly, but feel them. She closed her eyes. She felt cold and dark. Was that what Calliopia was feeling? Where could she be in Florida that she was feeling cold? A freezer or meat locker?

The cut on Reg's hand burned. She opened her eyes and looked at it. It had opened up again and was wet with blood.

"Are you okay?" Jessup asked, starting to rise.

Reg motioned her down. "It's nothing. It's fine. Let me just get a wet washcloth." She retreated to the bathroom and ran a cloth under the cold water. She dabbed the blood away, and then held the cloth against the cut for a few minutes, soothing it and, hopefully, taking down the swelling.

"Did you… have any luck?" Jessup asked tentatively.

"I could feel something… but nothing clear. Maybe if you

could get me something of hers?" Reg studied Jessup's smooth, unlined face. "Or maybe I could go with you to her house, if you're going to go there."

Jessup nodded. "I was planning to go there next, actually. I was hoping to have an idea of what to look for when I get there."

"If I can go with you... maybe I'll be able to find something. I can't promise, but... there's a better chance if I'm surrounded by her things than if I'm just here thinking on a name, or holding one thing that belonged to her."

"Okay. I guess. You'll have to leave the cat here, though. They're... allergic."

Reg wondered how Jessup happened to know that Calliopia's family was allergic to cats. That seemed like an awfully specific thing to know about someone who, presumably, she had only just met when they reported their daughter missing.

"I wasn't planning on bringing him with me. Are they really sensitive? Will they react to the fur on my clothes?" Reg looked down at the black and white hairs that seemed to cling to all of her clothes since she got Starlight.

"No, that much shouldn't bother them," Jessup said, making a waving-off motion.

"Okay. I'll just grab my bag and we can go."

Jessup hadn't been urging her to hurry, but since Reg had reached out to Calliopia, she had a growing sense of dread. What if Calliopia weren't just a runaway? What if someone had taken her and she was in danger? They were just sitting around, talking and something could be happening to her.

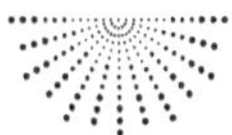

CHAPTER THREE

Detective Jessup had a normal car, which Reg appreciated. She didn't really want to be riding around town in a marked police car. She was still building her reputation and didn't want people to think she was a felon.

It wasn't long before they had left the part of Black Sands that Reg was familiar with and were into large estates or acreages. Reg tried not to gape at the huge houses in the brilliant green landscape. They drove up to a barred gate and waited for the security guard who must have been watching the surveillance camera to open the gates remotely.

Jessup drove on. There was a long, winding path up to the estate, flanked by beautiful gardens lush with colorful flowers and lazily floating butterflies. The house itself was the size of a hotel, with medieval-looking turrets and embellishments.

"That's incredible," Reg murmured.

Jessup looked over at her and nodded. Her expression was masked, giving nothing away. She wasn't telling Reg whatever it was she knew about the family and their situation. No gossip about how they had made their fortune or what their standing in the community was.

They parked in the drive in front of the house and were met at the door by a butler. He was tall and slender, very pale with an almost blue cast to his face. Reg thought that his uniform might have been silk, but was afraid to say anything. He seemed to know who they both were, even though Jessup hadn't introduced herself or Reg, and ushered them into an airy hall with gold upholstered furnishings and lots of potted plants and trees. Reg thought she saw a hummingbird dart around one of the plants, but she blinked and couldn't spot it again. She turned to Jessup to exclaim about it, but Jessup gave a tiny shake of her head. Reg zipped her lip.

They were joined in a few minutes by a tall, stately couple, much like the butler in appearance, but dressed even more richly. Neither shook hands or greeted Jessup and Reg directly. The woman, her hair done up in a complicated updo of golden curls, was carrying a swaddled baby in her arms, and attended to it after sitting down across from them. Reg couldn't see the baby among the blankets, and it kept quiet and still throughout the interview, obviously fast asleep.

"Mr. and Mrs. Papillon," Jessup greeted. "How are you holding up?"

The couple looked at each other, then back at Jessup, not answering her query directly.

"Have you found anything out, Detective?" Mr. Papillon queried.

"We're working on it. Believe me, this is the most important case that we have on our plates right now. We're putting all of our resources into it."

"So you have not discovered anything yet?"

"I'm actually here to have a look at Calliopia's room. I know the crime techs have already been through there, but Ms. Rawlins and I would like to have a look over it, if we could."

"Of course," Mr. Papillon agreed. He looked at his wife for a moment, cuddling the infant, then stood. "I will take you there."

Jessup and Reg stood. Reg studied Mrs. Papillon with the baby for a few seconds before following Mr. Papillon. She seemed very young to have a teenage daughter, perhaps not even thirty herself. Was she the second wife? A new wife and baby in the home might have made things untenable for Calliopia. Had the wife been jealous of Mr. Papillon's firstborn? Had Calliopia been jealous of the new baby getting all of the attention and of the woman who had replaced her mother? Had one or both of the parents been abusive or negligent of the daughter who was no longer wanted?

She watched for any change in body language or facial expression from either of them, and reached out with her mind, trying to identify their thoughts and feelings around their missing daughter. They had reported her missing, so that was at least some indication that they cared about her.

They walked up a grand staircase and down a long hall into another wing of the house to reach Calliopia's bedroom. The house was not as ostentatious as she would have expected from the exterior and the rich finery of their dress. There were fewer paintings, sculptures, and antiques and more greenery and flowers than Reg would have predicted.

Calliopia's room was large, with floor-to-ceiling windows lining one wall of the room. Yet there were heavy blue velvet drapes pulled across most of the windows blocking out the light, so that the room was illuminated by just one panel open in the middle. Mr. Papillon gave a little shrug.

"You know kids," he said. "Up at all hours, trying to sleep during the day. Callie didn't like the sun in her eyes."

Jessup nodded understandingly. She and Reg both looked around the room, letting their eyes adjust to the dimness and taking everything in. Reg felt the girl's presence very strongly. She wanted Mr. Papillon to go away so that she could be left to feel Callie and try to tell Jessup what had happened to her.

"If there's anything you need… if you have any more questions…" He left the sentence hanging.

"We'll let you know," Jessup agreed.

Mr. Papillon looked at Reg one more time, as if trying to figure out who she was, then turned and left them to search

Callie's room. Jessup closed the door behind him, leaving them in the cave-like darkness of the room. But Jessup didn't immediately reach for the light switch or go and open more curtains.

"Can you sense anything?" she asked in a low voice.

"Yes. I'm going to… if you want to just be still and quiet for a minute… I'm going to see if I can find her."

Jessup nodded.

Restless, Reg went to the bed and sat down.

She wanted to find Calliopia and to help her, but she was afraid that when she reached out, she was going to find nothing. She didn't want to let down Detective Jessup and Calliopia's parents. She didn't want to let down Callie. She needed to find her, even if it were just to verify that she had run away and didn't want to live in the mansion with her parents anymore.

And she didn't want to reveal to herself and everyone else that she was just a fraud. A lucky guesser. Good at cold readings, but a fraud nonetheless.

She took a long, deep breath, and closed her eyes.

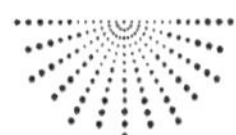

CHAPTER FOUR

The transition from the dark bedroom in the castle to the dark room where Calliopia was being held was an easy one. But the contrasts between the two were disturbing. The soft, luxurious bed that Reg was sitting on in Calliopia's room was completely opposite to the one Calliopia sat on. The thin pad that separated Calliopia's tired body from the springs of the bed was more like a thick quilt than a mattress. She could feel every bump and broken spring right through it. She would probably have been more comfortable wrapping it around herself and lying on the floor. But it was bare earth. The cold and damp of the room penetrated Callie's bones.

She was younger than Reg had expected, or at least she looked younger, maybe fourteen, still slim with a round, little-girl face.

There were movements around her, sometimes in the surrounding rooms and sometimes in her own room. A cockroach crept out from under the bed and sat in the middle of the floor staring at her with glittering green eyes for a long time.

Florida bred big roaches.

Reg didn't know whether the shudder was her own or Callie's, but she couldn't repress it. She drew the air in sharply through her teeth, trying to stay calm and focused. If the police were going to find Callie, they would need to know the details of where she was. She looked around the room, looking for any clues. She sank deeper into Callie's mind and memories, trying to remember everything that had happened to bring her there.

"Calliopia," Reg whispered, "beautiful voice."

The girl started to sing. It transformed her from the plain, muddy-haired, sullen teen to an angel, glowing in the darkness. All movement around her ceased as every creature in hearing stilled and listened to her lilting song. Reg wasn't sure what language it was. Latin, maybe, or French. Definitely a Romance language.

* * *

"Reg! Regina!"

Reg became slowly aware of the hand tight on her shoulder, shaking her, the low voice trying to hush her. She opened her eyes and looked at Detective Jessup, trying to find her footing. She opened her mouth to ask a question, but was startled by the opening of the bedroom door.

Mrs. Papillon had thrown it open and stood framed in the doorway with light behind her.

"What was that?" she demanded. "Who was singing? How did you know that song?"

Her eyes alit on Reg. They burned with a strange light.

"Who are you? What do you know about my daughter?"

Her daughter. She wasn't the step-mother, then. Or maybe she was, but she had accepted Calliopia as her own.

"This is Reg Rawlins, ma'am," Jessup advised her. "She's a… consultant that I've brought in on the case."

"A consultant? What does that mean?"

She held the baby at her shoulder, her posture rigid. There was no movement or protest from the infant.

"She's… a psychic," Jessup answered reluctantly. "She's very good, she recently helped us to break a major case—"

Jessup didn't mention that Reg hadn't been hired by the police department for that case. She obviously didn't want to reveal that they had never hired Reg before and had just brought her in on Calliopia's case without knowing if she'd be able to do anything for her.

"That is my daughter's song. How do you know that song?"

"She was singing it. What do you mean, it's her song? Did she write it?"

"She was singing it? When did you hear her singing it? She never performed for anyone."

"She was… she was singing it now, when I saw her."

Callie's mother stepped into the room, towering over Reg, who was still sitting on the bed.

"Where is she? You must tell me."

"I don't know. The room was dark, I could barely see. There was nothing to indicate where it was she was being held." Reg looked at Jessup. "I'll work with the police department to try to figure it out. And I'll try to make contact again. If I could… take something with me from this room. Something that will help me to find her when her presence isn't so strong."

"Take anything," the woman said, making an abrupt gesture to indicate the room. "Nothing is of any value to us without Callie."

Reg nodded. "Okay. I'm… sorry I can't tell you where she is. We'll try to find her."

"She is being held?" Mrs. Papillon asked. "She is being kept there against her will?"

Reg nodded. "Yes. She doesn't want to stay there. She wants to come home."

Tears glittered in the corners of the woman's eyes. "She wants to come home," she repeated. "She needs to come back *here*."

Reg was startled by her vehemence. She nodded mutely. Mrs. Papillon strode into the room and started to yank the curtains open, flooding the room with bright sunlight.

It was a pretty room, a princess room, white with gold and

pink accents. And yet, Reg didn't get the feeling that it had suited Calliopia. She was a strangely sad girl for living in a house that was so magnificent, with parents who obviously cared for her. Maybe Reg was mistaken. She hadn't talked with Calliopia and had been connected with her for only a few moments. She could be sad simply because of the circumstances. Maybe she had been perfectly happy before the kidnapping.

"Can I… stay here a little longer?" she asked Mrs. Papillon tentatively. "Just… to see if I can pick up anything else."

Callie's mom looked around. She didn't make any comment on the state of the room as her husband had, writing it off as Calliopia being a teenager.

Like the rest of the house, Reg found the room strangely bare. All of the necessary furniture was there, clothing hanging in the closet, and a few plants near the window where they would occasionally be able to get some light. The walls were bare of decorative paintings or teen idol posters. The top of the dresser was bare, not littered with the usual clutter teenage girls collected. Quick to dust. Easy to leave behind.

"Take as much time as you need to," Mrs. Papillon allowed, shrugging. She gazed at Reg for a moment, then turned away and left her and Jessup alone in the room once more.

"Picking anything up?" Jessup asked.

"Just… I don't know. I feel like this is a front. This isn't who Calliopia really is."

"You think it wasn't her room?"

"No, I'm sure it was. Her presence is pretty strong here. But I thought… I don't know how to explain it. She wasn't the one who decorated it. It's… someone's idea of what a girl's room should look like. But not all little girls are into princesses and pink. And when they grow into teenagers… how many teenagers do you see being happy with a room like this?"

"Okay… so she's probably outgrown it. Even if she wanted the pink theme when she was a little girl, it probably doesn't suit her anymore. But her parents don't want to redecorate, or don't realize that she wants something different."

Reg nodded. That felt right. But did it get them any closer to finding her? Did that help them to figure out who was holding her?

"There wasn't a ransom?"

"No ransom. No contact from anyone saying that they have her or know who does. Or anyone saying that they saw her taken or that we shouldn't look for her because she doesn't want to be found. It's the ones who disappear without any fanfare or ransom call that are the most difficult to find… the ones who stay lost for years."

"Well… she is alive. For now, anyway."

"What did you see? Did you see the people who took her? Anything distinctive about where she's being held? Smells? Sounds?"

"I didn't see any other people. Not clearly. Just shadows in the darkness. Cockroaches. It's… a cold room. Dirt floor. Other than that… I really don't know. Nothing identifiable. She doesn't want to be there."

Jessup moved around the room, peering into the closet, opening the drawers of the dresser to look over the contents. Reg reached out to the clothes in the closet, looking for something that might help her to connect with Calliopia again later and to learn more about what she had been through.

Her hand landed on a long black dress, silky to the touch and practically vibrating with the girls' energy. Reg slipped it off of the hanger and closed her eyes, feeling and imagining.

"What did you find?" Jessup demanded.

"I don't know. Just a dress." Reg opened her eyes and looked at it. It was less a dress than an overcoat. Something meant to be worn over top of her clothes, but was not particularly warm or weatherproof. Almost a cape. Reg shrugged. She held it up for Jessup, and then draped it over her arm. "It just has a strong energy. I'm hoping it will help…"

"Can you find things that are hidden?" Jessup asked abruptly.

Reg blinked at her, thinking back to many lost and found objects. "Yes, sometimes I help people find things that are lost. It wouldn't be any harder to find things that were intentionally hidden."

"Teenagers have secrets. Everybody has secrets. She's bound to have hidden something in here." Jessup looked around. "The crime guys have already been through it, and they didn't find anything. No diary. No pictures of boy or girl friends. No drugs. So what were her secrets, and where did she hide them?"

* * *

Reg looked around the room with new eyes this time. Where would Calliopia have hidden something? If, as she had suggested to Jessup, the room didn't reflect Callie's personality, then where were the objects that did? What were the things that made her comfortable with who she was when she was alone? Her energy was strong enough in the room that there had to be things that were imbued with her energy. Just like the cloak.

Reg made a slow circuit around the room, letting her imagination guide her.

It was only recently she had discovered that what she had always been told was an overactive imagination was more than that. Not her own invention, but psychic powers. The ability to see into the world of the unseen. Her disrupted childhood had been peppered with imaginary friends, the souls of those who had gone on before. She was still getting used to the idea that paranormal phenomena were actually real, something that she could control or interact with.

So she still called it her imagination, envisioning what Calliopia had done in her room when she was by herself. Reg opened a few of the drawers and pulled out objects that called to her, assembling them on the dresser. It still didn't look like anything but a random assemblage of junk. Something anyone could have produced. Nothing mystical about it.

Jessup eyed the items with a frown.

Reg focused on the collection as a whole. An empty crystal bottle which had probably previously held perfume. A small silver disk that could be a coaster or ashtray. A silver brush and comb set with a few dull brown hairs clinging to them. A fountain pen. And the black dress in Reg's arms. There was something missing, but as many times as she looked through the drawers and walked through the room, she couldn't seem to find the missing object.

"What is it? What are you looking for?"

"I don't know. There's something else that goes here."

"What is this supposed to be? Some kind of shrine?"

"I don't know. I just know that these things are important." Reg looked down at the assortment. They were the simple treasures that any child might accumulate. Pretty, everyday objects that kids collected and developed an attachment to. Like crows gathering glittery things that they had no real use for.

"There's a pen, but still no journal," Jessup pointed out.

"Maybe she keeps it on her…" Reg trailed off, looking around in realization.

"On her…?"

"Your crime guys must have already taken her phone and computer."

Jessup scratched her temple. "Not that they mentioned to me. They said they hadn't found anything of interest. I'll double-check…" Jessup pulled out her own phone and called in.

Reg continued to look at the objects while Jessup followed up. Eventually, the detective ended the call and shook her head.

"No. No phone or computer."

"Nothing? What kid these days doesn't have a phone or a computer? Not even a tablet?"

Jessup shook her head. "It might be her… the culture here," she explained. "These people—this family—tends to eschew technology. They wouldn't have encouraged her to get a phone or tablet."

Reg hadn't realized until then that she hadn't seen a single TV or electronic device as they had walked through the house. No wide screen on which to watch the latest sports or movie. Her parents hadn't had phones in their hands, lying on the side tables, or bulging in their pockets.

"They must have something. How could her parents work without computers or phones?"

"It's a different world," Jessup said.

It was a lifestyle Reg could hardly even imagine. Surrounded by luxury, but without any of the forms of entertainment she was used to. She could picture Calliopia's parents reading together as they sat by the fire in the evening. Though, in Florida, who needed the fire?

Reg would go crazy without TV or movies. Reading was not something she had ever learned to enjoy. Reading for entertainment was as foreign to her as running for fun. Both equally painful.

She went to the bed and checked under the mattress for a journal. Of course there wasn't one there; that would have been one of the first places the crime techs would have checked. She and Jessup checked all of the usual hiding places. Under the clothes in her drawers, on the bottoms and backs of the drawers. Hidden under other miscellany in the closet.

Reg went back to the treasured items and stared at the pen, searching mentally for its mate. What good was a pen without paper? She picked it up and turned it slowly in her fingers, waiting for it to give her a clue. She went back to the drawers that they had already checked. The drawers had all been checked multiple times, by the crime guys, Jessup, and Reg herself. But Reg was following the tug she felt from the pen. On TV shows, Reg had seen them trace bullet trajectories, and that was what it was like. Like a string was being pulled from her belly button to the pen and projecting past it.

"We already looked there," Jessup objected.

"I know," Reg agreed. But she looked again anyway, removing each article of clothing and folding it neatly to place on top of the dresser beside of the treasures. When the drawer was empty, Reg put her hand in against the bottom and felt a sort of pulsing heartbeat. The wood was warmer under her fingers than it should be.

"Is it a false bottom?" Jessup asked, tapping the bottom of the drawer and looking at it from several angles. "The tech guys would have noticed if it wasn't as deep as it should be."

It didn't appear to be any shallower than any of the other drawers. Reg felt around the bottom and the edges of the drawer, looking for a release. She couldn't find any kind of catch. Finally, she pressed down lightly on the bottom of the drawer, where it was warm. There was a click, and the wood rose up to reveal the hidden compartment.

"Well, I'll be..." Jessup breathed, looking over her shoulder.

Reg didn't touch the diary. She didn't want to destroy any fingerprints or any other trace evidence. She moved out of Jessup's way. Jessup put on a pair of gloves and pulled an evidence bag out of her pocket. Before transferring the journal to the evidence bag, she turned the pages, eyes skimming over them quickly.

"Anything?"

"Usual teen stuff," Jessup said. "I don't see anything that would indicate anyone was stalking her or causing her other problems." She turned a few more pages.

Looking at the book, Reg wondered how Jessup could even read it. Print was difficult enough for Reg. Cursive was that much more difficult. The script that Calliopia had written with the fountain pen wasn't the same cursive that Reg had been taught in school, but was an older-style hand. Tall and angular and squeezed close together.

"She was interested in a boy," Jessup noted.

"That's not surprising. Where did she go to school? Did she

bus to public school? Get driven to some private school? Or tutored?"

"Private school, but not as elite as you would think. A good mixture of races and classes."

"So there were boys."

Jessup nodded, her eyes on the handwriting in the journal.

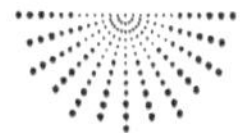

CHAPTER FIVE

*R*eg was tired going home, even though it was just mid-afternoon. She had said that she was only going to do less strenuous work as she recovered from the Warren Blake case to give herself time to get caught up on her sleep and get her energy back. But the work she had done for Jessup had not been easy and she knew there was more to do if they were to have any chance of finding the girl. Finding the journal was helpful; it might even be the key to finding out what had happened to her, but while Jessup and the police department were reading and analyzing it, Reg would need to see what else she could discover.

She unlocked the door to the cottage without first looking around the yard and making sure she was alone. Maybe because in the past, the people she had been most threatened by had been the police, but this time she was helping them, so she knew they weren't going to be waiting for her there.

She hadn't been thinking about Corvin or any other threats to her safety.

"How did it go?"

She jumped at his voice and whirled around. "What are you doing here?"

"You said I could come by today."

"No, I said you could call today," Reg corrected. "I specifically said to phone me."

Corvin gave her a slow smile, exuding warmth and whatever pheromones Reg had come to associate with him.

"Not the way I remember it," he said.

"Then you're remembering wrong. Shouldn't you be brewing potions or something?"

"That type of thing is usually more efficacious if done at midnight, or at least under the moon. During the day… my time is more open for other pursuits, barring emergencies."

"You have witching emergencies?"

"Don't you have psychic emergencies?"

The trip to see Calliopia's home had been pretty urgent, and it wasn't the first emergency job Reg had been called on to perform within her new career as a medium.

"Well, okay. Yes." Reg rubbed her eyes, still standing on the doorstep with the key in her hand. "Now is really not a good time, Corvin. I'm tired…"

"So the job for Detective Jessup went well?"

"How did you get that out of me feeling tired?"

"You've obviously expended a lot of energy. I assume that is good news."

"Well… I don't know. It might be. I didn't have anything that could direct the police right to her, but…" Reg trailed off. "How do you know about this case?"

"I hear things."

"Yeah? What do you know about it?" She couldn't speak to him openly about the case if he didn't really know anything about it. It was a police matter, and she assumed she needed to keep quiet about it with anyone who wasn't already in the know.

"Missing teenager," Corvin said. "Part of that lot," he made a vague directional gesture.

Reg raised her brows.

"Part of the Papillon family, I think," he offered.

Reg nodded grudgingly.

"And…?" he prompted.

"Like I said, I couldn't do anything that would point them directly to where she was being held, but I did get some impressions. I found her journal for them. Maybe there will be something in there that will help them to figure it out. If it wasn't just some random kidnapping…"

"And this…?" Corvin indicated the cloak Reg hadn't yet had a chance to take into the cottage.

"Just… a piece of clothing to help me to reach her again, if I can."

"So, no location clues for the police? Being held near a large body of water?"

Reg couldn't help laughing. "Everything in Florida is near a large body of water."

"So that would be a pretty good bet."

"No, nothing like that. I could see where she was, but only from the inside, nothing that would be helpful to the police in figuring out where she was." Reg leaned on the doorframe. "I really am tired."

"I could come in," Corvin suggested. "Help tuck you into bed?"

Reg shook her head at his audacity.

Reg did not allow Corvin to tuck her in. She left him outside where he belonged and went into the cottage on her own. Already unnerved by one unexpected guest, she checked all around the cottage to make sure there were no burglars lurking under beds or behind doors before deciding she could safely go to sleep. Having been assaulted by Hawthorne-Rose in the cottage, she couldn't help feeling a little overanxious, double- and triple-checking locks to be sure she couldn't be taken off-guard.

Starlight followed her from room to room, obviously

wondering what she was looking for. When she satisfied herself that it was safe and headed toward the bed, he nipped at her calves.

"Hey! Cut that out!" Reg whirled on Starlight, and he jumped back, retreating far out of her reach, then sitting down and watching her as she glared at him angrily. "What was that for? Just because I'm going to bed, that doesn't mean it's time to eat. You don't need anything right now. If you do, you can eat your dry kibble like cats are supposed to!"

He licked at his back where his fur had become ruffled.

"If you're going to bite me, I'm going to start carrying a spray bottle around with me. Or maybe a whole glass of water. How would you like that?"

He stopped licking and stared at her steadily.

"Don't give me attitude."

He didn't flinch or blink.

"Fine, I'm going to lay down now. If you don't like it, that's too bad. I'll shut you in the bathroom."

She turned back to her bedroom, but looked back over her shoulder once to make sure he wasn't coming after her again. He stayed where he was, watching her departure.

Reg sighed as she climbed into bed and got settled in. The day was warm, even with the air conditioning running, so she peeled off her socks and didn't pull on the covers. Her brain felt fried after the mental work she had done looking for Calliopia. As soon as she lay down, she could feel her consciousness slipping away.

* * *

She slept soundly for a couple of hours, but then she started to dream. She found herself once again in Calliopia's room. The drapes had been pulled closed again, so the room was only dimly lit through the cracks between the panels.

Calliopia was sitting at her desk. In her hand was an item that they had not turned up in her bedroom, maybe the object that Reg had sensed was missing. A glittering silver knife. The handle was ornately carved, and it felt warm and well-balanced in Callie's hand. She drew the point down her arm several times, not cutting the skin, just running the blade over it. She whispered something to herself, but Reg couldn't understand what it was. As with Calliopia's song, she had reverted to another language. Her family must have retained their native tongue when they had emigrated to the United States, however far in the past that had been.

Reg didn't know what she was saying, but it sounded like a question. The same thing repeated over and over again.

She seemed to be working her way up to something. As she repeated the question in a whisper, she ran the blade down her arm again, the cutting edge positioned against her pale skin. She moved it down, and Reg felt the bite of the blade and gasped in shock. She tried to put her hand over the cut or over Calliopia's hand to stop her, but she had no control over the situation. She was only an observer.

Blood welled up in a line. It was a shallow cut, nothing serious, but Reg knew enough about self-harming to know that was the way it started. Shallow cuts at first, hesitation marks. Testing how difficult it was and what kind of relief it might bring before proceeding further. Then deeper cuts, other locations, and maybe a suicide attempt.

She tried to call out to Callie in her mind, telling her to stop and to talk to someone, to get help before it proceeded into something more serious. In the vision, Calliopia sat there staring down at the blood welling up on her arm, still repeating the question in a voice that was breaking and getting quieter.

People love you. Reg tried to get the message across the abyss between them. *People love you and want you to be healthy and happy. Don't do this.*

But she was seeing the past, not the present. Reg couldn't change the past, and she couldn't see what it would lead to. But whatever had happened next, Reg had been right. Calliopia was not a little girl anymore, playing princess and ponies in her pink and gold room. She was a teenager, dangerously depressed.

Who knew what sequence of events she had been about to trigger.

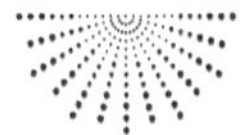

CHAPTER SIX

When Reg woke up, Starlight was standing on top of her, kneading with his paws, purring up a storm. Reg considered this strange behavior for a few minutes, still groggy from her afternoon nap, before rolling over to tip him off.

Starlight snorted and righted himself, stalking around her to confront her nose to nose.

"What are you doing?" Reg demanded.

He yowled, drawing the sound out like a plaintive query. He snuffled at her hand and Reg realized from the coldness of his breath that it was once again wet with blood. She checked to make sure she hadn't bled on the pillow or bedsheets, then got up to take care of it.

"I don't know why it keeps opening back up," she told Starlight crossly. "It should be starting to heal by now."

Apparently deciding that she was alright, Starlight rubbed against Reg's legs, curling his tail around them like a snake.

"I suppose you're ready for something to eat now. Me too. Let's see what we can find in the fridge."

One benefit of Sarah coming and going as if she owned the place—which she did—was that she had taken it upon herself to make sure Reg was taken care of, and that included the occasional restock of her fridge. Reg checked the fridge but didn't find anything new and interesting there, so she pulled a box of macaroni and cheese out of the cupboard and started the pasta boiling.

"This is not cat food," she told Starlight. "You need to eat the food that's actually made for cats. Look at this." She took the box of dry cat food out of the cupboard, shook it, and showed him the box. "Look, it has a picture of a cat on it. Like you. That means it's for you. And listen: 'promotes smooth and luxurious fur' and 'scientifically balanced nutrition' and 'great meaty taste.' Doesn't that sound good?"

He stared at her inscrutably.

"Listen to the ingredients. It has…" Reg scanned the dense ingredients list for familiar words, "…uh, chicken and pork byproducts. That sounds good, doesn't it?"

He didn't seem the least bit impressed. Reg was a little irritated at the cat food company for burying the meat under a lot of other polysyllabic chemical names. Shouldn't food for cats actually be filled with meat? She might have to replace the cat food with another brand that had more real meat in it to see if it were more appetizing to him.

When the macaroni was soft and Reg had mixed the bright orange cheese into it, she spooned some into Starlight's dish. He immediately went to work on it, making slurping and chawing sounds as he went. Reg made a face at him.

"Eat politely."

He stopped to look at her, then went back to eating, even more noisily.

"You're as bad as a kid."

* * *

Reg called the number on Detective Jessup's card and told her about the dream she'd had.

"And are you sure this was a vision of something that

happened to Calliopia?" Jessup asked, "It wasn't just a random dream because you were thinking about her?"

"No. I'm sure it really happened. You could ask her parents about it, but a lot of times, parents have no idea when their kid is cutting."

Jessup *hmmed*. "They might know if she was depressed, though. They never said so, and she didn't have anything… dark on the walls or in the journal."

"What *was* in the journal?"

"She did have a boy she was interested in. Not obvious from the journal just how close they were. Unless a girl is explicit, it's hard to tell the difference between a crush from a distance and an actual physical relationship. It is worrying, though."

"Worrying how?"

"The boy that she was interested in… was not someone her parents would have wanted her to see."

"Why? Was he older?"

"I haven't checked his age. But the two families… are not friendly."

"Oh," Reg stretched the word out several syllables, understanding. "Romeo and Juliet, huh?"

"Something like that."

"Have you told her parents? Asked them if they knew?"

"If they'd known, they would have told us when they made the initial report. Hopefully, it was just a crush and she never actually got together with him. You know how silly girls can be."

"Are you going to go back to them with it?"

"I will, but not yet. I want to check it out quietly first."

"You don't think that this boy had anything to do with her disappearance, do you? If she's being held against her will, then it's not by him, right? If she was with him, I wouldn't have seen her locked in a dark room."

"You didn't actually see that it was locked. You said there were other people coming and going. Maybe she was just sleeping there and that's why the room was dark."

"No. She wanted out. She was being kept there against her will. And *he* wouldn't be holding her against her will."

"How do you know that? She liked him, yes, but if she decided she didn't want to stay with him anymore and wanted to go home, and he wanted to keep her there…"

Reg's stomach clenched and felt queasy, suddenly regretting that she and Starlight had polished off the entire box of macaroni.

"I hope not."

"I'd rather that than some of the alternatives. But we don't know yet. No point in jumping to conclusions."

Reg made a noise of agreement.

"I want you to talk to Corvin," Jessup said.

Reg felt her jaw drop. She looked at the phone for a minute, as if it were the phone's fault for sending the wrong message.

"What?"

"What you saw with Calliopia. I want you to talk to him about it, tell him what you saw."

"About her cutting?"

"Yes."

"Why? What is Corvin going to know about that? He's not a doctor or psychiatrist."

"He has expertise in some areas. I'd like you to give him your impressions and see if it triggers anything for him."

Reg shook her head. "I don't want him coming here."

"Understandable," Jessup agreed. "I wouldn't want him in my house, either. How about at the police station?"

"I'd prefer not to go there, either. Isn't there somewhere neutral we could meet? A coffee shop? As long as you're there, I don't have to worry about…"

Reg wasn't sure how to finish. Just how much did Jessup know about who Corvin was and what he did? Just because she was familiar with some of the magic that was practiced in Black Sands, that didn't necessarily mean she knew all of the details. It would be hard for anyone to know all of the players and how they were involved in the magical community. If Jessup knew a lot of practitioners, she wouldn't have called on Reg to consult on Calliopia's case. She would have had other psychics on retainer already.

"I'll keep Corvin in check," Jessup agreed. "Between the two of us, we can manage him."

* * *

Reg left it with Jessup to make arrangements with Corvin. She wanted to have some time to herself before meeting with him again face to face, to make sure she was calm and ready to see him again. If she were tired and stressed, he would work on her weaknesses and might be able to overcome her defenses. She knew what he was now, and hopefully that meant that she would be able to keep her head and not be drawn into his snares like an insect into a Venus fly trap.

She had no intention of losing her powers to him again. Next time, she knew there would be no getting them back. That had been a one-time thing. But she wasn't going to let him steal them again.

Reg tried to meditate and achieve a state of calm, but the meditation thing wasn't working for her. She had such a busy brain that she could never seem to focus on one thing for long enough to achieve any sort of Zen state.

She tried patting Starlight instead. She could feel the calming, soothing energy coming off of him like the warmth from a fireplace. As soon as she touched him, her heart rate started to slow.

Why did Jessup want her to talk to Corvin? She closed her eyes and tried to remember every detail that she could of the dream. Callie and her knife. Tracing lines down her arm, and then starting to cut. The words were almost a chant in her mind. Was she thinking about the boy she had a crush on? Were they a couple or did she admire him from afar? Did he have a girlfriend, and that was what had upset her so much that she had cut herself? Was the cutting to relieve her pain or was it leading up to a suicide attempt? Or both?

Starlight purred and Reg refocused on him. She would do everything she could to help Calliopia. The cutting was in the past. Reg wanted to prevent anything bad from happening to Calliopia in the present or the near future. Reg owed Callie that much.

CHAPTER SEVEN

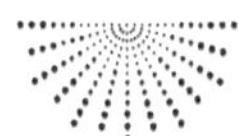

*J*essup met Reg outside The Crystal Bowl so that they could go in together and neither would be left alone with Corvin.

"It's a public place, so there's not that much he can do," Jessup said, "but we'll stay together anyway. Better safe than sorry."

"He can still turn on the charm in a place like this, and lead on to other places," Reg agreed.

Jessup looked Reg over thoughtfully. "Is that what happened before?"

Reg shrugged and looked away. "Pretty much, yeah. We went out for dinner, drinks, dessert… which led to other things… I took him home…"

Jessup winced.

"I know. Stupid," Reg acknowledged. "I should have listened to Sarah. Used some common sense. I didn't think he would do anything."

"Not really your fault. That's what he's genetically programmed to do. Charm and seduce to feed on others' powers. You were lucky."

"I know. They don't usually give them back."

"They *never* give them back. There's something special about you."

Reg shook her head. "It was the only way to get the upper hand over Hawthorne-Rose. It was just the logical solution. But now Corvin seems... even more obsessed with getting them back again."

"He's fed recently, so he should have some self-control. I'll be there to make sure nothing happens. I really do need his opinion on this."

"I want to get Calliopia back too. I know... how scared and vulnerable she's feeling. She just wants to get out of there."

Jessup nodded and patted Reg on the shoulder. "We'll figure it out. This is the fastest way."

The two of them entered The Crystal Bowl together. Reg felt Corvin's presence before she even saw him. She led Jessup to a back table. There were no private dining rooms at The Crystal Bowl, which was good. She would be safer with everything out in the open and plenty of distractions.

"Ladies," Corvin greeted. "You have no idea how delighted I was to get your call."

Jessup placed a small box on the table. Corvin's eyes followed it. He put his hand over the box as if checking its temperature. His pupils dilated.

"Not yet," Jessup said, sliding the box away from him. "You help me first."

Corvin nodded, giving a strained smile. "Regina," he greeted, reaching out to shake her hand.

Reg didn't touch him. She pulled out a chair and sat down. "Let's get this over with. The longer we draw out the small talk, the longer it's going to take to find Callie."

Corvin motioned to the teapot in the middle of the table. "A drink?"

"Is it safe?" Reg looked first at Corvin and then at Jessup.

"You think I would poison you?" Corvin demanded.

"I think you would… magic me. Or maybe something else that would let you control me."

Corvin looked at Jessup. "No spells," he promised. "Just tea." He looked back at Reg. "Just regular black tea, no hallucinogens or special ingredients. Something to refresh yourselves and to focus your awareness."

Jessup nodded. "Go ahead," she told Reg, and poured herself a half teacup. Reg followed suit. She took a sip of the tea, took a deep breath, and let the air out slowly.

"Okay. Tell me what it is you need to know."

Corvin raised his brows at Jessup. "You'll have to take that one, I don't know what it is you needed my expertise on."

"Just tell him what you told me," Jessup told Reg. "I want to see what he thinks."

Reg related the dream she'd had about Calliopia, trying to be as specific as possible about what she saw and heard and about her impressions at the time, her certainty that it was a memory, not just something her brain had conjured.

Corvin's eyes were quick and bright, focused on Reg's face throughout the story. He nodded a few times and scratched his whiskers, thinking about it.

"Your focus was on Calliopia cutting herself," Corvin said. "I want you to widen your perceptions to the rest of the room, or whatever else was in view."

"Hmm." Reg closed her eyes and recalled the vision, frowning. "Okay. She was in her bedroom. The drapes were pulled, so it was mostly dark, but I could still see."

"Where in her room was she? Sitting on the bed? On the floor?"

"No, at her desk."

"What else was on the desk?"

Reg pressed her fingers into her temples. The cut on her hand throbbed. Reg concentrated.

"The things I took out of her drawers." She could see them out on the desk in front of her, and it all started to come together. A vial of liquid. Burnt herbs smoking on the salver, their acrid sweet scent hanging in the air. The pen laid across a couple of sheets of parchment, with a recipe or incantation written in Calliopia's old-style script, indecipherable to Reg. "Oh."

"Yes…?"

"It was a spell, wasn't it?"

"Tell me what you saw."

Reg told him what she could about each object. Corvin nodded.

"I don't know what spell she was performing without more details, but it certainly sounds like it."

"Blood magic," Jessup said.

Reg looked at her. "Is that… like human sacrifice…?"

"Human sacrifice would be a different kind of blood magic. Blood is used to strengthen some kinds of spells. Especially love potions. The caster uses her own blood, not blood from another victim. Putting some of her own life force into the spell."

"Modern-day practitioners don't generally use ceremonial daggers," Corvin said. "That's a bit… dramatic. Most today will use a finger lancet, like a diabetic uses for glucose testing. You only need a drop or two."

Reg pressed her thumb into her palm, aware her cut was bleeding again. Cuts on fingers and hands were so problematic. It kept opening again every time she moved. She tried to ignore the pain. "A love potion. For the boy she wrote about in her journal?"

Corvin took a sip of his own drink, which was definitely not tea, and raised a questioning eyebrow at Jessup.

"What boy?"

Jessup sighed and didn't answer. Reg realized she probably shouldn't have mentioned him. She looked down at her tea, trying to imagine what kind of a boy Calliopia had been attracted to. Was she drawn to him just because he was the forbidden fruit? Was he good-looking? Did they have any common interests?

Corvin's eyes were dancing as he looked at Reg. "A Rosdew?" he suggested.

"A who?"

Jessup looked daggers at Corvin. "Where did you get that from?"

"Miss Rawlins." He smiled at her.

"I don't even know what a Rosdew is!" Reg protested. "And I didn't say a word!"

"You didn't have to. It was written all over your face."

"You were never telepathic before," Jessup growled at Corvin. "A little intuitive, maybe, but nothing like that."

"After holding Regina's powers, I've retained a small measure of her abilities. And I've done the best I could to enhance them through whatever other sources I could." Corvin eyed the box that Jessup had placed on the table.

"You are here to consult, not to pry."

He just smirked.

Reg looked away, determined not to be pulled in by his charm. Even knowing what he was and what he had done to her, she struggled to see him for what he really was. He constantly drew her in with whatever pheromones or magical glamour he exuded.

"Let's not fight," Corvin crooned to Jessup, leaning closer to her. "Marta."

"I'd rather fight," Jessup snapped back, inching her chair away. "You have not been asked to take part in this investigation."

"I've been asked to consult. I'd say that was invitation enough. I can help you." Again, the inviting croon entered his voice. He enveloped them both with his offer. "I know how girls think."

Reg's mind was muddled for a minute. Girls?

Calliopia!

She was letting him distract her. Distract both of them. Calliopia was in trouble, and they couldn't afford to while away their time with Corvin Hunter.

"So who or what are the Rosdews?"

Jessup put her teacup down with a clatter that made Reg jump, sure it was going to shatter. But it didn't.

"Magical folk," she said brusquely.

"And Calliopia's family are too? And the two families have some kind of... magical feud?"

Jessup and Corvin both nodded.

"You really think this boy might have... kidnapped her? It doesn't sound very likely to me. People don't kidnap because of feuds or love... If he liked her, then it's more likely that they would have just run off together, isn't it? And if he didn't... I don't know. He'd reject her. Make fun of her. But kidnap her? Why?"

Jessup looked steadily at Reg. "You said she was being held. You said she wanted to get away and couldn't."

"Yes... I know..." Reg again felt the chill and dread that had been present in Calliopia's prison. She hadn't run away there with a boyfriend. Had the boy coerced her into going there, and then they'd kidnapped her? Had he lured her into a trap? "Are these Rosdews like you?" she asked Corvin.

"Like me?"

"I mean... do they have..." Reg cleared her throat uncomfortably. "Charms? Glamour? Whatever it is you attract people with?"

"Ah." He smiled. "No, they don't have the natural attraction that I do. But they do have... their own brand of magic. Their own ways of... luring prey."

Goosebumps stood up on Reg's arms and sweat started dripping down her back. The classification of Calliopia as prey—and Reg too, if she extended the words to Corvin's own behavior—was unsettling.

"Then that's where we should go. To the Rosdews."

"We?" Jessup repeated. "In case you forgot, this is a police investigation, and you are not part of the police department. Neither of you is. Before the police can go beating down someone's door, they need a little thing called a warrant and probable cause."

"Even here? In a case like this?"

"Yes. Even a case like this. Sure, some police have played fast and loose with the law here, but they don't last long if they won't follow the rules."

"Isn't the journal reason enough to question the boy?"

"It's enough to ask him some questions about Calliopia, but not enough to make him a suspect. There's nothing to indicate he's done anything wrong. I can't arrest him or force him to answer anything. He would just laugh and walk away."

"And then you'd have tipped him off that you know he's involved."

"Yes. We could put surveillance on him, see where he leads us… but in a community like that, surveillance can get *complicated*."

"He can't turn invisible, can he?" Reg asked with a laugh.

"It's not as impossible as you might think. Camouflage, distraction spells, wards, a sense of where people are looking…"

"But not actual invisibility, right?"

Jessup shrugged and didn't say one way or the other.

"Then what's the next step?" Reg asked. "That's it? I'm done?"

"For now, yes," Jessup agreed. "Submit your invoice and I'll get the payment processed for you. This isn't a partnership. I asked you to perform one task and you've done that. Above and beyond, having a second vision of Callie and meeting with the warlock about it. But that's all there is. It's all just plain police work from here on in. Feet on the ground, chasing down every available lead."

Reg looked at Corvin, who was watching her with half-closed eyes. He didn't agree or disagree with Jessup's analysis. Reg supposed it was in their best interests to just let the police do their jobs. If Jessup called one or the other of them occasionally for a consult, that was a nice extra paycheck, but they weren't about to become Mystery Incorporated and solve all of the spooky crimes around Black Sands together.

And that was good, because channeling people in magical comas or remote viewing people who had been kidnapped was exhausting work.

"You look like you could use some distraction," Corvin told Reg. "You've been working too hard."

"I'm just tired. A good night's sleep…"

"You keep shutting yourself up in that little cottage. You need to get out and meet some people. For business development as well as your emotional health."

"I suppose," Reg admitted. "I'm usually more social. I just never knew how tiring it could be to work with something that's… so ephemeral."

"You'll adjust. Your body will get more used to it, just like with any other kind of exercise."

"I don't know. It doesn't feel the same. When you've had a good workout, your muscles are tired and sore, but you still feel… that extra boost. But after something that uses a lot of my… psychic energy… I just feel like sleeping for three days. I know I should get out in the community, but I don't know…"

"There's a community newsletter that gets published around here," Corvin said. "If you haven't seen a copy of it, I could get you one. There are meet-ups between practitioners of various arts, community mixers, sports, sales and fundraisers…"

"Yeah, Sarah's left me a calendar and some flyers. But… I'm just not really ready to go to anything. Maybe when I know a few more people."

"That's how you get to know them! By going out to these things. Come on." He touched her hand. "Pick something out and I'll go with you."

His hand was warm and soothing, like something she could curl up in and be kept safe and protected. He hardly even knew her, but he was willing to take that on himself. He had told Reg that he was duty-bound to protect her, after what had happened between them. She wanted nothing more than to just cuddle up into him.

CHAPTER EIGHT

*R*eg."

Reg was lost in Corvin's eyes. Swimming out to answer the call was an arduous task. She wanted to just stay where it was safe and warm.

"Rawlins. Reg. Hey!"

Reg winced. Not just at Detective Jessup's raised voice, but at the sharp jab in the shoulder. She pushed Jessup's hand away clumsily.

"Don't." It was like her mouth was full of toffee. Shaping her mouth and pushing out even just one word was almost more than she could manage.

"Let her go," Jessup snapped.

Corvin withdrew his hand, leaving Reg's cold and tingly. A little of the haziness lifted.

"You're here on business. You're not supposed to be entrancing Reg."

Corvin raised his brows in an expression of innocence. "She's tired. She needed a boost. I'm just trying to help. You're the one demanding her services without giving anything in return."

"She'll be paid."

"Money is poor recompense for her pouring her life's energy into your case."

Reg looked around, breathing more deeply and realizing that the contact with Corvin had, in fact, left her invigorated. It seemed counterintuitive that the comfortable, drowsy feeling that had come over her would give her more energy, but once her contact with Corvin was broken, it had.

"You should not be touching her. She doesn't know the ways you can enthrall her. This is a business transaction, not a date."

Enthrall. To make into a thrall. A slave.

Yet somehow enthralling had come to mean something fascinating or exciting. How long had men of Corvin's ilk been enticing women into their power?

"If our business transaction is complete, then I believe you owe me that," Corvin said dryly, his eyes on the little box.

Jessup slid it across the table to him, looking repulsed. Corvin closed his hand around it, purring.

"What is it?" Reg asked.

"A morsel," Corvin said. "A small token of thanks for my expertise."

Reg looked at Jessup and back at Corvin. She probably didn't want to know the details. An organ from one of the animals that Uriel Hawthorne and his cabal had been poaching and trafficking? Some magical artifact that had been used in another kind of blood rite? Or maybe it was something that seemed completely innocuous, and Jessup was just disgusted at having to deal with Corvin Hunter.

"We should go now," Jessup told Reg, rising to her feet.

"Yeah. Okay."

Reg stood up from her chair. She felt like she had run a long race and then sat down, her legs wobbly and shaky as the tiny kittens Reg had once found in a cardboard box in a back alley. Jessup put a hand on her arm, steadying her.

"Don't move too fast. You'll be fine once we get out of here."

Reg nodded. She held on to the table for a minute, trying to draw in strength and stabilize herself. She'd get home to Starlight. She'd feed him. She'd go back to bed, and in the morning she would feel more like herself again. She just needed a good night's sleep.

"Look at the community calendar," Corvin told her again. "Pick out what you'd like to go to, and I'll go along with you so you won't be alone. Nothing is going to happen to you with other magical practitioners around you."

"Like here, right?" Reg demanded, thinking of how he had bewitched her again, even when she was on guard, even with Jessup sitting right there. Sitting in the middle of a restaurant full of other community members.

"I didn't do anything to harm you. I took nothing from you. I only gave."

* * *

Jessup said little once they were out of the restaurant, escorting Reg to her car.

"You're okay?" she checked.

"Yes, I'm fine. Feeling a lot better, actually." Maybe she'd watch some TV before bed. She no longer felt like she needed to fall right into it.

"Don't go back in there," Jessup warned, nodding to The Crystal Bowl.

"Why would I do that?"

Jessup straightened, looking across the parking lot toward the building. As if she could still see Corvin, sitting at his table, coolly sipping his Jack Daniels. "Because a lot of women would."

"Well, I'm not like a lot of women. He made a fool of me once, but that's not going to happen again."

"You're vulnerable and he's in there getting stronger. Just go straight home. If you forgot your pocketbook or lost an earring, forget about it and just go home. Stay away from him tonight."

"I will," Reg insisted.

"Okay. Take care of yourself."

* * *

Back at the cottage, Reg let herself back in and yawned widely. It was as if her fatigue and Corvin's restless energy were both present, yet separate like oil and water.

"Starlight! Here, kitty, kitty."

Reg walked to the fridge to get something out for him, expecting him to bolt out of the bedroom and reach it before she did. But there was no sight or sound of him. Reg frowned. She went ahead and got out the tuna anyway.

"Kitty, kitty?"

But once again, opening the tuna and spooning some into Starlight's bowl didn't bring him running. Reg went to her bedroom and looked in, expecting to find him curled up asleep on the bed. But he wasn't. Reg looked around. Under the bed? On top of the dresser? She checked the bathroom to see if he'd gotten shut in there. The spare room door stood open, and there was no sign of him there. Reg went back to the living room and checked on and under the furniture, behind the drapes, and inside every other hiding place she could imagine. It didn't make any sense. There weren't that many places a cat could hide in the cottage; and why would he? He always came racing to her if there were food being offered, or just close at hand.

"Starlight?"

Finally, she went to the door of the cottage and opened it, sticking her head and out looking around.

"Starlight? Starlight?"

She had a cold, scared feeling in the middle of her stomach. What could have happened to him? He couldn't let himself out of the cottage. Her mind went to kidnapping, but that was only because of her involvement with Calliopia. Who would steal a cat? It wasn't like Starlight was a rare and valuable breed. He was a cat with considerable psychic powers, but who would care about that?

He wouldn't align himself with just anyone. His powers wouldn't be of any worth to anyone unless he shared them willingly.

Unless, like the poached animals, his power remained in his body after his death and someone could put it to use. Her stomach roiled at the idea. She thought of Corvin and his box at the restaurant. She'd said before that what he did was reprehensible, and he had countered that his predatory nature was beyond his control, just part of his nature, like red hair was part of her physical makeup. How could it be wrong to be what he was born?

"Starlight…?"

The back door of the big house opened and Reg saw Sarah silhouetted against the indoor light.

"Reg?"

"Have you seen Starlight? I can't find him?"

"Oh, Reg! I'm so sorry!" Sarah hurried down the path across the yard. "I don't know what happened. I just went into the cottage to check on things, and he shot out the door as soon as I opened it… I called him and called him, but he wouldn't come back. I shook his food, I tried to explain to him that it wasn't safe for him to be out wandering around… but he wouldn't come back."

"He went outside? Where?"

Reg looked around, hoping to spot Starlight sheltering under a shrub or sneaking up on a bird. It would serve Sarah right if Starlight ended up hunting one of the birds in the garden. She should have called Reg. She shouldn't have been in the cottage in the first place. It was Reg's rental. She was supposed to have peaceful enjoyment of the property, not to be interrupted by the witch who owned the place multiple times a day.

"I don't know where he went. He raced by me, and then he was gone. I looked for him and I called him… I'm so sorry…"

"I'm sure he'll come back," Reg said, though she wasn't at all sure. Dogs and pigeons returned home, but cats? If Starlight had decided he wanted to be wild and free, what was going to make him change his mind and return? Cats were well-known for their independent attitudes and Starlight's recent conduct hadn't been particularly compliant.

"He will," Sarah repeated. "Of course he will. I just don't know what he was thinking." She shook her head. "I never could understand cats!"

"Well…" Reg looked around once more, feeling empty and alone. "I suppose he'll be back when he's hungry."

Sarah nodded and patted Reg on the shoulder, murmuring to her. Reg withdrew and shut the door, hot tears prickling in her eyes. She didn't need Sarah's sympathy and apologies. She didn't need anyone or anything else in her life.

CHAPTER NINE

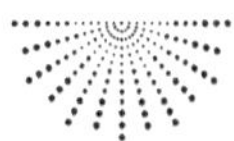

$\mathcal{R}$eg expected Corvin to show up any time, but he didn't. She kept startling at every sound, not used to how quiet it was without Starlight around, and certain that the cat was just outside or was going to come to harm.

Was it possible that Corvin had something to do with Starlight's disappearance? He and the cat had been particularly antagonistic toward each other. Not like Sarah, who was willing to make friends with Starlight and was kind to him even though she didn't have a natural attraction to cats. Corvin had made it plain from the start that he and Starlight were on opposite sides. Starlight had been able to see through Corvin's exterior to the kind of person he really was inside. Reg should have paid more attention to him.

Morning came, and there was still no sign of either Corvin or Starlight. She supposed it was good news that Corvin was staying away. Unless he'd had something to do with Starlight's disappearance.

But he couldn't have. He had been at the restaurant with Reg and Jessup when Starlight had taken off.

Reg was determined not to spend all of her time and energy worrying about the whereabouts of the cat. She could, after all, go back to the shelter and pick out another cat any time she wanted to. And maybe the new cat would be more normal and behave appropriately. He'd eat cat food and sleep in a cat bed and not act like he was a human or thought himself superior to humans.

Reg wanted to help find Calliopia. She'd had a number of restless dreams, some to do with Callie and some not. Jessup didn't want her help, but that didn't mean Reg couldn't do a little investigating of her own.

Jessup hadn't given her the boy's name, but Corvin had told her the family name. Rosdew. There couldn't be a whole lot of Rosdews around. Reg had never even heard the name before. Reg asked her phone for directions to the public library, and there a librarian helped her find a stack of school yearbooks for the area. She didn't have to read them, all she had to do was to look in the index for any Rosdews. Even if there were a few of them, she'd have some idea of where to start. If she were lucky, Calliopia's name would be in the same book.

* * *

Not too shabby for an amateur detective. An hour later, Reg was outside the private high school that both Callie and Ruan Rosdew attended.

She had studied each picture that Callie or Ruan had appeared in, looking for any indication of the relationship between the two. But they were not in any of the same organizations; in fact, both of them had a serious lack of after-school clubs or sports. There were no pictures of them hanging out together, or of friends they appeared to have in common. They were a grade apart, Ruan being the elder.

And then there were their looks. If someone were making a movie about the kidnapping and their relationship, they would have cast a beautiful, fresh-faced girl and a dark, handsome, brooding boy, something like a younger version of Corvin. In real life, Calliopia was a girl with plain features, muddy brown hair, and a weedy figure. Ruan, far from being a dark and handsome Romeo, looked like a ten-year-old. He was shorter than any of the boys he appeared beside in the year book. Maybe the shortest one in his grade. His face was child-like, as if he had not yet reached puberty. Both had watery blue eyes. Neither showed up on the honor rolls and certainly neither one would ever be prom king or queen. They would probably be lucky to even get asked to the prom.

And maybe that was the one thing they had in common. Maybe they were both outcasts, the bottom of the barrel, without a hope of ever measuring up to society's measurements of success. They'd grow up to be office clerks, dentists, or social workers, good respectable jobs with little praise or chance at achieving social standing.

Reg waited for the lunch bell to ring. In the chaos that followed, she could mix with the crowds and ask people if they knew Callie or Ruan. If she were lucky, she would find Ruan himself, and see if he knew anything about Callie's disappearance. Since she wasn't a police officer, there was no danger in spooking Ruan. He wouldn't have any idea that he was a suspect. Reg was just a friend of the family trying to find out what had led up to Callie's disappearance.

Before the bell rang, the door nearest Reg opened, and she watched Ruan walk out alone.

In her old life, she would have dismissed it as a coincidence. A highly unlikely one, but a coincidence nonetheless. She was used to such things. Unlikely things did happen to her. Serendipity. Synchronicity.

In her new life, she knew what Sarah or Corvin would tell her. It was part of her psychic gifts. An intuition that told her which doors Ruan was going to come out of and when. She needed to meet him, so she was standing there when he decided, of his own accord, to leave the building before the dismissal bell had even rung. She watched to see which way he would go. He walked straight toward her. Reg waited until he was close to her before calling out.

"Ruan."

He turned his head and looked at her. His expression was blank. If he were surprised at being addressed by name by a stranger, he didn't show it.

"Ruan Rosdew. That's your name, isn't it?"

He looked around as if making sure she wasn't accompanied by someone else and that they had not attracted anyone's attention. "Who are you?"

"I'm a friend of Calliopia Papillon. Or rather... a friend of the family."

He rolled his shoulders in a shrug. "So?"

His clothes, Reg saw close up, had been well-tailored at some point. But they were old and worn and had been mended numerous times. Like clothes that had been passed through a long line of boys, even though he was the only Rosdew she had found in the recent yearbooks. He carried a damp, earthy odor. Not sweat or body odor, but a musty scent. His hair appeared to be uncombed. That was a teenage boy for you. Some of them went to excessive lengths to look just right, with not a single hair out of place, and some refused to attend to any personal hygiene at all.

"Did you know that Callie is missing?"

He considered her for a moment before nodding. "Yes. I heard that."

"You two were friends, weren't you?"

He shook his head. "No. I never had anything to do with her."

"She liked you."

His eyebrows went up, making him look even more childlike. "No one likes me." He didn't say it in an angry or depressed way, but as if he was simply stating a fact. As if he would have been surprised if someone did like him.

"Callie did. She wrote about you in her diary." Reg bit her lip after saying that. She should really not have revealed such a thing. If they rescued Callie and she ended up going back to school with

Ruan, she would be mortified that he knew she had written about him.

Ruan didn't act as if this were a revelation to him or of any interest. He just shook his head.

"You know who Callie is."

"Yes."

"Did you like her?"

"No." Again, a simple fact. Ingenuous. Unconcerned. Not that he'd hated her because of the feud, or loved her in spite of it. No embarrassment or teenage drama. As if he'd never given Calliopia Papillon a second thought. Maybe he never had. She didn't detect any signs of deception from him and she was usually a pretty good lie detector.

Was the whole idea of star-crossed lovers a false trail? Maybe the kidnapping had nothing at all to do with Ruan or the Rosdews. Just because their families had a feud going on, that didn't mean that the Rosdews had been the ones to take her.

Jessup had said that Callie was interested in the Rosdew boy, but Reg couldn't see any reason she would be. It was possible she had admired him from afar and he had never known it, but what would she admire him for? How short and childlike he was?

Or maybe… Reg flashed back to her own days in high school. Maybe he had just said a kind word to her. Something that he didn't even remember, but she did. School could be a cruel place, full of bullying and scorn. For someone like Calliopia, it could be a very lonely place.

Reg had hated school. She was always the new kid, poor, a weirdo foster kid who didn't fit in. She made friends quickly, but they weren't the kind of friends she'd keep for life. They were friends that she worked hard to entertain, so that if she were lucky, she wouldn't have to sit alone for lunch. It wasn't about who she was, but about giving them what they wanted so that she would be accepted.

Maybe Ruan had just not been mean to Calliopia. Maybe he had bumped into her in the hallway and apologized for it. Or had given her a compliment or asked her opinion. For an outcast, such a tiny thing could mean everything to her.

"Did you guys take the same bus?" Reg asked, trying to find the thread between them and hoping to discover how Callie had disappeared.

"We do not take the bus." Ruan shook his head and laughed. "No."

"When was the last time you saw Callie?"

"I do not know."

He made no apparent attempt to remember and Reg felt suddenly cold. Any normal person would have at least been curious enough to think back on the last time they had seen a missing person. And a normal person talking to someone investigating a kidnapping should have at least made some show of caring and giving himself an alibi.

Maybe there was a reason Reg wasn't getting any tells from Ruan.

Not because he was innocent, but because he was a psychopath. He didn't have to cover his guilt; he didn't even feel it.

But Reg had a new weapon in her arsenal. She didn't have to look for those infinitesimal physiological changes. She could use her psychic skills to test whether he were telling the truth and find out what he knew. She focused her attention on Ruan. First on the space around his body, his aura. His spiritual energy.

It was dark and cold. Like the smell he carried, it felt damp and musty. No, not a boy who had once said a kind word to Callie in school. He had no warmth about him. Reg brought her attention down to skin level. He was pale, but not as blue-white as Calliopia's parents. Their paleness reminded her of starlight, but his of the squirming white maggots that lived under a stump or rock.

Reg delved into his mind, taking care, not wanting to alarm him or to go into a trance that would give him some indication of what she was up to. He was, she sensed, older than she had thought. There was nothing boyish about his mind. Was it a case of possession? And older spirit imposing itself on Ruan's mind? She wasn't sure if she believed in such things, but she hadn't been sure about other psychic phenomena either, and had not believed in real witchcraft or the other things she had recently had to come to terms with. Maybe demonic possession was real and Ruan was under the control of some older, angrier spirit.

She was thrown abruptly out of Ruan's mind with a violence so palpable that she staggered backward. He looked at her, eyes wide and innocent. But she could now see beyond his outward appearance, to the cunning craftiness behind those wide, childlike eyes.

"Do you not know it is rude to enter one's mind without permission?"

"I'm… sorry. It was an accident. I'm still learning how to use my… gifts. I was curious and I… I'm sorry, I breached the barrier without meaning to."

He took a step back from her, his eyes never leaving hers. Reg felt mesmerized by his gaze. Not like she felt with Corvin; she felt no physical attraction to him, but he held her there, unable to move. Corvin's words echoed in her mind. *They do have their own brand of magic. Their own ways of luring prey.*

She tried to look away from him or to close her eyes.

"No," Ruan said aloud, still holding her.

"I said I'm sorry," Reg said. "It was a mistake."

"It was a mistake," Ruan agreed in his prepubescent voice. "This isn't any of your business. Stay out of it."

"But if you've taken that girl…"

"You don't know anything about it."

With an enormous effort, Reg managed to pull herself away from his gaze. He made a grunt of protest and took a step closer to her. Reg kept distance between them, being careful not to look back into his face. She felt half-blind not being able to meet his eyes to read his expression and body language, but she wasn't about to let him get control of her again.

"Kidnapping is wrong," she told him.

"Yes."

Reg was thrown by his agreement and caught herself just before she met his eyes again. She was sure it had been a ploy to get her to do just that.

"Yes?" she repeated. "If you know it's wrong then why won't you tell me what you know?"

"Stay out of piskie business."

"What?"

"Human creatures have no business getting involved in piskie dealings. You and the rest of your people must stay out of it."

"I thought your name was Rosdew."

But maybe they were part of a larger clan. Jessup hadn't mentioned it to her, because she hadn't wanted Reg to get involved. She had misjudged how helpful Reg could be to the investigation.

"If you want to know what happened to the girl, I will tell you."

Reg looked at him. His offer appeared to be genuine. His gaze met hers unflinchingly. She realized her mistake too late.

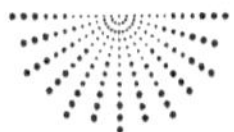

CHAPTER TEN

The eyes are the windows to the soul.

She had spent so many years reading people's faces, looking for danger and deception while carefully guarding her own expression to protect herself and get what she needed, that looking into the boy's eyes was her natural reaction to his surprising offer. She wanted to gauge his expression and see what he was trying to pull. Ruan was a convincing liar, but she knew he wasn't telling her the truth. She immediately wanted to verify it in his eyes.

And he had a hold on her again. Stronger this time. He wasn't going to let her go or be taken off guard. Rather than pulling away, Reg went for the opposite. He'd pushed her away once when she had looked into his mind. He would do it again. She looked past his eyes, delved again into his brain. She felt for any sign of Callie and his recollections of her.

They wrestled, gazes locked on each other. A battle of wills. Reg had been told that her powers were significant, but struggling with Ruan, she didn't feel like it. She had needed the assistance of Starlight to break Uriel Hawthorne's spell, and she wished she had him with her in her fight against Ruan. But Starlight was gone and she was too far from the cottage to hope that he might feel her need and come to her aid.

Holding her paralyzed, Ruan stepped forward and grabbed her by the arm. His fingers were like iron, far too strong for his diminutive body. Reg grabbed him to pull his hand off of her. There was initial resistance, and then Ruan gave a cry and let her go. He rubbed his arm where she had grasped him, looking at her with those wide, childlike eyes. He broke his gaze and looked at her hand. It throbbed and Reg knew she was bleeding again.

Ruan muttered something she didn't understand, turned in a full circle, and then ran, ducking behind a low stone wall and disappearing from sight. Reg stood frozen for a moment, then ran after him. She jumped over the wall to pursue him, but he was gone.

There was no sign of Ruan Rosdew.

* * *

Reg searched up and down the length of the wall, looking into the trees that surrounded the private school, but she could see no sign of the boy. The school bell rang, and students poured out the doors. Not wanting anyone to see her lurking in the woods and think she was a danger to the students, Reg walked briskly back to her car and sat down.

For a few minutes, she just sat in the car with the air conditioner blowing on her, running through what had just happened in her head. Ruan had as much as admitted that he knew what had happened to Callie, despite his earlier denials. If he didn't know what had happened, he wouldn't be able to claim that it was family business. She needed to let Jessup know that there was definitely a connection between the kidnapping and the Rosdew family.

But even as she reached for her phone, Reg knew she couldn't tell Jessup her discovery. Not only was she not supposed to be investigating on her own, but she had done exactly what Jessup had said that she wanted to avoid, spooking Ruan and sending him running.

Blood had soaked through the bandage on her hand and Reg didn't have bandages or any kind of first aid kit in the car. If she had been Erin, she would have been prepared. Erin was always obsessing over planning and making lists, and she would have had everything she needed right there at hand. Reg, on the other hand, always seemed to be lacking for something.

Her hand was throbbing and she was shivering with cold. She turned the air conditioning off and waited for her body to warm up. In a few minutes she was again sweating in the Florida heat and decided she'd better head home. Halfway there, she was shivering again. She swore to herself. Either she was coming down with the flu, or her wound had become infected.

She'd been careful to keep it clean, but maybe there had been something on the knife and she hadn't been quick enough to get antiseptic on the wound. She swore at Hawthorne-Rose. She really didn't have anything to complain about, considering he had put Warren into a magical coma and could have done the same to her, but she was still irritated with him for not keeping his blade clean.

* * *

Once home, she looked around again for Starlight, calling his name up and down the street, but it would seem the cat was gone for good. She walked back into her cottage, feeling lonely and abandoned. It didn't make any sense; she'd lived alone all her adult life but had only had a cat for a short period of time. So why should she miss him so much? He'd been nothing but a bother during the time she'd had him, biting her, complaining, and giving her all sorts of attitude. But she had gotten attached to the furball and missed having him around.

On the kitchen counter there was another flyer, this one about a community celebration, which apparently included a potluck, a dance, and some business development opportunities. Reg stood looking at it.

Sarah kept giving them to her. Corvin had also pushed her to start attending some of the community events. Maybe they were right. It would be good not only for her business, but for her personally. She wouldn't feel so lonely if she knew more people in the neighborhood and could find some people she had something in common with. And maybe she wouldn't be so strongly attracted to Corvin if there were someone else in her life.

There was a knock at the door. Reg turned to see Sarah open it, but she remained on the doorstep instead of entering as she usually would have. Her body language was tentative.

"I saw you out looking… but no sign of Starlight?"

"No," Reg sighed. She made an inviting motion to Sarah. "You can come in."

Sarah didn't need a second invitation. She entered, shutting the door carefully behind her. Locking the barn after the horse was gone.

"I'm so sorry," she apologized again. "Have you called the pound to see if he was picked up?"

"Yeah, I did that earlier. They put me on a list, but I'm still supposed to call in every few days in case someone forgets to call me back."

Reg carefully removed the sagging, blood-soaked bandage from her hand to examine the cut. Sarah got closer to have a look at it.

"Oh, that looks bad." She took Reg's hand gently to look at it close up, turning it in the light and giving it a couple of light prods. "That must really hurt. You should go to Letticia. She is very expert in magical healing. She could tell you just what to do."

"I already know what I need to do. Clean it, bandage it, and let it rest. It's just so hard when it's a hand. And my dominant hand too. I can't stop using it."

"If you don't, this might get a lot worse," Sarah said darkly. "I really don't like the looks of it. It didn't look like this when you first got it."

"No. It's infected. I'll put some antibiotic cream on it and take an aspirin. It will be fine."

"You should have Letticia look at it. I'll give her a call."

"You don't need to do that."

Sarah glanced over at the flyer Reg had been looking at, maybe detecting that it had been moved a quarter of an inch away from its original position.

"Are you going to go?"

"Maybe. I guess I should start getting to know more people in the community."

Sarah nodded her agreement. She tapped the flyer with on finger. "This is at one of those big houses out by the sanctuary. They're always so lavish. It's fascinating to see how the more... elite of our community live."

"Out near the Papillons' house?" Reg asked, immediately interested.

"Yes, one of their closest neighbors. Just terrible to hear about their daughter, wasn't it? They must be going crazy with worry."

"If they're a magical family, why can't they just cast some kind of spell to find out where she is? Or to bring her back home?"

Sarah gave a little laugh. "It's not quite as easy as all that," she said, shaking her head. "The books and movies always overstate things... they make magic look like a circus act. But that's not what it's like. It's far more subtle than that."

"But they should be able to do something, shouldn't they?"

"They probably are. But that doesn't guarantee anything, especially if... there were other practitioners involved."

And Reg happened to know that it was, in fact, the case.

"You know the Papillons?" she asked.

"Yes, of course. They've been around here as long as I have, maybe longer. That doesn't make us best friends, mind," Sarah cautioned. "Most of the time, we do our own thing and they do theirs. But we do have some contact." She motioned to the flyer.

"Some social events. With what's going on with their daughter, I don't know if the Papillons will be there. But others from their clan will be."

"What are they like?"

"What are they like...?" Sarah hummed, thinking about it. "They are... powerful... haughty... reserved... that makes it sound like I have something against them, but believe me, I don't. I'm just being honest and plainspoken... they wouldn't want me to suggest they had qualities that they don't. They prefer to be thought of as distinct. It's not bad to consider them different than we are. They are what they are."

Reg nodded slowly. "They were very beautiful and so was their house. Their castle. Although Calliopia..."

"She hadn't yet come into her own. She would, in time." Sarah leaned closer to Reg. "I haven't been inside the castle before. What was it like?"

"Very big... spacious... When I think of a castle, I always think of all of the art work and fine things, but there wasn't really a lot of decoration. There were beautiful plants and gardens."

"Ah," Sarah nodded. "There would be! They are very close to nature. It doesn't surprise me that they would want to bring the outdoors inside."

"I think maybe I'd better go," Reg said, looking down at the flyer. "Maybe..." She didn't complete the thought. Maybe she could solve the case. Maybe she could find out vital bits of information from the guests at the party and figure out what had happened to Calliopia and where she was being held. It was best not to tell Sarah that. Let her think that Reg was just going for the social aspect.

"What you need to do now is go dress that wound. Come up to the house after you have had a rest and I will help you to get ready for the party."

CHAPTER ELEVEN

Going to the old crone's to get dressed for the party might not have sounded like much fun, but Reg knew from Sarah helping her to get ready for a date with Corvin that Sarah had a treasure trove of gowns and jewelry that would have put a fashion designer to shame. Never mind that Sarah was an overweight, grandmotherly woman. She apparently hadn't always been. Or else she collected clothing as a hobby. Reg did as she was told, taking care of her hand and having a nap to prepare for being out most of the night. As the afternoon drew on, she headed up to the big house.

Sarah already had several gowns picked out and was fluttering from one place to another looking at various accessories and accouterments. "See what you like, my dear, and tell me if you want something different. It will be full formal, but that still gives you plenty of latitude. Floor-length skirts are best, but what shape you prefer is up to you, jacket or bare shoulders, hair up. No masks."

"Masks?" Reg repeated.

Sarah nodded. "No incognito," she said, as if that were a perfectly normal thing to specify for a community dance.

Reg picked a shimmering gold dress and held it up, first in

front of her and then pressed against her body. It was beautiful, but a bit more showy than she wanted. She didn't want to blend in with the background, but she didn't want to be the focal point of the room either. A satiny red dress caught her eye, and she picked that one up next.

"I wouldn't normally recommend a red dress for a redhead," Sarah commented. "But your hair is dark enough I think you can pull it off."

"I don't think I've ever had something this color before." Reg held it against her. The luxurious feel of the fabric drew her to it even more.

"Try it on."

Reg took the mounds of cloth to one of the bedrooms to try it on. As before, it seemed like Sarah might have a little magic on her side, since the dress fit Reg like a glove. It was off the shoulders, with crossed straps over the bust and long drapes of sheer cloth that pooled on the floor. At the waist that fitted to her like it had been altered on the spot, was a gold dragonfly embellishment.

She gathered up the train and went back to where Sarah was muttering over hair accessories.

"Ah, beautiful," Sarah exclaimed, clapping her hands together. "You have the perfect figure. Dresses love you. Really, it's too bad that trousers are *de rigueur* for everyday wear now. You really are made for gowns."

Reg had to admit that she liked the way she looked in a dress and frequently chose one when pants would have done just as well.

"Now let's put your braids up and find you some jewelry. And shoes."

"Are you going to go?"

"Oh, certainly."

Reg glanced at the clock on the wall. "Then you'll need time to get ready too. I can do my hair myself, if you have a few bobby pins."

"Nonsense. I don't take any time to get ready. Come sit down and we'll take care of it."

Reg would just have formed the braids into a quick knot or bun, but Sarah fiddled and fussed, winding them into a coil and weaving them around each other, until she was satisfied with her creation. There were gold pins holding it together, one with a dragonfly that was almost a duplicate of the one on her dress. As if they'd been made as a set. Maybe they had.

Her shoes would rarely be seen under the trailing draperies of the dress, and Reg was already a good height, so the shoes Sarah suggested were not too showy or too high.

"Dress shoes are never comfortable," Sarah sighed. "But these are as close as you're going to get. You can stay on your feet for several hours in these, dance as required, and not have blisters or numb feet by the end of the night."

They felt good when Reg put them on, but she knew that as Sarah said, her feet would be sore by the end of the night anyway.

Reg knew gloves were going to be way too warm in the Florida heat, but Sarah insisted they were necessary to cover up her bandaged hand.

Sarah provided a few choices of necklaces and other jewelry. Reg looked them over.

"And have you put spells on any of these?" she demanded. "It was a bit of a shock last time."

Sarah had the grace to blush. She fanned her pink cheeks with her hand. "I figured you could use every protection you could get against Corvin's glamour," she said. "Maybe I should have told you, but..."

"As it turned out, you were right," Reg admitted. "I should have listened to you and not even gone out with him."

Sarah's eyes were downcast. "Perhaps I should have told you more. But... such things are just not discussed in polite company. Men like Corvin... well..." She shook her head. "What they do is unspeakable."

Reg wouldn't have understood that before, but after going

through what she had with him, she had to agree. She was loath to even put it into words. Of course, that compounded the problem. Not talking about him to other women could put them at risk with Corvin.

But as everyone seemed to know more about him than she did, she didn't have to agonize over how to warn anybody else about him.

"Let's not talk about that right now," Sarah said, demonstrating her distaste for the subject. "We are getting ready for a party. There are no spells on any of these pieces, although some of them have a small amount of power themselves." Her hand hovered over a necklace with a large blood-red crystal. "Just pick what you like."

Reg looked again at the clock. "Why don't I try some of these things on while you go change. I don't want to hold you up."

Sarah seemed to hesitate.

"I'm not going to steal anything," Reg said sharply. "You know all of what's here. If it goes walking off, it's not like you wouldn't know where to find me."

"I would never suggest such a thing. No. I just thought you might have more questions or need help deciding."

She withdrew, going to another part of the house to do her own magical transformation. Reg swallowed and watched her go, feeling anxious. There had been many times in the past when bits of jewelry or heirlooms *had* disappeared when she'd been in the same room with them. Maybe it was the fact that she wasn't planning on taking anything from Sarah that had made her hesitance sting. If Reg had been planning to take something, she would have just laughed it off.

She tried to push the anxious thoughts and feelings to the side, shoving them to one corner of her mind where they wouldn't bother her, and tried on each piece of jewelry in front of the mirror, making her choice slowly and methodically.

* * *

It seemed like Sarah could only have been gone for five minutes when Reg heard her returning. She looked up to see if Sarah had forgotten something she needed in order to get changed.

But Sarah's boast that it would take her no time at all to get changed was true. She wore a floor-length gown with a deep forest green pattern. It had a square neckline and long sleeves, and she wore a simple pendant of the largest emerald Reg had ever seen. Reg moved closer to get a look at it.

"That's amazing. It's real, isn't it?"

"Of course it's real, Reg dear. What would be the point of wearing glass?"

"It really is incredible."

The emerald hung from a thick gold chain woven like a rope. It caught the light and reflected it back, making it look like it was glowing. It even seemed to be radiating warmth and a feeling of calm. Sarah smiled and patted it like it was alive.

"One of my greatest treasures."

"And you have it just laying around the house? I would have it in a safety deposit box in a bank. One with a really good vault. I'd be afraid to wear it anywhere."

"Hiding it away in a bank would defeat the purpose of owning it," Sarah pointed out. "Are you ready to go?"

Reg nodded, displaying her jewelry selections for Sarah. Sarah nodded and took Reg by the arm. "Then we're off."

"Do you want me to drive?" Reg offered. Her car was smaller, and might not be comfortable for an older lady, but Reg wasn't particularly comfortable with Sarah's driving skills. She wanted to get to the party in one piece, preferably without a bloody nose.

"No, I've arranged for transportation."

Reg's heart sank. Sarah placed Reg's hand on her arm as if Reg were escorting Sarah somewhere rather than the opposite. She took Reg down the wide stairs of the grand staircase to the great room, and then out to the curb. But rather than Sarah's black jeep, there was a stretch limo. Reg couldn't have been more surprised if it had been a pumpkin carriage with six white horses.

"You hired a limo?"

Sarah just smiled.

"Are we picking anyone up? Do you have a date?"

"Just us, Regina."

The driver got out and held the doors for them. Reg slid in beside Sarah. Lots of leg room. Sumptuously upholstered seats. Drinks available. TV screens and tablets. Reg sat back, sinking into the seat, and just enjoyed the ride. No worries about getting her long train dirty or tangled up around the pedals of her car. No worries about Sarah's maniacal driving. She could just sit back and enjoy.

CHAPTER TWELVE

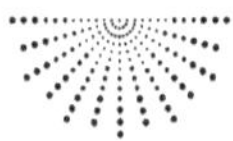

*S*arah wasn't the only one who had hired a limo service for the party. There was a long line of limos queued along the driveway, inching forward to drop off their passengers and then turning around to find a place to park while they waited for the revelries to end.

Reg's mouth dropped open when she saw that there were a few horse-drawn carriages making their way to the party as well. She peered out the window in amazement. It was like prom, only better.

Actual horse-drawn carriages!

The limo crept down the drive. Reg and Sarah watched everyone who got out ahead of them, admiring the gowns and costumes on show. It was so different from the community potluck that Reg had imagined, she could hardly comprehend it. She'd half-expected burgers on a grill, casseroles, and salad mixes being heaped onto paper plates while everyone stood around chatting in jeans and t-shirts. Even though Sarah had told her that it was full formal. Even prom had only been cracker canapés and punch in plastic cups, despite the formalwear and limo services some of the kids had been wealthy enough to hire. Reg had said she wasn't going to go to prom, but at the last minute had put on a thrift store gown and made her way to the school to check it out. For all of the planning and anticipation the other girls had put into it, it had still just been high school kids sweating in the gymnasium.

Along the driveway leading to the mansion, there were white twinkle lights adorning all of the trees. The lights alone must have taken days to string up. Unless, of course, there had been some kind of magic involved.

When they reached the mansion, footmen opened the limo doors and offered a hand to the women to help them out of the car. Reg gathered up her skirts, but it was only a few steps from the car to the red carpet, and then she didn't have to worry about her train dragging in the dirt.

She and Sarah walked side by side to the house, and at the door to the ballroom, their names were announced to the room, though neither of them had given their names to the herald. They joined the group that had gathered there ahead of them, chatting pleasantly while waiters circulated with drinks and dainties.

Reg stuck close to Sarah. She was there to mix—and to see if she could find anything out about Calliopia's kidnapping—so she'd stay close to Sarah and get her to introduce Reg to everyone.

Sarah nodded and smiled at a few people before heading toward a tall, pouchy-faced woman in a green turban.

"Marian," she greeted warmly, holding her hand out. The two women started out looking as though they were going to shake hands, and then embraced, cheeks pressed briefly together in an air kiss, then drew apart again. "I want you to meet Reg Rawlins, a new talent in town."

"Oh yes," Marian said, looking Reg over and giving her a cool nod. "I have heard of Ms. Rawlins' talents."

Sarah smiled, acting as though she didn't hear the bile in Marian's voice. "You're both in the same business. Mediums."

"Ah." Reg nodded, understanding. Marian was the competition. She'd heard about Reg and maybe she was afraid Reg was going to steal her business. The story about Warren Blake had made some waves around town. And there had also been Amy Calvert, a woman who had made the rounds to all of the psychics in the area, who had been singing Reg's praises nonstop. "It's a pleasure to meet you, Miss Marian."

"Yes, it's lovely that you could make it. Always nice to meet someone in the business. These events are so important to keeping up on what's going on in the community."

Marian grabbed a drink from one of the trays circulating around the room. Reg was suddenly thirsty herself, a strong craving hitting her in the gut. She took a drink from the same waiter and looked at Marian speculatively. Was the craving for drink emanating from her? If so, was it because that was what she was feeling, or because she was hoping to push Reg into drinking too much and making a fool of herself?

She turned to Sarah indicating the drink with her eyes. "Is it… safe?" she asked in a murmur. Who knew what kind of drinks they served a such a party. The food and drink she'd had with Corvin had been intoxicating, and she wasn't sure it had been just his influence. She didn't know what kinds of drugs or mind-altering ingredients might be considered acceptable in the paranormal community.

Sarah surprised Reg by taking the glass from her hand to examine it and give it a sniff. She handed it back. "Safe," she pronounced, "but very strong. Best consumed by the thimbleful."

Reg looked back at Marian, who, in apparent defiance of Sarah's advice, threw back almost her entire glass, then wiped her mouth with the back of her hand. Reg watched a red flush rise from Marian's boxy bosom up her neck to suffuse her cheeks. Her eyes rolled up and Reg thought for a moment that she was going to pass out on the spot. But Marian regained her equilibrium and stared at Reg. Reg again felt the wave of thirst and desire. It was definitely coming from Marian, and she was doing it deliberately. Reg returned her glass to another waiter's tray, determined not to take any intoxicants. Let Marian make a fool of herself; Reg was going to stay grounded.

"Oh, you must try these," Sarah nearly squealed, indicating a tray of desserts circulating nearby. "If you get nothing else from this party, you have to taste the cakes."

Sarah helped herself to one colorful, delicately decorated morsel with each hand. Reg selected a delicious-looking fairy cake for herself.

"They look too beautiful to eat."

"And they taste even better." Sarah pointed to the tiny rosebud decorating Reg's cake. "That is an actual rose, crystallized in sugar. You'll never find anything like this in a bakery."

Reg examined the beautiful decorations before taking a small bite. The light, airy cake melted in her mouth, filling it with a tangy sweet lemon flavor.

"Delicious!"

Sarah nodded, her mouth too full of cake to respond.

"Hello, ladies."

Reg knew from the voice and the warm flush who it was before she turned around.

"Corvin."

Sarah looked at Corvin, scowling. "What are you doing here?"

"It's a community party. I'm part of the community."

"You'd better behave yourself."

He smiled, touching her arm. "Is that any way to treat a fellow guest?"

Sarah's expression softened and her eyes lost focus. She smiled.

"Really, Corvin?" Reg challenged. "Charming Sarah?"

"Jealous, Regina?" He removed his hand from Sarah's arm.

Reg stepped back before he could touch her.

Corvin frowned. "What's wrong with your hand?"

Reg looked down at her injured hand, which looked perfectly normal with the glove pulled on over the bandage. No blood had seeped through the glove and for once it was not throbbing.

"What do you mean?"

"It's..." he searched for a word, "darkened. What have you been doing?"

Reg bent her fingers into a fist and straightened them again, testing the pain level. It was still painful to move. "It's the one Hawthorne-Rose cut."

He swore.

Reg gulped. "What does that mean? What's wrong?"

"I don't know. The blade he used—do you still have it?"

"No. The police took it when they arrested him."

Sarah's voice was far away. "What are you talking about?"

"The wound on her hand. Have you looked at it?"

Corvin shook Sarah, trying to bring her back to earth. "Sarah! Pay attention. Come back."

Sarah blinked owlishly. She turned her head back and forth, then shook it. "Don't touch me."

He withdrew his hand. "I'm not charming you, I'm trying to wake you up."

"I'm awake. I'm fine."

"Reg's hand."

Sarah's eyes dropped to Reg's injured hand, then she looked back at Corvin. "What about it?"

"Have you looked at it? What's going on?"

"It's infected. I told her to see Letticia. She put antiseptic on it. It's an allopathic remedy, but it should work."

"No. That's not going to solve the problem. You can't see how it's changed?"

"Changed?" Sarah echoed. She looked at Reg, eyelids partially closed. "No… changed how?"

Reg held her right hand in her left, looking at it, panic starting to rise. "Are you kidding? You're just trying to scare me, aren't you?"

Corvin must be having a little fun with her. Seeing if he could fool her.

"It must have been a magical blade," Corvin said. "It had some kind of power. Had been used for some kind of ritual. And it's… causing a reaction. It's not just the physical infection. It's affecting you on a higher level."

"Higher?"

"Psychic. Spiritual. A higher level."

"That's not real." In spite of all of her experiences in Black Sands, Reg tried to make it all go away. There were no psychic powers. No spirits. Nothing could affect her on a more profound level than her physical body. Not without her choice.

Corvin look at her hand, frowning. He breathed out heavily, and masked his expression. "Well, nothing is going to change tonight. We can talk to Letticia tomorrow. See if we can get the blade from Jessup to examine it. Tonight, you're here to have fun."

Reg deliberately relaxed her shoulders. Her hand wasn't going to fall off or burst into flames. It would be just fine until they had a chance to investigate it further. She could go back to enjoying the party until then.

"You scared me!" She gave Corvin a little shove with her other hand. "Don't do that!"

"I'm sorry, Regina," he apologized humbly. "How can I make it up to you?"

She braced herself against the wave of warm feelings and the heady scent of roses that swept over her.

"A dance?" he suggested.

Reg had been eyeing the dance floor, watching the graceful couples in fantastic costumes floating around it, following the cadence of the orchestral music. She'd always liked to dance. And who else was she going to get the chance to dance with? Corvin was one of the few men she knew in the community. Who else was going to ask her? Bill, the bartender at The Crystal Bowl?

"Come on," Corvin encouraged. "Let's make this a night you'll never forget."

Tempting, but she'd already had one such night with him, and didn't wish to repeat it.

"I can't. You'll enthrall me."

He looked at her with dark, glittering eyes. "Not without your permission."

"If you use your powers on me, then that's not giving permission. It's no different than if I was drunk or drugged."

He gave her a pout. "You don't understand the rules of our community. It's allowed."

"No. Not with me. I'm telling you right now, the answer is no. And if you magic me, it's still no, even if you can trick me into saying yes. You use your powers, it's an automatic no."

Corvin scowled. "That's not playing fair."

"*You* don't play fair."

"You can't say that."

"You said it's a contract, right? Well, that's the first clause of my contract. No magic or the rest of the contract is void."

He stared at her for a few long seconds, then turned and strode away. Reg felt his absence immediately, like a hole in her gut. She wanted him to come back. She wanted to fill that hole, and for him to be there with her every day. But she couldn't let her loneliness rule her.

CHAPTER THIRTEEN

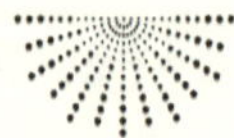

Sarah chuckled softly. "Well, you told him," she said with admiration. "Let him chew on that for a while. Meanwhile, you and I have more partying to do!"

Reg tried to lose herself, focusing on the music and the food and the fabulous outfits. While everyone who came in gave the appearance of being human, there were a few Reg found herself wondering about. Skin tones that crept into the blues and greens, just vague enough for her to attribute it to the lighting. Tattoos. Pointed teeth. Bizarre body modifications that must have cost thousands of dollars in surgery.

But most looked just like anyone else. It all seemed like a game, Sarah identifying them as witches, mediums, fortune-tellers, or practicers of other arts. It couldn't really be true. Not all of it. But it was fun.

Reg had met a few of the partiers before, at The Crystal Bowl or other places she had visited. A lot more people seemed to know who she was than she recognized or had heard about. It made sense, considering she was the newcomer and her recent exploits had been discussed around the community. Maybe they had even been written up in one of the community newsletters Sarah was forever dropping off for her. Reg hadn't taken the time to read them. The magical community of Black Sands didn't seem to have fully adopted the internet. There were those like Letticia who didn't even approve of phones. She probably would have preferred the community newsletters to be hand lettered on parchment rather than photocopied at the nearest office supplies store.

"Is Letticia coming tonight?" she asked Sarah.

Sarah raised her brows, shaking her blond head. "No, I wouldn't expect so. Why? Is your hand bothering you?"

"No, I was just wondering. I don't know a lot of people, so I wondered if I'd see her."

"Some witches are very… introverted. Letticia keeps to herself. She wouldn't have any interest in an event like this. Way too many people."

Reg nodded, remembering Erin's friend Adele, who preferred to spend her time hidden away in the woods in the summerhouse she rented or wandering around looking for herbs or doing whatever magical things a witch did when the moon was full and high in the sky.

"Oh, look…" Sarah nodded toward the entrance, and Reg turned to see what she was looking at. A group of tall men and women, pale blue, had just come in and were consulting with each other before being presented to the company.

"Is it the Papillons? Calliopia's family?"

"Not her parents, but her kin." Sarah sighed, looking at them. "Always so stately and graceful. Even in my finery, they make me feel dumpy."

"You're not! You're beautiful. Especially tonight."

"Yes." Sarah absently rubbed the emerald at her throat. "And I think so… until I look at them."

"Well, stop looking at them then. They're unnaturally pale. In the Florida sunshine? I'm pale, and they put me to shame!"

Sarah laughed and turned away slightly. The small group approached the hall, and Reg listened to the herald announce Lord and Lady Bernier and the other members of their party. She watched them covertly, not wanting to draw Sarah's attention back to them. They did not mix with the crowds, but stayed together in a tight grouping as they moved through the room. They were, as Sarah had said, very stately.

A witch named Kathleen was talking to Sarah about recipes or potions, or recipes for potions, when she broke off from their conversation, looking past Reg.

"Well, here's trouble," she commented. "Who invited him?"

Sarah followed Kathleen's gaze. "He's back," she warned Reg.

Reg turned around, knowing who 'he' would be. Corvin was again approaching. He gave Reg a sweeping bow and offered to take her hand.

"Will you give me the honor of a dance, my lady?"

Reg shook her head, wondering whether he had been drinking and had forgotten their earlier conversation. "No, Corvin. Sorry."

He didn't withdraw his hand. "I agree to your terms," he informed her. "I will not glamour you. I will," he looked at Reg's escort, "as Sarah says, behave myself."

"Do you really think you can stop yourself? I thought it was instinctual. Built in. How are you going to just turn it off?"

"I *can* control myself. You know I have before."

"When our lives depended on it. But in an environment like this? With all of the partying and flirting going on around us? With drinks and other indulgences?"

He gave a curt nod. "I am able to abstain. I'm not an animal."

Reg stared at him steadily for a few long seconds. She did not venture so far as to enter his mind, but she did search his face and his eyes for the truth. He didn't mesmerize her like Ruan had. He raised an eyebrow and waited, hand still held out to her.

Reg looked over at Sarah. "Do you think it's safe? What would you do?"

"Corvin has as much honor as his kind are able. If he says he won't charm you… If it were me… I wouldn't go far. I'd be sure to stay within sight."

Reg swallowed and nodded. "Okay," she told Corvin, finally

giving her hand to him. "You remember your promise. No magical temptations."

"I am a man of my word," Corvin mocked Sarah's words, "as much as my kind is able."

"I want to stay where I can see Sarah and she can see me."

He gave her a little tug and separated her from her escort. "Just relax and enjoy yourself. Let yourself go."

"No way. Not this time. I'm keeping a firm grip on myself tonight."

He just smiled. "Your loss."

The crowd on the dance floor parted in front of Corvin, and in a minute, Reg was swept away by the music and the rhythm. She tried to watch the other dancers to see what they were doing, but Corvin shook his head, pulling her close against him.

"Don't try to copy everyone else. Just make it your own. You know how to waltz. Just focus on me."

Reg stopped looking at the other dancers and looked at him instead. Whether it was her psychic powers, his expressive eyes, or his hands gently leading, Reg was able to anticipate Corvin's movements and changes of direction, keeping her feet moving smoothly in rhythm with music she didn't know, never stepping on him or stumbling.

"Beautiful," Corvin complimented. "You are very talented."

"Dance was one of the few phys-ed units that I actually enjoyed."

"You're a natural. I would have assumed you'd taken more than just a few school classes."

"No, that's it. No training. I would have loved to have taken ballroom dancing privately, but foster parents... they don't have the money for things like that. You're lucky if you can get new clothes."

"Foster parents. That's who took you after your mother's death."

"Yeah. I didn't have anyone else. Or if there was anyone else, I never knew them."

"That's too bad. I would be very interested," he leaned his face ever closer to her ear, "to know who your family was."

"Why? You think they were… like me? You think they had gifts?"

"These things tend to run in families."

"Well, I can tell you that my mother never had any magical powers. If there's a word for a person who is completely normal, without any hint of paranormal powers, that's my mother."

"I thought you didn't remember Norma Jean."

Reg let Corvin spin her and bring her back into his arms, their movements perfectly coordinated.

"If she'd had the ability to see into the future, don't you think she would have provided for me? At least found someone who would have been able to take care of me instead of leaving me all by myself? Or maybe not gotten herself killed?"

"Even those who can see the future can't always see their own," Corvin advised. "Nor does seeing your own future give you the ability to change it." He stared past her, off into the distance. "You would be surprised how little ability earthbound spirits have to change their own fates."

He dipped her at the end of the song, and there was polite clapping. Corvin drew Reg back upright, nestling her close against him, far more intimate than was necessary for a waltz. He brushed her cheek with a kiss as the next song started, breathing on her neck and ear. Reg could feel his body heating up with their movement and proximity and tried to position herself a little farther away from him.

"Regina…"

"Just give me a bit of space."

"It's a dance. We're meant to be touching."

"Hands, yes. But not pasted together. Give me some more room."

He relented, letting her move more freely, but Reg had lost her sense of synchronization with his movements. She tried to lose herself in the rhythm of the music again. She was getting too warm.

"Let's take a break," she murmured.

Corvin didn't protest, but led her off the dance floor. As if he sensed what she wanted, he led her outside onto a porch. Though it was getting quite late, the moon was out, and the trees and arches of the porch were lit by tiny lights. There was a cool breeze blowing. Reg took a deep inhale, smelling the fresh tang of the ocean.

"It's a gorgeous night."

"Mm-hmm," Corvin agreed, gazing down at her. "The kind of night you wish would go on forever."

He had put a wish into her mouth the last time. Reg wasn't going to let him do it again. She didn't know what might get her into trouble.

"Everything comes to an end. Let's just enjoy this. Where we are now."

The wind changed direction and Reg's nose was suddenly filled with the scent of roses, cloying with its heady sweetness. Startled, she tried to withdraw. His hands kept her corralled.

"Corvin." She fought against the overwhelmingly pleasant feeling of his nearness. She wanted nothing more than to swim into it once again. To be surrounded and enveloped by his warmth and safety and desire. "You said you wouldn't."

"I'm not." His voice was huskier than usual.

Reg put her hands against his chest. "You are too. Let me go. I need to find Sarah."

"We don't want Sarah."

He bent down to her, and Reg couldn't remember why it was she wanted Sarah, or what it was she didn't want Corvin to do. He'd promised to keep her safe, and that's just what he was doing.

CHAPTER FOURTEEN

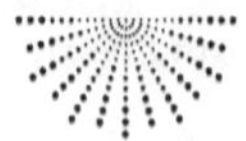

*R*elease her!"

Corvin jolted, crushing Reg against his body instead of letting her go. Reg blinked, trying to clear her mind, but she couldn't remember why she was there or what she was doing.

"Release her, or face the wrath of the kin," a tall, fair-faced man ordered, his face stern.

Reg tried to parse the words. The wrath of the kin? What kind of sense did that make? And why did the man care whether Corvin held her in his arms? Reg didn't mind, so why should he?

"This is none of your business," Corvin growled. "You don't have any say in our doings. We've agreed not to interfere with one other."

"She is protected."

Corvin's body went rigid. He looked at the tall man, scowling and shaking his head. "What do you mean, protected?"

"She has the protection of our people. It is not a matter for discussion. We will not allow you to seduce her."

Seduce? Reg almost laughed at the word. What a strange word. She didn't know why he cared what she did while in

Corvin's company. There didn't seem to be any reason for inter-ference.

"Do you hear her asking for help?" Corvin asked, as if he had read Reg's thoughts.

"She is in your thrall, unable to ask."

"She was tired of dancing. She needed some air. We're just out here to enjoy the fresh air."

"Release her, then. She can enjoy it without your hold on her."

Corvin slowly let go of Reg. Her legs were a little weak, but she steadied herself on the short wall surrounding the porch and was able to keep her feet. Corvin said she needed air, so she took breaths of clean, fresh air down into her lungs. Her mind cleared enough to wonder why she was so befuddled. She looked around, frowned at Corvin, looked at the stranger.

He was one of the men in the Bernier party, but he had sepa-rated from his friends, and until they caught up with him, the three of them were alone. Reg brought her hands up to her pounding head.

"What's going on?"

"You must not allow yourself to be alone with this witch," the stranger warned.

"No. No, I wasn't."

His eyes were blue as ice, penetrating her confusion. "Will you let me help you?"

"You already have." Corvin was no longer holding her, and that was what the stranger had wanted. What he had said Reg wanted. So all was well.

"Let me help you."

"Uh… okay."

He raised one hand and passed it in front of Reg's eyes. She blinked, awareness slowly coming back. Where was Sarah? Where was the party and the safety in numbers? She had been told not to be alone with Corvin. He had promised not to use his magical powers on her. But she knew by the scent of roses that still lingered on the porch that he had betrayed her trust. The stranger again waved his hand past Reg's face, as if blowing away the smell or brushing away the confusion that surrounded her. Things became clearer. Reg stood without the support of the wall. She looked at Corvin, anger rising up through the fog.

"You promised me. You said you wouldn't!"

"I didn't—"

"I know you did! And this guy, whoever he is, knows you did. Don't give me that crap! You did it after you said you wouldn't."

Corvin's face crumpled. He reached toward her. "Regina. I swear to you, I was doing my very best to resist. But *you* are so intoxicating, so…"

"I asked you if you could resist and you said you could."

"I thought… I thought I could. I just wanted to dance with you. I didn't think…" In spite of the fact that she wasn't trying to enter his mind, she suddenly felt his gnawing hunger, that emptiness that could only be filled if she gave her powers to him. He had tasted them before and he desperately wanted them back. Despite the fact that he'd been given powerful objects by Jessup, they hadn't been enough to satiate him. Not when Reg was right before him, so tempting and vulnerable, mere moments from ceding to him once more.

Reg clutched at her stomach, the shared sensation causing her physical pain. Nausea threatened to overcome her. She almost fell to her knees, but the strange man put his hand on her arm and helped to support her.

"Put him out of your mind," he told her. "You do not share this hunger."

Reg wanted to curl up in a ball and cry. She didn't have the strength to fight back against the horrible emptiness. In her mind, she saw Corvin as he'd been as a child, so overcome by the hunger that all he could do was writhe on the floor in the corner of the kitchen and cry, begging his mother to feed him, to make the emptiness go away. But she couldn't fill that need for him. A bowl of oatmeal wouldn't take the pain and emptiness away. A hundred bowls of oatmeal would never fill that hole.

"No," Reg cried, her knees giving way, "no, no, no… please…"

The stranger put his hand on her arm but it didn't stop the pain. He turned on Corvin. "Take it away now or I will cut you down where you stand!"

"She should know what it's like," Corvin growled. "She wouldn't deny me if she knew how I feel!"

The stranger reached into his waistcoat and drew a dagger. He advanced on Corvin. "You will release her or you will die. She is protected."

Reg sensed other movements around them, but she couldn't take her eyes away from Corvin and the tall stranger. She wanted to tell them to stop, but the pain had her retching on the ground, overcome.

"Not exactly sporting," Corvin said, looking around at the others of the Bernier party like a trapped animal.

The other man held the dagger to Corvin's chest. "Sporting?"

Corvin growled deep in his chest. The pain and longing drained out of Reg. She was on her hands and knees, long drapes of red fabric pooled around her on the white stone of the porch like blood. She breathed heavily, trying to regain her equilibrium.

A woman was at her side. One of the Bernier women, maybe Lady Bernier herself. She steadied Reg with one soft hand and brought the other up to Reg's mouth. A tiny crystal vial of red liquid.

"Drink," the woman prompted. "Take this. Take strength from us."

Reg drained the few drops into her mouth, figuring there wasn't enough there to cause her any harm, though she didn't expect it to do her any good either. It burned like acid all the way down, making Reg break out into a sweat. A chill and a shiver followed, and then warmth spread from Reg's stomach outward, strengthening her limbs. She rose awkwardly to her feet, the Lady still attending to her, encouraging her.

"Regina," Corvin spoke to her again, his voice still husky,

broken. "I swear, I never intended…"

"You broke your promise to me," Reg said. She wiped her mouth with the back of her gloved hand. The bitter taste of bile remained in her mouth. "And your… desire isn't an excuse for attacking me. It's your responsibility to control yourself."

"Yes," he agreed. "You're right. I know. I just…"

"You will be brought up before your coven for this," the stranger said, tapping his dagger against Corvin's chest. "Broken covenants. Using force. Giving her your pain. You will be cast out."

Corvin's lips pressed together. He swallowed hard. "I'll answer for my actions."

"Yes." The man withdrew his knife. "That you will."

Corvin's hands hung loosely at his sides. He made no movement toward Reg or to the man who had intervened. Lady Bernier patted Reg's cheek as though she were a little child. "You are feeling better?"

Reg gazed at her, unsure what to say. Her face burned with embarrassment. The Lady reached out and touched the dragonfly figure on Reg's dress, looking thoughtful.

Sarah pushed through a line of gawkers to get a clear view of Reg. She joined Lady Bernier at Reg's side. "Reg! Are you okay? What happened?" She looked at the Bernier party gathered around them, confusion in her eyes. She looked at Corvin. "What happened here? Is Reg sick? What are you doing out here?"

Corvin shook his head, looking down at the ground. His obvious shame answered her question.

"You and your appetites," Sarah said scathingly. "You stay away from Reg. I don't know what's gotten into you, but you can't seem to control yourself around her."

Corvin gestured toward Reg, opening his mouth to explain, but words failed him and he dropped his hand back down again.

Sarah gave a tight nod. "That's right." She looked around again at the Bernier party, her brows drawn down. "And what…?" She gave a little curtsy to the woman. "Lady Bernier…?"

The Lady made a little flutter with her fingers. "We came to the child's assistance. She was clearly ensorcelled by the warlock, at his mercy."

"Well, thank you. It is much appreciated. But… why did you?"

"She is protected."

"Protected…? But how?"

Lady Bernier raised her eyebrows. "That is of no concern."

"Well…" Sarah looked for a way to argue the point, but she couldn't come up with a reason she would need to know how Reg had obtained this protection. She shook her head. "Again, our thanks for your assistance. Reg…?"

Reg looked at her, preparing herself for the criticism that would surely come.

"Are you ready to go home?"

Reg let out her breath. "That would be… really good."

"You look like you've been through the wringer. I'm sorry, I never thought that…" Sarah looked at Corvin. "I mean, I believed that it would be okay. I'm sorry. I'm not a very good guardian."

Reg massaged her temples. "Guardian? You're not my guardian. I'm an adult. I'm big enough to take care of myself." She winced. "At least, I'm supposed to be."

"But you are a novice, living under my roof. I'm not exactly your mentor, but… I do have a responsibility to watch over you."

It seemed odd that Reg could have multiple protectors, and yet still keep getting herself into situations she needed to be rescued from. She looked at the Bernier clan, not sure what to say to them by way of appreciation. If they had not intervened when they had, she surely would have fallen prey to Corvin's wiles again, and she would not have gotten her powers back a second time.

"Thank you, sir," she told the tall stranger.

He bowed his head in acknowledgment.

Reg took Sarah's arm, and they walked back out to the front of the house, where their limousine was pulling up to the red carpet to take them home.

CHAPTER FIFTEEN

$\mathcal{S}$arah was quiet on the way home, her brooding silence unusual. Reg would have tried to fill the uncomfortable silence if she'd known what to say. She didn't want to discuss what had just happened, but she didn't want to talk about the party as if nothing had happened, either. She didn't feel like the same person going home as she had on the way there. Cinderella returning from the ball tattered and shoeless.

Reg removed her shoes in the car and rubbed her feet with her good hand. Dancing with Corvin had been incredible, until things had gotten out of hand. She'd never been to such an event before.

And she'd never known a man like Corvin. Not quite.

The car eventually pulled up in front of the house. The driver opened the doors for them, and Reg walked up the sidewalk without putting her shoes back on. The long trains of gauzy red fabric swirled around her in a breeze off the ocean.

"I'm sorry," Sarah said. "Do you want to spend the night at the house? So that you're not alone?"

Reg thought of how alone she had felt when Corvin had pushed his pain onto her. Nothing could compare to that. She preferred being by herself to having Sarah hovering over her.

"No. I'll be fine. I'll just go straight to bed anyway."

"Are you sure? I'll come back with you, make sure you get settled."

Reg didn't have the mental energy to argue with the old witch about it. She was going to accompany Reg one way or the other; there was no point in Reg wasting time and energy arguing with her.

They walked around the big house into the back yard where the guest cottage nestled in the trees. The stars were shining brightly and fireflies sparkled in the night.

Home.

Reg's eyes teared up. She didn't know why she should feel so weepy after everything was over and done. She hadn't cried while it was happening. She dabbed at her eyes, trying to be careful not to transfer mascara onto her gloves.

There was a plaintive yowl as they approached the door. Reg looked around. Starlight sat to the side of the doorstep, sounding irritated that she had stayed out so late, abandoning him outside.

"Starlight!" Reg swooped down to pick him up. She wasn't sure whether she had moved too fast or he was spooked by the billowing red cloth around her. He jumped out of the way and ran halfway across the yard. "No. Don't go away. Come inside. Come on. I'll give you some tuna."

Sarah unlocked the door and pushed it open, making inviting clicks with her tongue. "Come on, Starlight."

They both went inside, leaving the door open in the hopes that he would follow them in. Sarah went to the kitchen and shook Starlight's bowl. She opened and closed the fridge, trying to make it sound like a meal was being prepared.

"Trust a cat to come home at the most inconvenient time!"

It wasn't the most inconvenient if it meant that Reg could cuddle up with her cat for the night instead of sleeping alone, the memories of the evening replaying themselves over and over again, hearing every creak and groan of the house settling around her.

In a few minutes, she could see Starlight's eyes shining in the darkness. She watched him out the corner of her eye while getting out a can of tuna to tempt him back in. Starlight's movements were erratic, and she couldn't figure out what was going on. Then she saw that he was carrying something, dragging it into the cottage. Reg's stomach turned. The last thing she needed was Starlight dragging some dead or injured rodent in to present to her. Or worse yet, a bird, which would send Sarah off the deep end. She had made it clear when Reg had brought Starlight home that she had an affinity for birds, not cats. If she were forced to make a decision between the welfare of the birds that lived in the area and the cat, she would undoubtedly choose the birds.

But it wasn't an animal. It was some kind of plant. A tall spray of flowers, greenery, even the clump of dirty root. Had he stolen it from someone who was planting their garden?

"What are you doing, you crazy cat?" Reg asked him. She bent down and picked up the plant, examining it. Sarah moved quietly to the cottage door and closed it so that Starlight could not make another escape.

Starlight sat back on his haunches, looking at Reg. She was relieved that he was home and unscathed. She really had been worried by his disappearance. She pulled her gloves off. They had already taken enough abuse, she didn't need to get dirt and greenery ground into them as well. She checked the bandage, which seemed to be staying in place well enough. Maybe it was finally on the mend.

Starlight jumped up on the counter and Reg turned to the water faucet to flick water at him. He meowed a protest that was almost as clear to her as human speech and she turned back to him. He pressed his face into the plant, sniffing it.

"Is it catnip?" Reg asked. "Why would he drag that home?"

"Cats are strange," Sarah said with a philosophic shrug. "You can't expect them to make sense." She picked up the ragged plant, frowning. "It's certainly not catnip. I think it is yarrow." Her brows drew down farther. "I'm not a great healer, but yarrow is a well-known remedy for the healing of wounds."

Reg looked at her hand, then at Starlight, who was looking at her with strange intensity. "Do you think he brought it to me because of my hand? To heal it?"

Sarah tutted. "He's a cat. Cats don't know anything about herbs and healing. We'll leave this here for the night. I'll call Letticia to come tomorrow to take a look at your hand, and if she wants to use it…"

Reg nodded. "Yeah. Okay. Should we put it in some water?"

"It's not like it's cut flowers," Sarah pointed out. But she went to the cupboards and found a tall vase that was just right to hold it. She filled it with water and pushed the root ball down into the vase.

Starlight sniffed at the plant and looked at Reg.

"I don't know how to use it," Reg told him. "Letticia will know what to do."

Apparently satisfied with this, he jumped down from the counter and started yowling about how hungry he was.

"You're the one who ran away," Reg pointed out. "If you're hungry, you've got no one to blame but yourself."

Even so, she gave him a larger than usual helping of tuna and watched him eat it, a lump in her throat.

* * *

Reg dreamed of Calliopia again. She hadn't expected to. Calliopia's troubles had been driven out of her mind by the events at the party. But it all melded together in the dream. Calliopia was still in the cold, dark room, unable to find sleep on the uncomfortable cot, listening to all of the strange noises around her.

"I'm not one of you," she protested. "Please, let me go back."

There were arguments held just out of earshot. Reg couldn't tell what they were saying and knew only that they discussed Callie's fate. If she wouldn't cooperate with whatever they had planned for her, would they return her? Or would they do something to ensure her silence?

"She is protected." Reg heard the whisper more clearly. "If we harm her, we will answer to the council."

Just like Corvin was going to have to answer to his coven for the community laws he had broken. They would have to answer for whatever things they did to Calliopia. She lay there in the dark room, languishing, the energy slowly draining from her. Had they given her food and water? Or was she starving while they looked for her and while Reg went to parties and entertained herself as if she had not a care in the world?

Calliopia started to sing, silencing the whispers in the nearby rooms. They seemed hypnotized whenever they heard her voice. But she couldn't go on singing forever.

CHAPTER SIXTEEN

*M*orning came too soon. Reg had known it would. She'd stayed out half the night, but the sunshine still woke her up in the morning. She got up before she was ready to face the day, and washed off the sweat from tossing and turning all night. Starlight followed her into the bathroom and was sitting on the mat outside the shower waiting for her when she stepped out. He rubbed against her wet legs, pasting cat fur to her skin and making his coat stick up in little peaks.

"Feeling a little insecure this morning?" Reg asked him, trying to wipe all of the fur off with her towel. "Did you miss me? It's your own fault, you know. You're the one who went running off. I don't know why you did that. I thought you were hit by a car and never coming back."

He rubbed against her some more, making her attempts to brush the cat fur off useless. Reg got dressed and then picked him up for a cuddle. He rubbed the top of his head against her chin, purring loudly.

They were just finishing their breakfast when Sarah knocked on the door and poked her head in. "Oh, you're up, good. Are you ready for company?"

Without waiting for an answer, she opened the door and

entered. Letticia, a tall, black-haired, severe witch followed behind her. She was the leader of Sarah's coven, despised technology, and didn't give the impression that she approved of anything, including Reg herself.

She nodded to Reg. "Sarah said you have an injury that needs to be treated."

Reg unwrapped her hand and laid it on the counter for Letticia's examination. Letticia stared at it coldly for some time, and then held both hands in the air over it, tipping her head back and closing her eyes. Starlight jumped up on the counter.

"Starlight," Reg protested, and moved to push him back off.

"Leave the cat," Letticia ordered. "And stay still."

Reg put her other hand back down and waited for Letticia's verdict.

"It is bad," Letticia said baldly. "You were right to call for me."

"I know it's infected, but I put stuff on it. Antibiotic cream. It's actually looking better today." Reg dabbed at it with the bandage, grimacing. "It opened again last night. I don't understand why it won't scab over and start to heal."

"How did you do this?"

"How did *I*...? It was Hawthorne-Rose, a policeman. He was threatening me and Corvin, trying to get me to... give up the memories that Warren Blake had given me." Reg shuddered, remembering him digging the knife into her palm.

"Where is the blade?"

"The police have it. Corvin said—" Reg choked on Corvin's name, the memories of the previous night becoming too clear. "Corvin said he'd ask Detective Jessup about letting us see the knife. But I don't know if she'll allow it. It's evidence."

"It's evidence, alright," Letticia agreed. "We will need to examine it to understand what happened and properly treat this wound. We need to know why it is responding like this. And we need to know as soon as possible, before more damage is done."

Reg looked at Sarah. "Do you know how to contact her?"

"Certainly, dear." Sarah patted her pockets. "I've left my phone in the house, can I use yours?"

Reg pulled it out and slid it across the counter to Sarah.

"In the meantime, we'll do what we can for this," Letticia said. "For a magical injury like this, the first line of defense is milfoil."

"Milfoil?" Reg had never heard of it. Certainly not something in her medicine cabinet.

"Yarrow," Letticia said, "Woundwort? Staunchweed?"

Sarah and Reg both looked at the plant they had put in the vase the night before. Letticia followed their eyes.

"Good. You are prepared." She removed the plant from the vase and rinsed it under the tap, examining it closely. "You did well to keep the plant intact, including the root. Most people use just the flower, leaves, and stem, but the root is also very powerful. We have lots here to work with."

Starlight walked along the counter, purring, running his tail under Reg's nose.

"Nothing like rubbing my nose in it," Reg said. But she patted him with her uninjured hand. "You're a very smart cat, aren't you? Much smarter than your owner."

He purred louder, rubbing his jowls and fangs on her hand. Reg laughed, her mood lightening.

"I would say most cats are smarter than their owners," Letticia said without turning back around. "But most still do not have the gifts that this one does. He is very aware of you. Very concerned with your injury." She used her fingers to separate and scrub the stringy roots of the yarrow. "Most cats are not healers, other than their instinctive knowledge about wound cleanliness."

"He ran off," Reg explained, "he was gone for two days, and he brought back that yarrow plant with him."

Letticia turned and looked at Starlight, who sat back on his haunches, stretching himself up tall, like a cat in ancient Egyptian art. He twitched his whiskers at her.

"Did he indeed?" Letticia asked, but there was no doubt in her voice. "As I said, he's a very wise cat."

Sarah put Reg's phone back down on the counter as it started to ring in speakerphone mode. After a few rings, it was picked up.

"Detective Jessup."

"Marta, it's Sarah Bishop and Reg Rawlins," Sarah announced. "We are calling to ask about the knife—"

"Reg Rawlins," Jessup's voice was displeased. "I was going to call on you today."

"Uh... yes?" Reg wasn't sure what to say about that. Her heart immediately started pumping faster and she wondered whether it was time to put Black Sands in her rear-view mirror. She did *not* like attention from the police.

"From my inquiries, I am led to believe that you showed up at Calliopia's school and talked to Ruan Rosdew yesterday."

"Um..."

"I don't know a lot of other women with red hair in cornrows in Black Sands, Ms. Rawlins."

Reg thought of all of the students pouring out the doors of the school as she hurried to get back to her car after Ruan's disappearance. How many of them had seen and described her?

"Yes," she admitted.

"And what happened during that meeting?"

"Not really anything... why?"

"I think we'd better meet."

"We were hoping to be able to see the knife that Hawthorne-Rose had," Sarah interjected.

There was silence for a few seconds as Jessup pondered this. "Why?" she asked finally.

Reg was relieved that Jessup hadn't immediately said no.

"Reg was injured with that knife and it apparently had magical properties," Sarah said. "Letticia needs to examine it to treat the wound properly."

"I'll bring it with me," Jessup agreed. There was no warmth in her voice. "Where are you now? At home?"

"At the cottage," Sarah agreed.

"I'll be there shortly."

Jessup disconnected. Sarah looked at Reg, raising her eyebrows.

"Well… it's good that she's coming right over…"

Reg looked at the door. There was no point in running, but she couldn't deny the impulse she felt to make herself scarce. They needed Jessup and the knife, if Reg were to believe what Letticia and the others said. Her injury wasn't just infected and it wasn't going to heal on its own. If she left without the proper examination of the knife and whatever incantation was required over the wound, who knew what would happen. She didn't want to end up losing her hand. Or worse.

CHAPTER SEVENTEEN

Letticia was busy with the yarrow, methodically shredding and chopping it into fine bits. Reg watched her, wondering whether she was going to have to drink a tea made of the concoction or whether it would be made into a poultice that went directly on the wound. She hoped that Letticia knew what she was doing and it would not end up like the case Erin had told her about, where foxglove had been used instead of something called boneknit in a poultice, resulting in the death of the patient. Reg suddenly wished that she lived closer to Erin and her witch friend Adele, who seemed to be very knowledgeable about herbs. Reg had to rely on the words of Sarah and Corvin that Letticia was a competent healer. She obviously couldn't trust anything that came out of Corvin's mouth. She wasn't sure Sarah's judgment was much more reliable.

"Here she is," Sarah announced, watching out the front window.

Reg decided she was safe to move away from the examination table to answer the door and let Detective Jessup in.

For a small woman, she looked remarkably menacing. She didn't bluster and threaten, just stood there in the doorway until Reg motioned her in, feeling like she'd been called before the school principal. She'd had female principals, and they were always worse than the men. A man might be swayed by doe eyes and weeping, but not a woman.

Jessup looked around the cottage. She went to the kitchen island and laid down an evidence bag containing a dagger.

"You can look at it, but it stays sealed in the bag," she informed Letticia. "It's evidence, and if it is out of my sight or removed from the bag, it will be compromised and we won't be able to use it in the court case."

Letticia nodded. She left the mass of green bits on the cutting board and studied the knife through the plastic. Reg couldn't see it clearly from across the room, but its mere presence made her hand throb. She flashed back to the incident and once again she was pinned to the wall by Hawthorne-Rose, the knife cutting into her. She'd been terrified, unable to give him what he'd wanted no matter how he hurt her. But the torture had worked on Corvin. He had, luckily, come to her rescue.

Reg closed her eyes, trying to wipe away the memories.

"Sit down," Jessup snapped, gesturing to one of the chairs. Reg did sit, but chose the other chair to assert her independence. Jessup hovered over her, forcing Reg to look up at her.

"Where is Ruan Rosdew?" Jessup demanded.

"Where? How would I know?" Reg shook her head. "I have no idea."

"Don't get smart with me. You were the last one to see him. So what happened? Where is he now?"

"I don't know. He ran away from me… I didn't see where he went. I looked for him, but then the kids were getting out for lunch, and there were too many people for me to keep looking for him. So I just… went back home."

"He ran away."

"Yes."

"Where? Why?"

"I told you, I don't know where he went. He ducked down behind a fence, a sort of a stone wall, and I followed him. But when I got there, he was gone. There was no sign of him. I don't know, I guess he ran into the forest, but I didn't see which way he went and I certainly have no idea where he would have been going."

"He just disappeared."

Reg shrugged. "Not poof in a cloud of smoke, but he might just as well have done. Either way, there was no sign of him."

"What did you say to him? Did you accuse him? Why was he running away?"

Reg shifted uncomfortably. She made a noise to call Starlight to her, stalling for time, trying to sort out in her mind what she was going to say.

"I did… ask him if he knew Calliopia and what had happened to her."

"Why would you do that? You're not a cop. I told you your involvement was over."

"I just thought I'd help. I couldn't bear to sit back and do nothing when she is in such danger. I had to do something. So I found out where they went to school and went to look for him. I didn't know I was going to talk to him, not for sure. I just wanted to see him, maybe to follow him… I thought he might lead me back to Callie."

"And you didn't think that maybe the police already had that under control? Don't you think I know the suspects better than you?"

"But you're a police detective. I know kids; he wouldn't talk to you. But he could talk to me. If it was just a regular person asking him questions, he might be more likely to have something to say."

"And did he?"

"No." Reg patted Starlight when he brushed by her chair. "He said he didn't know anything about it."

"That's no big surprise."

"But he did know something. I'm sure of that."

Jessup stared into Reg's eyes. "And how do you know that? Telepathy?"

"He blocked me from his mind. He was very adept at that. Why block me unless he had something to hide?"

"Because it's an invasion of privacy. Because no one wants someone else poking around in their head. Did you see anything? Not that I could use it if you did."

"No. He knew something. He denied it, and he didn't have any tells, but I knew he was lying to me. And then he said it wasn't any of my business, that it was his family business. How could it be his family business if he didn't know anything about it?"

"How do you know he was lying if he didn't have any tells and you couldn't read his mind?"

"Because... he didn't try to pretend that he cared or try to establish an alibi. He acted like it was nothing that had anything to do with him. Like a psychopath, no appropriate emotion."

"What do you know about psychopathy?"

"Let's just say... I know."

"He said Calliopia disappearing was a family matter?"

"Yes... he used a name I didn't know, I guess maybe his wider clan..."

"It's a fairy blade," Letticia said.

Reg looked at her, pulled out of her conversation with Jessup, trying to understand this non sequitur.

"What?"

Letticia held the dagger up, still in its sealed plastic bag. "A fairy blade," she repeated.

Reg thought of the fairy cakes at the party. What did Letticia mean? That the blade was small? Delicate? Did it have fairies carved into the handle? Reg hadn't had a very good look at it. She'd been too busy trying not to scream in pain. It was sharp, that was all she'd noticed about it.

"How did Hawthorne-Rose get a fairy blade?" Jessup wondered. "They are very careful about letting them out of their possession."

"Who is?" Reg asked.

The eyes of all three women turned to her simultaneously. Reg squirmed in her seat.

"Fairies," Jessup said, as if Reg were being completely dense. "Fairies don't give up their blades. They don't sell them or give them away."

"Fairies."

There was silence in the cottage. Reg shook her head.

"There are no fairies. There's no such thing. They're make believe."

"Reg…" Sarah said tentatively, as if she thought Reg might have hit her head or lost her mind.

Reg looked from one woman to the other, seeing the same expression on all of their faces. Letticia still holding the knife up. Sarah with her mouth open. Jessup's brows drawn down and a scowl across her face. It was Jessup who spoke.

"Calliopia is a fairy."

"No."

"Of course she is."

Reg thought of Calliopia's parents, tall and thin, with their blue-white skin. The house full of living plants rather than treasures. The unfamiliar language Calliopia sang or chanted in. Even just the names. Calliopia. Papillon. Those weren't normal names.

"They're fairies?"

The women nodded.

"And those people at the party… her kin. They were fairies too?"

Sarah nodded.

They had touched her. Reg couldn't help the little tickle of excitement at the thought that fairies had touched her, spoken to her, and helped her.

"I thought that fairies were… tiny. Little people. With wings."

"Fairy tales," Sarah said with a shrug. "Just like the stories of witches riding broomsticks and forever walking around in ceremonial hats. Do I have green skin and warts? A cat who also wears a pointed hat? Did you see a big black cauldron bubbling in my kitchen?"

Reg blinked at her. Just like Reg didn't need a crystal ball or a head scarf to read fortunes, or a circle of people sitting in the dark holding hands to contact the dead. It seemed that the paranormal world was far more ordinary than she would ever have thought.

"There are really fairies."

"Yes."

Reg massaged her temples, thinking it through. "I'm not freaking out," she said aloud.

"No, you're doing just fine," Sarah agreed.

"You're telling me that fairies really exist, and I've met them, and I'm not freaking out."

"Maybe just a little," Jessup said dryly.

Letticia started working on the yarrow again, crushing it and releasing a smell that made Reg think of spaghetti. Starlight sniffed at the air, then started to wash his paws and coat.

"Why did Ruan run away from you?" Jessup asked. "What did you say to him?"

"Did his parents report him missing? Didn't he go home?"

"We have not been able to get in contact with his family. He did not go back to school after lunch and no one at the school has seen him since. Maybe he went home and is being protected by his parents. We don't really know."

"They won't let you in or talk to you on the phone?"

"Their homes tend to be… difficult to find. And they don't use technology."

"Right. Fairies worship nature and don't use electricity… do you think this is all part of their feud? When I told Ruan that Callie liked him, he didn't seem to think that was possible. And he didn't like her. So maybe we were wrong about it being a Romeo and Juliet thing…"

"I would much prefer an illicit romance."

Reg could understand why. It was much happier to picture Callie and Ruan trying to prove their love and reconcile their families than what Reg had sensed from the start. A young girl trapped in a cold, dark room, with nothing but whispering shadows and cockroaches.

"That was when he ran away?" Jessup pressed. "When you asked him if he was in love with her?"

"Uh… no."

"Then tell me what you said."

Reg reluctantly described being mesmerized by the boy, managing to escape his gaze, and then being caught again.

"Ruan grabbed me. And then… he yelled something and let me go, like I'd hurt him. He spun around in a circle, and then he ran off, and ducked behind that wall… and was gone. Just like that."

Jessup scratched her head, considering this. "You weren't carrying anything…? Iron… bells… bread…?"

Reg shook her head. "There wasn't anything. Just… it was my injured hand. It was bandaged. There might still have been… antibiotic cream or something on it…"

Letticia's hand hovered over Hawthorne-Rose's blade, her eyes closed and her head thrown back, the same as when she had searched Reg's hand for invisible signs of magical injury.

"It's fairy blood."

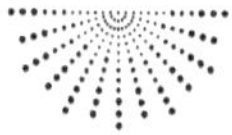

CHAPTER EIGHTEEN

*E*veryone turned and looked at Letticia.

"Fairy blood *would* have had that effect on Ruan," Jessup agreed. "But where would it have come from?"

Letticia tapped the knife. "From here," she said irritably. "The blade is contaminated with fairy blood."

"But I didn't have the knife," Reg pointed out. "The police had it."

"It was already contaminated with blood when Hawthorne-Rose cut you," Letticia enunciated slowly. "Transferring minute amounts of that blood into your wound. That's why the wound isn't healing properly."

"And that's why when Ruan touched your hand, it affected him," Jessup filled in.

"Because… fairies can't touch fairy blood? That doesn't make any sense."

Jessup shook her head. "Ruan is not a fairy."

"Oh. Well then… what is he?"

Reg wasn't sure she wanted to hear the answer. But this time, she wasn't going to be taken off guard. Obviously, he was some other sort of magical folk. He was burned by the fairy blood, he had practically vanished into thin air, and his people had homes that were difficult to find and they used no electricity.

"A pixie," Jessup said, as if Reg should have figured that out.

"Oh. A pixie. And pixies and fairies can't touch each other."

"Most beings can't touch fairy blood. Pixies are no exception."

"But people can. Human beings," Reg corrected herself, not wanting to discriminate against fairies or pixies or whatever other beings who might consider themselves 'people' too.

Letticia indicated Reg's hand. "That should be all the answer you need to that question," she said sternly. "If humans are immune to fairy blood, then why is your hand getting worse instead of better?"

"Oh."

"The yarrow will help," Letticia assured her. "We might need the addition of rowan berries as well, but I'll have to see if I have any dried berries in my stores. I might need to source them out…"

"Amazon Prime," Sarah advised. "Next day delivery."

Reg fought the urge to laugh.

"Come here," Letticia instructed. "We'll apply the milfoil directly to the wound and keep it covered. I'll also make you a tea to fight what's already in your bloodstream. Lucky for you, milfoil has a pleasant enough taste."

* * *

Reg looked out the car window as Jessup drove through parts of the town that Reg had never seen before.

She hadn't expected Jessup to ask her to ride along with her to meet with the Rosdews. After having scared Ruan off, Reg figured Jessup would want her to be as far away from the investigation as possible. But Jessup hadn't seen it that way.

"You were the last one to see Ruan that we know of. These are a people who will lie and deny everything, including that Ruan was ever at school that day. I want a witness as to what he said. Particularly that the kidnapping was pixie business."

"How will that make any difference?"

"Maybe it won't. But I'm getting worried about Calliopia. If the pixies have her… there's no telling what they might do."

"Like… what?"

Jessup looked at her sidelong. Her fingers tightened on the steering wheel. "They may look and act human, but don't be fooled by that. They do not have the same scruples as we do. They have human intelligence, but they don't have the same social constructs as we do. If you hadn't touched Ruan with fairy blood… there's no telling what he might have done to you."

Reg's stomach turned. The unseen world was full of dangers that she had no idea of. She'd thought that she was going to the school to talk to a human youth about the disappearance of his sweetheart. She couldn't have been much farther from the truth.

"Is it safe to talk to them?"

"I have certain wards. It's not one hundred percent, but when was police work ever one hundred percent safe?"

"Well, considering where you ended up on the last case… I'm guessing Black Sands isn't exactly Mayberry."

"No. Things can get pretty wild around here. You might not have the drugs and gangs of big-city USA, but believe me, we've got plenty to rival it."

"And a smaller work force."

"That's right."

The scenery outside Reg's window was getting more and more disreputable. They had left behind the retirement villages and single-family bungalows. They hadn't gone to the green country and mansions like when they had traveled to Calliopia's house. Instead, Reg saw slums that would have rivaled any of the big cities. Falling-down concrete buildings, shacks built from cardboard shipping boxes, cars that had probably last been driven in the seventies. There was no lack of people on the streets. Youths hanging around smoking and selling drugs or other goods or services. Old men and women with shopping carts piled high with everything they owned in the world. Children playing games or crouching in ditches, some of the little ones stark naked, a state of affairs that didn't appear to garner any special attention.

A rock hit the car. Jessup hit the brake, looking around for the culprit. No one appeared to be looking at them, but Reg suspected a group of youth huddled close together, talking and laughing with each other. Jessup shook her head and kept driving, deciding not to pursue it. She probably would have had to call for backup, and they had a job to do. At least it had been a rock and not a bullet.

"I didn't know..." Reg couldn't finish her sentence. She shook her head. She'd lived on the streets. She knew what it was like. But she'd never imagined that such a grim place existed right in Black Sands. When she'd been researching places to move to on the internet, Reg had imagined Black Sands to be an idyllic village. No poverty, no violent crime, a place full of rich marks and other people taking advantage of the opportunities.

"It's nothing to brag about," Jessup agreed. "On one hand, we have plenty of affluence and magically-enhanced lifestyles. On the other, we have..." she gestured to indicate the streets around her. "Dante's inferno. Misery on a grand scale."

"I guess there's no escaping it. You can't have one without the other."

Jessup concentrated on her driving, her eyes moving back and forth as she avoided potholes and detritus and watched out for other dangers that might lurk nearby.

"Most of the practitioners, at least the ones I know in Black Sands, will tell you there's no objective good or evil. But that's a cop-out. Believe me, good and evil are alive and well in Black Sands."

They reached a dead end. Reg expected Jessup to consult a map or GPS and to turn back around, but she didn't. She opened her door and got out.

"This is it," she told Reg, leaning down to look into the car. "Let's go."

Reg climbed reluctantly out of the car. She didn't like the looks of things. The buildings around her didn't appear to be apartments, but industrial buildings, most of them falling around. It wasn't so much a dead end as a place where debris had collected and never been cleared away. For all Reg knew, there had once been a through street, but it had long since been obscured.

"What is this place? People live here?"

"You'd be surprised at the conditions some beings live in."

Jessup led the way into one of the buildings. A door swung loose on its hinges, the latch long since broken and rusted. Reg felt a chill as they entered, and tried to tell herself that it was just the coolness of the building, concrete walls blocking out the heat of the sun. Jessup walked around puddles, her hand resting on her sidearm.

"You're sure this is where we're supposed to meet? You're sure it's safe?"

Jessup said nothing. Reg's mind started to crank through scenarios. What if Jessup were leading her into a trap? What if Jessup, like Hawthorne-Rose, was a dirty cop? She could be leading Reg to her death. Reg's body would never be discovered in the abandoned building. The rats and other vermin would eat her flesh and scatter her bones until there was nothing left of her.

"Is this the right place? Did you check the address?"

"Shut up, Rawlins. I need to be able to hear."

Reg zipped her lip and stayed as close as she could to Jessup without stepping on her heels. She strained her ears for any sound. Was Jessup expecting to hear something and hadn't? Or had she heard something and was trying to figure out what it was?

Reg could hear water dripping. Not an unusual sound some-where as humid as Florida. She couldn't hear any footsteps but their own, or any noises that sounded deliberate.

Jessup led her through a couple of doors, into stairways that went down below ground level, each level getting darker and cooler. Reg had heard that they didn't build basements in Florida because of the water levels, but there were obviously a couple of exceptions.

The halls turned into tunnels with rounded roofs and the temperature turned downright chilly. There was condensation on the rough-hewn walls, and a trickle of foul-smelling water running down the center of the tunnel. As they went farther, the stench grew worse. Reg was always glad in such circumstances that she wasn't Erin, a super-smeller who would have been doubled over retching by that point. Instead, Reg just breathed through her mouth and tried not to think about it. By her guess, they were in an old sewer network. Maybe an abandoned one that wasn't used any more, though she was sure it would fill up with water during a storm. Jessup stopped abruptly. Reg nearly ran into her.

"What is it?" Reg whispered.

"Wait."

Reg listened, wondering if Jessup had heard something. Water dripping, and maybe footsteps? She couldn't tell if someone was splashing through the puddles toward them or whether it was just the irregular dripping from the walls and ceiling.

Jessup tapped on an access panel on the wall. A voice answered, but it didn't come from behind the panel. It seemed to be all around them. Reg strained her eyes, but couldn't see any speakers.

"Who enters the realm of the piskies?"

"Detective Jessup. Making inquiries of Brannock and Demelza Rosdew."

"You have no jurisdiction here."

"Under treaties with your people, I do. This is an official investigation. You can't deny me entrance." Jessup said it with complete authority and certainty. If she had any doubts whether the pixies would let her in, it didn't show.

There was silence from the sentry. Reg waited for Jessup to make some sign as to what they would do next. Jessup waited. Time passed. Water dripped. The seconds drew into minutes; a long, silent interval during which Reg tried to stay focused and alert. Not an easy task with a mind that jumped from one thing to the next like a squirrel through the trees. Reg had often wondered what it would be like to live in the mind of someone who focused on one thing at a time and could live inside her head in perfect peace and serenity. It sounded like an impossible task.

Jessup reached over and knocked on the access panel. Loud this time, like a policeman normally knocked when rousing someone from their bed at two o'clock in the morning. A firm demand.

"Enter at your own risk," the sentry's voice sighed.

CHAPTER NINETEEN

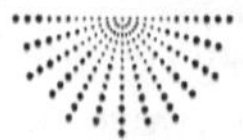

*C*ome on."

Reg expected the access panel to open up into another tunnel, or for some other hidden route to appear, but nothing changed. They continued to walk down the tunnel just as they had been, walking in the same direction as they had been. Reg looked around for some marker showing the boundary of the pixie's lands, but couldn't see anything that differentiated one part of the tunnel from another.

But in a few minutes, she started to hear voices, echoes bouncing back to them from somewhere farther down the line. Shadows flickered on the wall, but she couldn't see who cast them. Eventually, just as the babble of voices and laughter grew to a level where Reg could hardly stand it, they entered a larger room where several tunnels joined together, and Reg saw the pixies.

Like Ruan, they were mostly dressed in brown. Worn and tattered clothing, mainly, though there were a few new suits among them. The girls were dressed pretty much the same as the boys. They all appeared to be young. Some looked like Ruan, nine or ten years old, some like teenagers. No one over twenty, certainly.

Several of the older teenagers swarmed toward them. Reg saw Jessup's hand go to her weapon, watching them warily.

"You have no business here," one of the boys said.

"I'm here on an official police investigation. According to the treaty between our peoples, you are expected to cooperate."

"Not if police poke their noses into piskie business."

"This is not family business. A girl has been kidnapped. I want to know where Ruan Rosdew is and how he is involved."

"Kidnapped," the boy scoffed. "No one has been kidnapped. Fairies kidnap. We are piskies."

"Brannock Rosdew?" Jessup called, looking around at the pixies.

They looked stubborn, but eventually a young man appearing to be seventeen or eighteen stepped forward.

"I am Brannock."

Reg laughed. She looked at Jessup. Jessup had said that Brannock was Ruan's father, but the pixie wasn't old enough to be anyone's parent.

"Where would you like to go to talk?" Jessup asked.

The boy looked around at the other pixies, as if he would insist that they talk right there in front of everyone else, then he scowled.

"Follow me," he said grudgingly.

Jessup and Reg followed close behind him. He moved quickly, light on his feet, darting ahead of them.

"Try to keep up," Jessup warned.

They were out of breath by the time the pixie indicated a wooden door. Reg realized with a start that they were no longer in the round sewer tunnels, but once again the walls were straight and square. She guessed that they were handmade planks. But they were still underground.

"What happens when it rains?"

The pixie boy looked at her. "Humans drown."

Reg opened her mouth to argue with this unexpected answer, but then didn't know how to counter. She hadn't been asking what happened to humans when it rained, she'd been asking what happened to the pixie settlement, so far underground and apparently connected to the town's wastewater system. But the pixie's answer demonstrated that they had no concerns about this. When it rained, it was humans who drowned, not pixies.

The boy pushed the door open. Reg didn't see any latch or lock on it. They entered a small, square room. Cold, damp, and dark. The boy left the door standing open, letting in the dim light of the corridor. Reg gazed out at the corridor, her brows drawing down. There had been no windows, lights, or candles in the corridor. How were the halls being illuminated?

The answer would, of course, be pixie magic. But Reg wanted it to be explained to her in scientific terms she understood. Not just explained away as magic.

A young girl entered the room. Fourteen or fifteen, with a black kerchief around her head and red spots on her pale cheeks. She could have been no more than four feet tall.

She went to the boy, and they stood together, staring at Reg and Jessup with open hostility.

"Demelza?" Jessup asked.

The girl nodded her head. Reg looked at Jessup, confused. Jessup raised her brows.

"They all look like that," she said with a shrug.

"Like children?"

"Not like ugly old trolls," Demelza said.

Reg stood with her mouth open while Jessup laughed. "You did ask, Rawlins."

Reg decided she'd better keep her mouth shut, or the pixies were going to make them feel even less welcome than they did already. She noticed uneasily how sharp Demelza's teeth were.

"Sorry."

Demelza switched her gaze to Jessup. "You want questions answered, you ask, and be on your way."

"Your boy, Ruan, where is he?"

She shrugged. "We do not track our children like humankind."

"Does that mean you don't know where he is?"

Demelza looked at her husband and neither of them answered.

"He was at the school and then disappeared. I'm concerned with his safety. Something might have happened to him. After Calliopia, I'm concerned that he might have run into someone that meant him harm."

"Pixies take care of themselves."

"Something could have happened to him."

They both stared at her with their ice-blue eyes as if what she said were of absolutely no concern. Reg wondered if their emotions were different from human emotions, or were just expressed differently. They must have some kind of feelings towards their offspring. Otherwise, how would the race survive?

"How old is he?" she asked Jessup. "You could file a missing person report on him yourself, without their input, couldn't you?"

Jessup looked at her.

"Well?"

"We're talking about a race that lives hundreds of years," Jessup said. "Ruan might not yet be a mature pixie—I really have no way of knowing—but he might be decades older than you or me."

"Oh."

Jessup turned her attention back to Brannock and Demelza. "What do you know about Calliopia?"

Brannock scratched at a spot on his jacket. Reg was cold, wishing she had dressed more warmly for the adventure. She hadn't known that she'd be underground, far from the Florida sun.

"Fairy name," Brannock said. "Fairy girl."

"Yes, she's a fairy girl. And she was kidnapped. At this point, I'm thinking she was kidnapped by a pixie."

"Fairies steal children from their beds. Piskies… we do not do this."

It was interesting, Reg thought, that the pixie apparently knew that Calliopia had disappeared from her bedroom and not snatched off the street or at school. Was that because he knew something, or just from the rumors that were doubtless flying around?

"Pixies have been known to steal children too," Jessup countered.

Brannock shook his head. "Piskies take care of children who have wandered off. Showing hospitality." He spread his arms wide to indicate the bare, cold little room as if it were a palace.

"Luring children still qualifies as kidnapping."

"Children need to be cared for." He smiled, showing off his teeth, sharp like his wife's. Like a carnivore's teeth. Reg shuddered, hoping that she wasn't about to find out that pixies ate the children they stole.

"Where is Calliopia?"

"She is not here."

Jessup took a slow look around, but it wasn't like there was anything in the room that would tell them what had happened to Calliopia. It was a bare room with a dirt floor and plank walls. There was a table along one wall, with no chairs or other furniture.

"Where did you take her?"

"Why would we take her?"

"She liked Ruan. Maybe he liked her too. Maybe he asked for her to wife."

"Piskies do not wed fairies."

"It's been known to happen."

"Fairies and piskies are not compatible."

"I've heard stories."

"Fairy tales," he scoffed. "Fairies lie."

"Pixies lie too."

Brannock stared at Jessup. Jessup stared at him. She was tough. She didn't give up easily.

"Ruan liked Calliopia," Jessup said.

"He did not know her."

"They went to school together. He knew her. They probably sat together at lunch. Passed notes during class. Maybe… more."

"No," Demelza insisted. She shook her finger at Jessup. "This did not happen. Never."

Reg felt the first wave of pixie emotion radiating from Ruan's mother. She had not been angry before that. But the thought of her son and Calliopia together aroused hate and disgust, just as recognizable as human emotion. So maybe they *had* been Romeo and Juliet? Attracted to each other, but forbidden by their parents to have anything to do with each other? They had to hide their feelings for each other. Until what? Until Ruan had broken down and told his parents? Until she'd run away from her family to be with her boyfriend?

"Calliopia was making a love potion," Jessup told her. "We know that. If it wasn't for Ruan, then who was it for? He was the one she wrote about in her diary."

"What a silly fairy girl dreams is no concern of ours."

"Where is Ruan? I want to talk to him."

"If you want to talk to him then you must find him," Brannock said.

"Is he in the realm?"

Brannock considered the question. He looked at his wife. He looked back at Jessup. "He is not."

Jessup sighed. She pulled out a business card and held it toward Brannock. "When he returns, I want to talk to him."

Brannock hissed, making Jessup jerk back from him.

"You have no right to command here," Brannock said fiercely. "Take your edicts away from this place."

"It's just a—"

"We have talked, as required by the treaty. Now you are done."

Jessup withdrew the business card and put it back away.

"You will not return here on this matter."

Jessup gave Reg a tiny nod and they turned toward the door. Demelza was standing there, barring their path. Reg couldn't help looking over her shoulder to where she had expected to see

Demelza. How had the woman moved so fast? And without them seeing her?

"This one wears wards and cites authority," Demelza said, looking at Jessup. "But this one…" She considered Reg.

Reg held up her injured hand. "You don't want to touch me. I have a… I have fairy blood."

Demelza gave a low hiss and bared her teeth. Her ice-cold eyes held Reg paralyzed.

"She is protected," Brannock confirmed. "Touch her not."

Demelza moved out of their way. Jessup headed out the door. Reg followed closely behind her. She wasn't about to be left behind to test out her magical protection. She trusted that the witches were right and the fairy blood would protect her from the pixies, but she still couldn't be one hundred percent sure, and she wasn't about to stay behind to find out.

Brannock and Demelza didn't follow them, or at least if they did, Reg did not see or hear them. But she was starting to understand that the pixies couldn't always be seen and she didn't trust that they weren't close by.

"Do you know the way out?" she asked Jessup anxiously, unsure whether Jessup had memorized all of the twists and turns they had taken to get to Brannock's room.

"We'll be out of here in a few minutes," Jessup assured her. "Keep up."

CHAPTER TWENTY

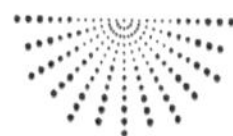

Reg breathed a sigh of relief when they stepped out of the last building and into the blinding sunlight. She covered her eyes, tears streaming down her face, and just soaked in the sensation of the sun beating down on her skin. She would never have guessed that it could be so cold just a few feet underground.

They both stood there for a few minutes, blinded and getting used to the light, before they were able to move and get back into the car. Jessup radioed in a status update. As they drove out of the dead end and again saw the people out on the street, Reg looked at them with new eyes. The children who played and laughed on the sidewalks and in the gutters might not be children at all, but pixies keeping guard, watching as they first approached and then drove away.

Jessup noticed her interest. "You'll never look at children the same way again. You'll always wonder, even when you're away from this place, how many of them are children and how many are pixies keeping watch or looking for new victims."

"Do you believe what they said?"

"Pixies lie constantly. I can't rely on anything they said."

"Then what was the point in interviewing them?"

"To observe them and see if they gave anything away. To see if Ruan was there. Or any sign of Calliopia."

"How would we know? It's like a rabbit warren down there."

Jessup turned her palm up in a gesture of surrender. "You don't know if you don't look."

"I suppose not. So did you learn anything?"

"I don't think Demelza knew that there was a relationship between Ruan and Calliopia."

Reg nodded her agreement. "That was the only time I felt anything from her. She really didn't like the idea of a romantic relationship between them."

"So whatever happened to Calliopia, it wasn't because Calliopia was lured here. Not by any of the adult pixies."

"Do you think she might have originally come here because of Ruan? Because he lured her here to be with him or she thought she could get together with him?"

"It's still a possibility. But I don't get the feeling that we have figured it out yet. I still don't think we've quite put our finger on what happened."

"Brannock knew that she had disappeared from her room."

"I noticed that too," Jessup agreed. "But I don't know if that's because the pixies had something to do with it, or just that they had heard about it."

"Is it true that fairies—"

Jessup put her hand over her hip and swore. She swerved slightly, making Reg grab onto the handle of the door for support, flashing back to Sarah's driving. They straightened out and she let the handle go, but Jessup kept swearing.

"What is it?"

"My badge! My shield! It was on my belt, so that it's handy if I need to use it to identify myself, and it's gone!"

"You think the pixies stole it?"

"It didn't just drop off of its own accord!"

"I'm sorry. Do you want to go back and get it?"

Jessup's fingers tightened on the wheel, and she considered for a moment. But then she shook her head. "Can't do that."

"Why not?"

"It's an old trick. Draw someone back to a place by keeping something they value. So they go back looking for it, thinking they're still protected by whatever wards they set originally… but they're not."

"So you really can't go back there?"

"No. You remember what Brannock said? 'You're done. You will not return here on this matter.' So if I went back, it wouldn't be covered by the treaty. I'd be going in with no official protection."

Reg shook her head. "It's all so complicated. All of these rules…"

"I imagine it is confusing. I've lived here almost all my life. My parents were practitioners, so even though I really don't have much talent myself, I grew up as part of the community, familiar with all of the rules and how things are done. For you… it must be like moving to a foreign country. You think that all of the customs and laws are going to be the same, but then you find out that they're not."

Reg nodded. "Exactly. Finding out that some of the fairy tale stuff is true… even if I don't understand all of it… it's crazy. I keep expecting to find out it's a joke or that I've lost my mind."

* * *

They were both silent for a while, Jessup seething about her lost shield and Reg trying to analyze everything she had seen and heard to figure out the realities of the new world she was living in.

"So is it true that fairies steal children from their beds but pixies don't?"

Jessup looked at her for a moment and pursed her lips.

"Good question… I suspect that it's only half true. Just enough to sound like it's true to throw us off the scent."

"So which half is true?"

"Fairies definitely have a history of stealing babies or very young children from their cots. It's a longstanding tradition in literature and fairy tales. The people who like to come up with explanations for folk tales suggest that the fairies stealing a child away was a way to account for infanticide, developmental delays, or negligent parenting. Just say that the fairies took him and that would explain everything."

Reg leaned back in her seat, closing her eyes and rubbing her temples and the space between her eyes. It wasn't like they had done a lot of physical work in walking down to the pixies' underground burrows, but she was exhausted anyway. Everything seemed to take more energy from her in Black Sands.

"Okay, so I get infanticide or children wandering off. But how do the fairies stealing babies explain developmental delays? You mean like autism?"

Jessup nodded. "These babies seem perfectly normal when they are born, right? You can't tell the difference. But then when they're not developing as expected or, worse yet, show regression in development, it could be explained by the fact that the fairies had stolen the true child and replaced it with a changeling. A changeling looks the same as the true child, but doesn't behave like a normal human child. No language. Flapping or spinning or other strange behaviors."

"I've heard the word before, but I never really knew what a changeling is. So it's... a fairy baby?"

"No, more like a counterfeit baby, like an automaton. Not a real human being. Which, again, makes it okay to commit infanticide, because it's not really a real human child. Just a replica made by the fairies to replace the child they stole."

"And what happens to the child that they stole? What do they do with it?"

"They raise it as their own. To become a fairy."

"Don't they have their own children?"

"Yes. But fairy children are few and far between. They might only have one baby every few hundred years. Even though a couple may be together for a millennium, they might only have one or two children, not enough to maintain the fairy population. So if they can't have them, they steal them."

"So the Papillons were lucky to have another child so quickly."

Jessup was focused on her driving, but after a few seconds, she turned and looked at Reg.

"Another child?"

"The baby."

"What baby?"

"Their baby. When we went to the house…"

"They don't have a baby. Calliopia was an only child."

Reg couldn't figure out what Jessup was saying. "Okay, then whose baby was it?"

"They didn't have a baby. What are you talking about?"

"The whole time we were there… Mrs. Papillon was holding a baby."

"No, she wasn't."

They looked at each other for a brief second, then Jessup had to refocus on her driving. "I don't understand."

"Are you telling me you didn't see a baby and I did?" Reg asked.

Jessup nodded. Reg felt the familiar knot in her gut. She had been in trouble so many times for seeing things that weren't there, she felt sick any time there was even a hint that her imagination was getting away from her.

"That doesn't mean you didn't see what you saw," Jessup said, glancing over at her again. "I'm not accusing you of making it up or being crazy."

"But I saw a baby when there wasn't one? What does that mean? She had a baby who had died and its spirit is still attached to her? Or she's pregnant and I saw the baby's spirit? What?"

"I don't know. What did it feel like?"

Reg thought back to Calliopia's mother and the baby she had held.

"It was strange. The baby didn't cry. She held him... awkwardly. Not the way that a mother holds a baby, more the way that a little girl holds a plastic doll. You know, held all stiff at her shoulder..."

Jessup thought about that. "I don't have a clue what that means."

"Is she Calliopia's mother? I mean... she seemed very young. I assumed when I first saw her that she was Callie's step-mother. A second marriage."

"No. As far as I know, she's Calliopia's real mother. Remember the pixies. You can't trust appearances. Some of these long-lived races look very young. It takes hundreds of years for them to age."

Reg closed her eyes, trying to recall it more clearly. She tried to see every detail and to hear and smell and feel everything that had happened.

"What if it was just a doll?" she mused. There was nothing in her recollection that would refute the idea. She hadn't had a clear look at the baby, it had only been a wrapped bundle in Mrs. Papillon's arms. But why hadn't Jessup seen it?

"Why would she be carrying a doll?" Jessup returned. "And more importantly, why would she hide the fact from us? If it was something from the physical world rather than a spirit, you saw through her concealment spell, but none of the rest of us saw it. It would have to be something of significance."

"Does that mean it was incriminating or just private?"

"Good question. Maybe we should go have a chat with her and ask."

We? Reg glanced over at her.

Jessup raised her brows. "Do you want to come?"

Reg was worn out after the encounter with the pixies. It would be nice to go home and have a nap and try the next day, but Calliopia might not have that long. If she were being held by the pixies—and the room Reg had seen her in was certainly consistent with the underground hovels of the pixies—she was running out of time.

"Uh… okay. I'll come along, if you want me to."

Jessup nodded. "Since you're the one who can see through her concealment, that would be helpful. She could have it right in front of me while I talk myself blue in the face saying that she had a baby the last time we were there, and I wouldn't know it."

CHAPTER TWENTY-ONE

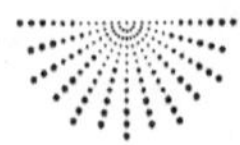

The Papillon estate was just as Reg had remembered it, lush and verdant, with the spires of the castles rising up out of the trees as if it had grown there instead of being constructed. There was a feeling of peace and serenity there that hadn't been present in the underground settlement of the pixies. Reg didn't know if pixies and fairies were related to each other; to her mind, they couldn't be more opposite. Other than that they were both magical, long-lived races.

Reg gave a sigh and breathed in the fresh air. It was invigorating and helped to counteract the anxiety the visit with the pixies had left her with. It was a place where she imagined she could forget all her troubles and live outside of time.

The butler took longer to answer the door than he had on their previous visit, obviously not expecting anyone. He looked them over and raised one eyebrow in inquiry.

"Did my lord and lady expect you today?" He obviously knew they did not.

"Are they in?" Jessup challenged without answering the inquiry. "We have some questions with regard to the investigation."

"I will see if they are able to meet with you."

"I'm going to have to insist," Jessup said, her voice hard. "If they will not make themselves available, we'll have to take additional steps, which they will not be happy about."

He looked at them for a few seconds longer, then withdrew to go talk to his masters. Reg studied a little oasis of plants and a water feature as they waited. The trickling sound of the water was soothing, unlike the constant dripping in the pixies' tunnels.

"If you will follow me."

Reg hadn't even heard the butler's approach and was startled by his voice. They followed him to a different room from where they had previously met. It appeared to be some kind of work room. Mr. Papillon was not dressed in the same finery as he had been on their previous visit, but in plain linens and an apron. He looked up from his workbench, where there was a line of planting pots, gardening implements, and bags of soil. Reg didn't know why it should surprise her to find him elbow-deep in gardening, considering all of the plants in and around the house. What did she think? That they just appeared there magically?

Mrs. Papillon was in the corner of the room, not working, but resting in a natural-colored wicker armchair, the baby bundle in her arms. She looked older than Reg remembered, tired and worn. If fairies took hundreds of years to mature, then Reg wouldn't have expected to be able to see any changes occurring over a few days. But apparently, even fairies could look bad after a few days worrying over a missing child.

"Detective Jessup," Mr. Papillon greeted. "We weren't expecting to see you today. I hope this means there has been a break in the case and you have come to tell us of your progress."

"We are making progress," Jessup said. "But it is difficult for us to do so when you withhold information from us."

He looked down at his pots, transferring rich-smelling soil into them one at a time with a small shovel. "We have told you everything we could. If there is something we neglected to tell you, I assure you it was an oversight."

Jessup looked at Reg, asking a silent question. Reg nodded at

Mrs. Papillon, confirming to Jessup that she was holding the baby. Jessup stared at the fairy, going nearly cross-eyed, but obviously could not see the baby that was so obvious to Reg.

"Ms. Rawlins has some questions for your wife."

Reg was startled. She had expected to listen and to affirm what Jessup had to say, not to take over the investigatory process.

"Uh… yeah." Reg walked across the room to talk face to face with Mrs. Papillon and, hopefully, to get a better look at the baby.

Close up, she saw the baby's face for the first time. She still couldn't tell whether it was an actual baby or an exquisitely well-made doll. The baby didn't stir, and Reg couldn't discern any rise and fall of the bundle of blankets with its breath.

"What's your baby's name?"

There was stunned silence from Callie's parents. Mrs. Papillon looked at Reg, searching her face. Then she looked across the room at her husband. His back was to her, but it was clear from his rigid stance that he was just as bowled over as she was.

"There is no baby," Mrs. Papillon finally said.

"Is it a doll, then? I don't understand."

Mrs. Papillon looked down at the sleeping infant in her arms. "It is… a shadow. Not a real child. Yet I am burdened with it until Calliopia returns to us."

"A changeling?" Reg asked.

Frown lines creased Mrs. Papillon's forehead briefly. She gave a hesitant nod. "Humans have their own names for things," she said. "I don't always know your words."

Jessup's eyes were alert, working the angles. "Can you reveal it to me, please?"

Mrs. Papillon looked reluctant to do so. She didn't make any special motion or whisper an incantation that Reg heard, but Jessup's eyes suddenly riveted on the infant. She also approached Mrs. Papillon to look down at the baby's face.

"It looks so real," she said. "It would have fooled me."

"I would not be fooled."

"Was this *shadow* left when Calliopia was taken?"

Mrs. Papillon looked at her husband. He nodded. She sighed and also nodded her agreement. "The shadow was in Callie's bed, where she should have been."

"But I thought a changeling was supposed to look like the child that was stolen to fool the family," Reg said. "It doesn't make any sense to leave a baby in place of a teenager."

Neither parent supplied an explanation.

"Doesn't the presence of a changeling tell you that Calliopia was stolen by other fairies?" Jessup asked.

"She was not stolen by other fairies," Mr. Papillon snapped. He took a moment to smooth the tops of each pot of dirt. "Fairies do not steal from fairies."

"Apparently they do. Unless you have a more logical explanation for the presence of the shadow child."

Mrs. Papillon shifted the baby from one side to the other. As she did so, Reg caught a wave of deep pain and exhaustion from her. Reg put her hand on the back of the chair to steady herself, just about knocked off her feet by the sensation.

"You said that the baby is a burden until Calliopia returns. What did you mean?" Reg asked.

"I am responsible to care for it until Calliopia comes back. She would not be able to return if the shadow that took her place was harmed or removed."

"And how do you take care of a shadow? Just like a real baby? Feed it, change it, rock it to sleep…?"

"Oh, no!" Mrs. Papillon objected. "You *must not* feed a shadow. If you do, it becomes yours permanently. Your child can never be returned to you."

"That's in line with the fairy tales I've heard," Jessup confirmed.

"But it won't starve if you don't feed it? Because it's not a real baby?" Reg couldn't believe that the pink-faced baby in Mrs. Papillon's arms was not a real child. It certainly didn't look like a robot or automaton. Its mouth opened a little when Mrs. Papillon moved it, and it smacked its lips in its sleep.

Mrs. Papillon nodded. "If you don't feed it, it will not develop like a child. But they do continue to get heavier." She made a slight movement toward Reg. "Would you like to hold it?"

Curious about it, Reg nodded and reached for the baby. She slid her hands under it to pick it up, but she found the baby to be a dead weight. Not just the ten pounds she expected, but too heavy for her to even pick it up. She stepped back and looked at Jessup, stunned. Jessup gave it a try herself. She raised the baby only an inch or so out of Mrs. Papillon's arms and then lowered it again.

"How could it be so heavy? And how can you keep holding it and carrying it around?"

Reg felt another rush of weariness from Mrs. Papillon, and this time understood it. Carrying around a hundred-pound dead weight for several days would have been more than any human could handle. It was taxing even to a fairy.

"If I want to get Callie back… I must. I must hold it and not let it go, for as long as it takes."

And judging by how tired she was already, Mrs. Papillon wasn't going to last much longer. They were all silent, considering the consequences.

"Have you found anything out?" Mrs. Papillon asked. "What have you found out about my Calliopia?"

Mr. Papillon laid down his trowel and turned to look at Jessup for her response.

"The best we can tell right now, it looks like the pixies were involved," Jessup said slowly. "But this changeling throws a slightly different complexion on the matter."

"It changes nothing," Mr. Papillon asserted.

"But changelings are something that fairies employ, not pixies. I've never heard of pixies swapping a changeling for a baby. Or an older child."

"There are many things you've never heard."

"That's true. Have you… heard anything from the pixies?

Have they sent a ransom note? A threat? If you knew all along that this was perpetrated by the pixies, why didn't you tell us that?"

"We could say nothing," Mrs. Papillon said, her voice tired and far away. "It would damage our chances of getting her back."

"So you just sit back and wait for us to figure out it was the pixies, knowing it the whole time."

They said nothing.

"So, how do you get your baby back?" Jessup asked. "I seem to remember boiling water in an eggshell, making it laugh, or injuring it somehow… obviously we can't do that."

"None of that will work. If it did, we wouldn't have had to involve anyone else. We could simply have done so ourselves."

"Then how?"

"*You* must find Calliopia and bring her back here."

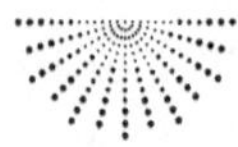

CHAPTER TWENTY-TWO

The pixies aren't going to just give her to us because we ask," Reg said, as Jessup drove her home.

"Obviously not," Jessup agreed.

"And with that rabbit's warren down there, I don't know how we could find her to get her out. Even if we didn't have to worry about being attacked by pixies." Reg paused, thinking about it. "What exactly will pixies do to you, anyway? I mean, do they turn you into toads, or kill you, or what? I know they can hypnotize you, or whatever they do with their eyes, but then what…?"

"There isn't a lot of information about that." Jessup pressed her lips together, thinking about it. "They're very reclusive. They don't mix much with humans or other races. It's only the last hundred or so years that we've had any kind of dialogue. Folk tales mostly have them luring humans underground, never to be heard from again. There are tales of parties and gruesome deaths, but mostly, being lost, squeezed, or buried underground."

"But they haven't done that to Calliopia. They're just holding her. Why haven't they done anything to her or asked for some kind of ransom? If they're that reclusive, why would they go to the fairies and steal her in the first place? Nothing adds up."

"We're still missing something. There's some key piece of information we haven't fit into place. Until we get it…"

"How long can Calliopia survive? They say you can't go without water for more than three days. In my dream, she hadn't had any food or drink since they took her. It's pretty damp down there, so she won't dehydrate as fast as she would in the sun, but sooner or later…"

"Fairy physiology is different than human physiology. I don't know what their physical needs are. I'm almost as worried about her mother as her. Carrying that changeling around or worrying about Calliopia—or both—are causing noticeable changes. Fairies are normally a very hardy folk. But emotional distress can kill them."

Reg's mind went to Calliopia, shut up in that cold, dark room. If emotional distress could kill fairies, then what effect would that environment have on her?

"Can you feel her?" Jessup asked, her mind obviously going down the same path as Reg's. "Is she still okay?"

Reg closed her eyes and reached out her mind to Callie. She repeated the girl's name in her mind. She pictured the place that Calliopia had been the last time Reg had seen her, checking to see if she were still there.

She could see Callie in her mind, lying listlessly on the bed, staring into the darkness. Like with her parents, her emotions were more difficult for Reg to read than human emotions, but Calliopia's were pretty raw after being stuck there for so long, and Reg could feel her singular yearning to go home.

Reg wiped her hand across her eyes. "She's still there. Still alive."

They drove for a while in silence.

"You must come from a very strong family," Jessup observed. "As far as their psychic potential, I mean. You've only been here for a little while, and still have so much to learn, but your abilities blow me away. Do you know how few psychics can actually do that? Reach out to contact someone they've never met before and have impressions that clear? It's practically unheard of. The reason you hear about psychics who are so vague and seem to be fishing for answers isn't because they are all fakes... it's because the answers are not clear, even for those who are legitimate."

Reg sucked in a breath and held it for a minute. Jessup shot a glance in her direction.

"Your parents? Were they psychic?"

"No."

"No? Nothing at all? Are you sure they didn't just mask it? A lot of people get beaten down for using their powers so much as children that they completely repress them as adults."

"No. Nothing."

"Grandparents? Extended family? Maternal grandmothers in particular—"

"Detective Jessup," Reg cut her off, putting a snap into her voice that she would never have used on a police officer normally.

Jessup stopped talking.

"In case you didn't know, I grew up in foster care. I don't have any family. I never knew any grandparents and barely knew my own mother. The only reason I know what I do about her is that she kept talking to me after she died. Otherwise, I'd have no memory of her."

"Oh. Sheesh, I'm sorry, Reg. That was classless. I guess I knew from your record that you ran into trouble because you didn't have a stable home. It completely slipped my mind."

Reg shrugged, looking out the window and trying not to show Jessup any emotion. Her hand was throbbing again, and she pressed her thumb to it, hoping it would settle down.

"But that means you really don't know what powers you might have gotten from your family," Jessup pointed out. "You don't know anything about them."

Reg didn't answer. She'd said all she was going to say about the matter. Jessup could believe it or not believe it as she chose. Reg would have known if her mother had been psychic. And her mother would have told her if anyone else in her family was. She would have been proud of the fact.

Of course, she had no idea about her father and his side of the family. She wasn't sure her mother even knew his identity.

"Is that the only way to get powers? They're always inherited?"

"No." Jessup seemed happy to steer the conversation back to more comfortable ground. "There are other ways. Some can be bestowed on you by someone who has them, like a gift. And there are parasites like Corvin, who take powers from someone or something else. Um… legendary objects that bestow powers, gifts by angels or fairies, being hit by lightning…"

Reg was fascinated. "Wow. Fairies can give powers?"

"Absolutely. Obviously, you got protection from the microscopic bit of fairy blood that contaminated your wound. That's just the tiniest fraction of what they possess. When they steal a human child, they actually turn it into a fairy with their magic. It is completely transformed from human to fairy."

"Instantly?"

"No, no." Jessup shook her head. "It's a transformation that takes place over years. Don't ask me to explain scientifically how it works, whether the body actually replaces human DNA with fairy DNA or what. I imagine if they tried to do it in an instant, they would kill the child."

"How do they do it?"

"Part of it is eating fairy food. I imagine there are many spells and enchantments that are involved, built up over the years, until the kidnapped child is completely transformed."

They reached the house, and both got out, Jessup walking Reg back to the cottage.

"What about other races?" Reg asked. "Could they transform other kinds of beings into fairies as well?"

"I imagine so, though I've never heard of it. I imagine some would be even easier than humans to transform, races that are already magical or long-lived."

"Like pixies?"

Jessup nodded as Reg turned the key in the lock. "Like pixies," she agreed.

They looked at one another, and as their eyes met, all of the pieces started to click into place.

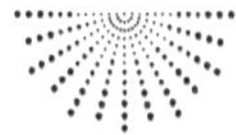

CHAPTER TWENTY-THREE

"She's taller than Ruan, but she has the same eyes," Reg said.

"She has that same muddy brown hair. Not curly, but that could have changed."

"When I told Ruan that kidnapping was wrong, he agreed with me."

"Because she was stolen from the pixies," Jessup finished. "She was taken away from *them* as a baby."

"Calliopia's mother said that if they didn't feed the changeling, it wouldn't develop, but it would get heavier."

"And the changeling was at least a hundred pounds. The weight of a teenager."

They walked into the cottage, both of them blind to their surroundings, sorting out all of the details that had appeared random before and now all fit together into a story.

"If the pixies knew enough about changelings not to feed it, why didn't they do any of the things they needed to do to force the fairies to swap back?" Reg asked.

"I'm not sure. Mrs. Papillon said that none of those things would work, so maybe they only work if it was a human who was stolen. With the pixies being magical, maybe they were barred from the usual methods."

Reg put the kettle on and prepared the tea things automatically, her brain far from what she was doing.

"Do you think Demelza was Calliopia's mother?"

"I don't know. That would be my first guess. But I don't know. It's going to take some investigating to get down to the truth." Jessup rolled her eyes. "More pixie interrogations. Oh, joy!"

"She didn't look like a woman who has been carrying a changeling around for sixteen years. Do you think the rules are different for every race? Maybe pixies don't have to hold on to the changeling."

"It's possible. But pixies are incredibly strong. They always make me think of ants carrying ten times their own body weight. Pixies don't use beasts of burden. Any hauling or building they do, it's pixie muscle. They carry rocks and beams on their backs that we would use cranes and trucks for."

"Then why now?"

The kettle started to whistle and Reg poured the water into the teapot. Her right hand hurt too much, so she handled it awkwardly with her left. Jessup didn't appear to notice as she took the tea tray over to the coffee table and set it down.

"Why now what?" she prompted.

Reg sat down slowly, feeling her brows knit. "Why did they swap the changeling and Calliopia now? They didn't do it when she was younger, but then they do it when she's a teenager? Almost grown up?"

Jessup took a sip of tea, thinking about it. "I wonder. Maybe she was stolen from somewhere far away and they didn't know where she was physically located. They didn't find her until now?"

"Yeah. Maybe. Brannock and Demelza didn't have accents, but then, they aren't necessarily even Calliopia's parents."

Starlight rubbed against Reg's ankles. She looked down at him. "Oh, hi, fur face. How are you?"

He sat back and meowed at her. Reg scratched his ears with

her left hand. He rubbed against her for a minute, then flopped over on his side, offering his soft belly. Reg stroked and scratched it. He only put up with it for a few minutes, then scrambled to his feet. He put his front paws up on Reg's knees and she sat back to make space for him to jump up into her lap.

Starlight purred and rubbed against her chin. He nuzzled Reg's left hand, and turned around on her lap, nudging her right shoulder and arm. Reg eventually gave in and stroked his ears with the fingertips of her right hand. He smelled her fingers and pushed his nose into her palm. Reg winced and let him smell it, realizing he wasn't going to be satisfied until he had fully investigated.

"Reg, are you okay?"

Reg looked at her injured hand. The bandage that had been so clean and crisp that morning was soaked with blood. She sighed. "I just need a new bandage."

"We need to get Letticia to look at it again."

"No, it just needs a new dressing. She left more of the yarrow in the fridge, I'll just put more on. It's not going to heal in a few hours. It just needs another application."

"Let me help."

Reg went to the kitchen to get the mushed yarrow out of the fridge, and Jessup helped to remove the old bandage, clean the cut, apply the poultice, and redress it.

"So what does this mean for Calliopia?" Reg asked, smoothing the bandage with her thumb.

"What do you mean?"

"The police are investigating Calliopia being kidnapped from the Papillons. But if the Papillons kidnapped her from the pixies, then you can't take her from the pixies and give her back to the Papillons."

Jessup stared at Reg for a minute, thinking it through. "Well… I don't know. The first thing we have to do is actually find Calliopia. She's a missing person. That's job one. Then… we'll have to unwind the whole story… if she was stolen from the pixies, then I guess that's where she'll go."

"She's been raised by fairies. How is she going to react to being told she's a pixie? Would she even know that? Does she think she was always a fairy?"

"Going to school with other races, she must have realized that she wasn't a natural-born fairy. But would she have known that she was a pixie? She had already changed enough that she didn't look like a full-blooded pixie either. The Papillons might have befuddled her, to keep her or anyone else from realizing what she was."

"So would she know? Would there be any way for her to figure it out?"

Starlight jumped up on the counter. Reg allowed him to smell the fresh bandage on her hand and satisfy himself that she was okay before shooing him off.

"Callie could have gone to someone skilled at scrying. Or she might have been gifted enough herself to cast a bloodline spell, to test her parentage."

She looked at Reg and licked her lips, as they both considered what she had said.

"A bloodline spell. What would that involve?"

"A sample of her blood… an incantation… a reagent…"

"So what I saw… maybe it wasn't a love potion. Maybe it was a bloodline spell."

Jessup nodded slowly. "If she did a bloodline spell and she tested it against a pixie relative, she might have broken the spell the fairies had used to hide her."

"So that the pixies could find her again and take her back."

There was a prolonged sigh from Jessup. "We're going to need someone who has more specialized knowledge about fairy and pixie magic. If we're going to go back to the pixies, I want an expert with us."

"Do you have someone at the police department who knows that kind of thing?" Reg envisioned going back to the pixies' burrows with a whole magical SWAT team. They wouldn't have to go alone again. They'd have backup.

"I have a consultant. Someone who has done a lot of research into magical history. He has published a treatise on the long-standing fairy/pixie war. He has a lot of knowledge that has been lost from the modern fairy tales."

Reg nodded eagerly, smiling. "Sounds perfect."

But Jessup was shaking her head, looking sour. "Not so perfect."

CHAPTER TWENTY-FOUR

Reg had a drink to fortify herself before Corvin got there. Jessup didn't know about the encounter between Corvin and Reg at the party. She didn't know that Corvin was going to have to appear before his coven for trying to force Reg's powers from her, and that Reg's antipathy toward him was greater than ever. Jessup knew their history from the Warren Blake case, but thought that they were reconciled.

"He's not coming into my house," Reg warned Jessup when she proposed to call him.

"No, I think that's a wise decision," Jessup agreed. "But I don't think we should meet in public, either. You never know when you might be overheard. Pixies are notorious for being able to hide themselves and go unnoticed in crowds."

"And in nature." Reg remembered how Ruan had disappeared, and the ability of the pixies to fade into shadows in their underground settlement.

"Yes. But I think if we meet in the yard…" Jessup pointed to Sarah's gardens outside, "Sarah will have the appropriate protections in place. We should be able to talk there without eavesdroppers there."

Reg nodded. Talking to Corvin in the yard was not the same

as inviting him into the cottage. She could do that without making herself vulnerable to him as long as Jessup was there to supervise.

They sat on deck chairs in the back yard. Reg couldn't help the throb of her heart when she saw Corvin, so handsome and attractive. She didn't want to look at him, but couldn't help looking into his face to gauge his mood. His face seemed paler than usual, with slight shadows under his eyes. His smile at Reg and Jessup was strained.

"How can I be of service to the police department today?" he inquired, without greeting Reg. "Is this still the kidnapping case?"

Jessup relayed their theory that Calliopia had been stolen from the pixies as an infant, and then kidnapped back by the pixies days before. She told him about the changeling left in Calliopia's place.

Corvin rubbed his bearded chin, thinking about it. "The pieces fit," he agreed. "Fairies stealing races other than humans is not unheard of. If Calliopia started wondering about her heritage… maybe the boy said something to her, got her wondering. He might have even suggested the lineage test and supplied a sample of his own blood. If she mingled her blood with his… the pixies would have been able to track her right back to her home."

"She was going to school with Ruan. If he thought she was a pixie, couldn't he have just snatched her from there? Why bother with a test and swapping her back for the changeling?"

"There are protections at the school. You couldn't have mixed magical races learning together without some pretty strong deterrents."

Reg closed her eyes, trying to see it in her head, testing out his theory. She'd been able to see Callie in the present, in her dark dungeon, and she'd been able to see her in the past, when she had cut herself. If she tried hard enough, maybe she'd be able to see Callie at the point when she had completed the blood test, or when the pixies had come for her. Had she known that they would come after her once she had completed the test of her parentage? Or had she been shocked to have the shadows suddenly swarm into her room to steal her away from the only family she knew?

She hummed, trying to remember how Calliopia's song had sounded. She couldn't remember the words of the incantation; it had not been English, and the words had been too foreign for her to recall them.

She reached out, trying to picture the knife again. Callie running it down her arm, pretending to herself that her hand wasn't shaking, drawing blood to complete the test. It was a test of her willingness as much as it was a test of her parentage.

Ruan had spoken to her at school. He stared at her with those intense blue eyes. "You're not a fairy. Why are you kidding yourself? You were never meant to live above ground in the harsh sun. You crave darkness."

She felt a jolt in her gut. She knew that was true. Her parents had always been frustrated by her attempts to block the sun out of her bedroom or the other rooms she spent time in. It hurt her eyes, burned her skin, left her feeling raw and unsettled. What had she been before? Was he telling the truth?

Reg forced her mind back to the knife. The key moment when Calliopia cut herself and mingled her blood with Ruan's. The moment she knew who she really was and the fairy spell that kept her hidden broke. But she couldn't bring herself to witness that private instant. She clenched her fists, frustrated and angry.

"Give me the knife," she blurted, opening her eyes and reaching her hand out toward Jessup.

Jessup stared down at Reg's palm, the bandage once more soaked with blood. "What?"

"The blade. Where is the fairy blade? I need it!"

"It's in my car. But…"

"Go get it," Reg insisted. She wiped at the sweat on her forehead with the back of her wrist. Her head was pounding and sweat was running off of her in long rivulets.

Jessup looked at Corvin, who gave a broad shrug. Jessup took another quick look at Reg. "Okay. Hang tight. I'll go get it."

She hurried away.

"Regina…" Corvin said lowly.

"Don't talk to me."

She could see he didn't like it, but he closed his mouth and kept his peace. He was frowning at her bleeding hand. The same way that Starlight would have looked at her, as if she were a child incapable of taking care of herself.

Jessup returned with the evidence bag. She held it just out of Reg's reach, tentative. "You can't take it out of the bag."

Reg leaned forward and snatched it from her, heedless of her injured hand. She closed her hand around the hilt, ignoring the thick plastic of the bag, and pointed the sharp tip at her left arm.

"Don't!" Jessup lurched forward to stop her, but stopped when Reg didn't actually attempt to cut herself right through the bag. Reg stared down at the silver blade, breathing shallowly. The others watched her.

"What is it?" Corvin finally asked, breaking the silence.

"This is the blade."

"The blade that Hawthorne-Rose used on you," Jessup agreed, her voice pitched low and soothing. "It was taken from your cottage that day."

Reg's eyes unfocused, seeing Callie in her mind, overlaying the images, comparing the minutest detail.

"This is the knife Callie used to cut herself."

"No, it's the one from Hawthorne-Rose."

"It's the same one."

"Letticia *said* it had fairy blood on it," Corvin reminded Jessup. "Normally, if a weapon sheds fairy blood, it is unmade. They will fire it and reforge it as something else."

"But they didn't."

"Maybe there wasn't time. Once she did the test, the spell broke, and they came for her."

"Then how did Hawthorne-Rose get it? He was already in jail when Calliopia was kidnapped."

"Was he? You only have her parents' word of when she was taken."

"Even if you ignore the timeline problems, Hawthorne-Rose still doesn't fit. How would he get the knife?"

Reg lowered the knife, looking at it. She was hot and dizzy. "I don't know, but he did."

"Are you okay?"

"Yeah. Just feeling a little… light-headed."

She felt herself slumping forward in the chair.

"Regina!" Corvin's hands were on her, steadying her and keeping her from sliding right out of the chair. Reg was a little startled to find him there so quickly. He hadn't shown real concern for her before. She believed that he had only pretended to like her or be kind to her so that he could get what he wanted. "Let's get her into the house."

"No." Reg objected. She wasn't going to allow him into her house for anything. "I'm fine."

"If nothing else, we have to redress that hand," Corvin told Jessup, pulling Reg's arm around his shoulder to support her back into the cottage.

"Stay out of my house," Reg insisted, taking care not to slur her words.

"I just put a fresh bandage on that," Jessup said. "And yarrow. I don't understand why it's bleeding so badly. It's worse every time I see it."

"Even so, she still shouldn't be responding like this to a little blood loss. It's not enough to put her in danger."

Reg did her best to pull out of Corvin's grip. "Let go of me. Don't touch me!"

"I'm trying to help you, Reg. I'm trying to give you medical care."

"No."

"You'd better let her go," Jessup advised. "Just let her sit here. I'll get the supplies. Letticia was going to get some rowan berries. You don't have any, do you?"

"Not on me." Corvin reluctantly settled Reg back into her chair.

Jessup retrieved the bandages and yarrow from the house and gave them to Corvin. He began to take off the blood-soaked bandage.

"Don't touch me," Reg repeated, pulling back.

"Let me change the bandage."

"No."

"Regina!"

How many times had she heard that tone from foster moms, thoroughly frustrated by Reg's behavior? She didn't care about his frustration. She hoped he did feel bad. He should.

"Let me." Jessup intervened and took over the first aid care. She looked at the injured hand, shaking her head. "We'd better start seeing some improvement in this before long. I was hoping the yarrow would work better." She tilted Reg's hand toward Corvin so he could see the wound. "It just keeps getting worse."

Reg's head spun as Jessup cleaned and redressed the wound. She kept seeing Calliopia cutting herself with the knife and then Hawthorne-Rose cutting Reg with it, trying to torture the information he wanted out of her.

"It's the same knife," she insisted.

"Okay, it's the same knife," Jessup placated.

"She could be right," Corvin said. "What are the chances that there would be two knives lying around with fairy blood on them? That's a pretty rare contaminant."

"I still can't fathom how he would have gotten his hands on it."

Reg saw Calliopia in her dungeon room and the wound felt like it had been cut anew. Reg caught it with her other hand, gritting her teeth and trying to get past the pain. Corvin moved in closer.

"What was that?"

"I just see her… waiting in that room. She wants to go home.

She doesn't want to be there. Even if she is a pixie, she doesn't want to live there, like that."

"You just saw Callie."

"Yes."

"And your injury hurt more."

"Yes."

"Has it been worse every time you've had a vision of her?"

Reg tried to sort her memories and identify whether there was a pattern. She nodded hesitantly. "Yeah. It throbs, and it bleeds more…"

Corvin nodded. He was too close to Reg. She could feel his breath. But she couldn't back away from him any farther.

"It *must* be Calliopia's knife," Corvin said. "It's her blood. It opened up a psychic connection between the two of you."

"That's why your visions of her are so clear," Jessup said, her tone suddenly eager. "Infecting your wound with her blood? That's pretty powerful magic."

"It's Callie's knife," Reg said.

"It's Callie's knife," Jessup agreed.

"Fairy blood."

"Yeah, Callie's."

They were all silent as Jessup finished taping the bandage securely in place. Reg let her hand lie in her lap, not bending or moving it so that she wouldn't hurt it any more. Corvin started to swear. Reg opened her eyes a slit to look at him.

"What is it?" Jessup asked.

"It's *fairy* blood."

"Yes… I thought we'd established that."

"Then Calliopia is no longer a pixie."

Jessup looked at Corvin, then at Reg. "You're right. That's going to complicate the pixies' claim on her, but we still have to find her and let the proper authorities work things out…"

"You *said* she could turn into a fairy." Reg wasn't sure why Jessup and Corvin seemed surprised and disturbed by this fact.

But it wasn't like an animal changing its DNA. Magic made things like that possible.

"Of course," Jessup agreed. "But… the timing is really bad. They wouldn't have stolen her back if they'd known she had already come into her own."

"She's still their daughter, biologically."

"But she's not. She's a completely different species. One that they are at war with. They could never live as a mixed family. It wouldn't be tolerated."

"We've got to get her out of there," Corvin said. "Before they kill her."

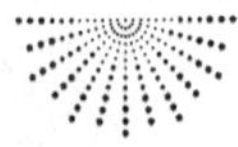

CHAPTER TWENTY-FIVE

When Reg tried to get up, her knees were wobbly and weak. She pushed herself up off of the chair, but she wasn't sure how she was going to stay on her own feet and walk to the car, let alone back down through the labyrinth of tunnels to where Calliopia was being held.

Corvin moved toward her. She could feel the warmth of the air around him as he got too close. Her mind and body fought, wanting him and yet needing to protect herself from him. How could someone so dangerous be so attractive to her?

She knew what he was doing, as he stood over her and she started feeling a rush of warmth and energy. He was almost touching her, and she could feel him inching forward, his breath becoming cloyingly sweet as he positioned himself right in front of her face.

"No," Reg protested, her body buzzing with the electricity of having him so close to her.

"I'm just helping you."

"Don't." Reg tried to catch her breath. "Don't touch me. Don't... so close..." Even as she tried to push him farther away, she could envision herself grabbing him, pulling him close until there was no space left between them.

Why did she have to be so careful of him? Why did she have to be the one to say no?

"Hunter," Jessup warned.

Corvin turned his head very slightly to look at her. Gauging her like an animal. Wondering if he could overpower both of them and get what he wanted.

Jessup put her hand on her sidearm. "You may be long-lived, but as far as I know, you're still mortal."

Corvin's eyes glinted red and then the animal look was gone. He withdrew a pace from Reg, giving her breathing room.

"I was just helping. Giving her some strength."

Reg found that she was able to stand without shaking. Her heart, pounding strong, pumped a newfound energy through her body. She could do it. She could help them to find Calliopia and bring her back to the fairies, where she would be safe.

"Don't trust 'em farther than you can throw 'em," Jessup said, still looking at Corvin darkly. "We need to find Calliopia and get her out of there now. We're only going to get one attempt."

"Take the knife with you," Corvin suggested, nodding to the fairy blade in the evidence bag. "We may need it."

"We can't go in there armed with fairy steel."

"We can't go in there unarmed. They're not going to let you just waltz in and take Calliopia. Even if they have decided they don't want her."

Jessup looked as if she agreed with this.

"Then we take it," Reg agreed, picking it up and handing it to Jessup. "What else? Do we have anything else we can use against them? Or protect us from them?" The thought of having to physically fight the powerful little child-faced creatures made her sick. Reg Rawlins was better at running from fights than facing the music.

"You've got fairy blood, which is helpful. Too bad we don't have the changeling. How about the cat?" Corvin wrinkled his nose. Reg knew he didn't like her familiar. "Could he come along? Fairies and pixies both despise *felis catus*."

Reg hesitated. It had been hard when Starlight had disappeared. She was used to having him around to talk to and for him to help her with her psychic work. She didn't want to somehow lose him in the winding tunnels of the underground. She might never see him again.

But when she thought of Calliopia and how she couldn't escape the dark, cold room on her own, Reg had to put aside her own selfish feelings about her cat. He was there to work. He was there to be a helper for her, so she would take him.

She went into the cottage to coax Starlight out and explain to him what was going on. "I'm sorry. I don't know what you think of all of this. I thought that you'd be a house cat and be nice and safe here all the time. I never thought I'd be taking you out as protection against pixies."

He rubbed against her, which Reg took to mean that it was alright and he wouldn't hold it against her. Reg picked him up and headed back out toward Jessup's car. Corvin wasn't yet in the car, but hovering nearby.

"Reg... just before we head out... I wanted to apologize to you. Last night at the party... I'd had too much to drink. I lost control, and I know there's no excuse for that, but... I'm sorry."

Reg said nothing.

"I said I'm sorry."

"I heard you."

"Aren't you going to accept my apology?"

"Like you said. There's no excuse for that. And I don't excuse it. You will pay for attacking me."

"I wouldn't have—"

"Get in the car."

"Regina. We can still be friends..."

"You're not here because we're friends. You're here to help get Calliopia back."

"I know that..."

Starlight hissed at him, bristling like a porcupine in Reg's arms.

Reg brushed by him to get into the front seat beside Jessup. She realized she shouldn't have taken the chance of touching him, but there was no time for him to react, and a second later she was in the car with the door shut.

"Aren't you coming, Hunter?" Jessup demanded, putting the car into gear.

"Oh, I'm coming with you." Corvin finally opened the back door and slid onto the bench seat. He shifted around uncomfortably. "You're not paying me enough to sit on the back seat."

"Good," Reg said. "You're right where you belong."

Jessup glanced at Reg, obviously wondering what was going on between the two of them. But it wasn't the time to air their dirty laundry.

Jessup told Corvin what she could of their previous visit to the pixies, describing each tunnel along the way. She told him about Brannock and Demelza and the words that had been exchanged. Then she asked Reg to tell her story of seeing Ruan in front of the school. Reg explained about how she hadn't felt any deception from him, even though she knew he was lying, and about when he had surprised her by agreeing with her that kidnapping was wrong. Corvin nodded.

"He would have grown up hearing all about fairies stealing babies. It would have been part of his family's culture, especially since they'd experienced a kidnapping themselves," Corvin agreed.

In her lap, Starlight stood up on his hind legs and put his front paws on the door of the car to be able to see out as they drove. He watched with interest, as if he were the navigator. As they got closer to the pixie settlement, he got more restless, alternating between looking out the side window and the front window. Then he was suddenly yowling and pawing at Jessup's arm.

"I think you took a wrong turn," Corvin suggested, smiling wryly.

"This is the way. It's the only way I know of to get into the kingdom," Jessup said irritably. But Starlight continued to paw at her, extending his claws so that he pricked and scratched her arm when she didn't stop and turn around as quickly as he would have liked. Jessup looked at Reg. "Do you really think he knows what he's doing? That he really has the intelligence to direct us a different way? I've lived here all my life and I don't know of any other way in."

Reg shrugged apologetically. "I have no idea. Sometimes I think he knows exactly what he's doing, and sometimes I think he's just being annoying. I really can't tell the difference between the two. I brought him along because Corvin said to, but I have no idea if he even knows what pixies are."

Starlight turned and nipped at Reg.

"Ow! Okay, okay. He knows what pixies are, and maybe he knows another way in. You choose. Follow the cat or go the way you know."

Jessup bit her lip. She slowed down and flipped a U-turn in the middle of the road, to the noise of irritated honks from the other drivers. Starlight settled down and watched out the window. Watching him carefully, Reg gave Jessup directions, until they had wound their way all over the broken-down neighborhood and stopped on a road at the edge of a grove of trees. They must have been the only trees in the whole subdivision, and Reg wondered if that was why Starlight had directed them there. Maybe he liked the little forest with its interesting smells and sounds.

They all got out of the car. Reg was holding on to Starlight, but he clawed and kicked with his back legs and she let him go quickly to avoid getting her arms ripped up. As soon as Starlight hit the ground, he was making a beeline to the other side of the clearing.

"Follow that cat," Corvin said with good humor. They all trailed after him, wondering where he was going to lead them. Starlight wound in between trees, then stopped at a fallen log, a big boulder, and a small hole in the ground leading to some small animal burrow.

"Uh… hate to tell you, cat, but there's no way any of us are making it down that hole," Corvin said. "Not even you."

Reg knelt down on the damp ground and put her ear to the hole, listening. Detective Jessup and Corvin both looked awkward, standing there while Reg knelt by the hole.

She could hear them. It was faint, but unmistakable. The drip of the water, the murmured voices, and when she concentrated hard on Calliopia, the thread of Callie's song, just reaching the surface.

"He's right. They're down here. But I don't know how to get down to them. I think they might notice if we get an excavator out here."

"There has to be some way," Corvin said. "Why would he bring us this way, otherwise? This is where Calliopia is, so this is where we go down."

He kicked at the boulder and the fallen log. He managed to lift the log up, and Reg saw the white, squirming grubs underneath.

"Ugh. Put it back down."

"Squeamish, Regina? They'd make a good breakfast."

"You can eat whatever you like for breakfast. I'm not surprised you'd like something disgusting like that."

He laughed, seeming pleased by her retort. He pressed his shoulder into the rock and grunted and groaned, trying to push it out of place. It wouldn't budge.

"I guess we dig, then," Jessup sighed. "Let's hope it's not as deep as it sounds."

CHAPTER TWENTY-SIX

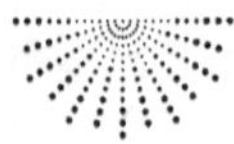

It wasn't easy. Jessup had a spade in her car trunk, but that was the only tool they had other than their hands or what they could improvise from the rocks and branches at hand. Corvin did most of the heavy work, deeming Reg too injured to do any shoveling, so mostly she stood around and watched for signals from Starlight and tried to see her way into the tunnels using her psychic abilities.

Eventually, Corvin hit empty space instead of rocks or more dirt, and nearly did a face plant. They helped to widen the hole and clear away any debris that could land on top of them once they went down.

The tunnel started right beside the boulder. The rock had shored up the walls, keeping it all from collapsing into itself over the years since it had gone into disuse. Jessup went first, all of them brushing dirt from their hands and faces.

"What's going to happen when they find out that we're in their tunnels without permission?" Reg whispered.

"I'm still going to claim the right to talk to them under the treaty," Jessup said. "It's a stretch, especially if we are not coming in through the official entrance, but I'm going to make it as hard as possible to ignore us and our demands."

They walked in silence, Starlight slipping to the front of the line to lead the way. He walked with his ears perked high, his pupils big and black in the dimness. Like the other tunnels Reg had been in, they were lit with a ghostly glow with no apparent origin.

And then their inconspicuous entrance was blown. Several male pixies stood in front of them, their childish faces angry.

"Who dares trespass on piskie land?" one of them demanded.

"We are not trespassing. We are here under the treaty," Jessup asserted. "I am here to take custody of Calliopia."

"Not a piskie name," one of them pointed out.

"A long time ago, she was a pixie. And I'm sure her mom and dad hoped that she still would be, and that they could finish raising her and she'd take her place in the pixie family. But things have not worked out that way."

The pixies exchanged looks with each other.

"Human beings are not welcome here. We have no need for a treaty."

"There is a treaty, whether you like it or not. This is an official investigation. A missing person report was filed by Calliopia's parents. We have determined that she is down here. You can turn her over to me. We will take care of the formalities."

The pixie men gave no indication that they planned to get out of the way. Reg clicked her tongue for Starlight. He looked back at her for a moment, but didn't go to her. The movement brought the pixies' attention to the cat, as if they hadn't noticed him before.

"The humans brought an offering," one of the pixie men chuckled. "A feast tonight."

"You are not eating my cat!" Reg snapped, outraged.

Starlight focused on the man who had spoken, headed straight for him. Looking alarmed, the little man stepped back to allow the cat passage. Starlight looked back over his shoulder as if wondering where his humans had gone. Reg started to follow, but the man stepped back in front of her, folding his arms across his chest.

"You are not here under the treaty," he accused. "You have no business here."

Reg reached her injured hand out toward him. "You know what this is? You want a closer look? You know I carry fairy blood?"

He looked nervously at the other pixies for their reactions. No one seemed too eager to challenge her. When they looked at each other for moral support, Reg thought she recognized one of the boyish faces.

"Ruan?"

The pixie ducked back to hide from her, but the others moved nervously away from him, so that Reg could see him clearly. It *was* Ruan. He made a warding gesture toward her. "The human does have fairy blood!" he confirmed. "She burned me without fair warning. Stay well back of her."

She couldn't have asked for a better reaction. All of the men took a step or two back from her. Reg was able to follow Starlight. Jessup and Corvin followed close after her, nearly stepping on her heels.

"Humans have no right to be here," one of the pixies howled, furious about the trespass. He came after them, sharp teeth bared, hands outstretched into claws in front of him. It took a moment for Reg to register first that he was a threat, and second, that he was unarmed, except for his nails and teeth. In the time it took for her to process both of those thoughts, Jessup had raised the knife in the plastic evidence bag in warning.

"Fairy steel!" she warned. "Who wants to test its edge? As a bonus, it's also been baptized with fairy blood."

There were hisses from the pixies. The one who was attacking slowed, but didn't stop. Jessup didn't stab him with Hawthorne-Rose's knife, but aimed a punch straight to his chest that knocked him back into the wall of the tunnel. The pixie fell to his knees, white face turning blue as he choked for breath. The other pixies laughed and swarmed him, kicking and hitting. For a moment, Reg was worried that they were going to kill him or even to eat him. Their sharp fangs glistened in the dark, and she had no idea whether cannibalism was a thing among pixies. They certainly looked vicious enough.

"Keep moving," Jessup whispered, giving Reg a little nudge forward. Jessup waited for Corvin to pass, then brought up the rear, holding out the fairy blade as a warning to other pixies. She should have been in the front. She was the cop. But instead it was the cat who led them while Jessup defended their rear. Ears pricked, Starlight kept a steady path toward Calliopia's cell, where every few minutes they heard her sing a line or two of her song. Then her voice would fade away, and Reg found herself holding her breath, worried every line would be Calliopia's last.

Each time they turned a corner, a few more of the pixies fell away, until they were on their own in the dim, dank tunnels.

Finally, they reached the small, dirt-floor room where Calliopia lay on the bed, her face pale and wan, staring into the middle of the dimly-lit room.

Starlight stopped outside the door and looked at them. Reg remembered how Jessup had said that Calliopia's family was allergic to cats, and wondered whether Starlight sensed that. She went into the room and approached Callie.

"Calliopia? We're here to take you home. Are you okay?"

Calliopia continued to stare into the middle of the room, not looking at Reg. The chill of the room washed over Reg and she shivered.

"Callie? Callie, we're here to help you."

Corvin followed close behind her and looked quickly around, as if expecting another attack from the pixies from within the room.

Jessup stopped at the threshold and looked down at Starlight.

CHAPTER TWENTY-SEVEN

*W*hat is it?" Reg asked.

Jessup didn't answer. Corvin looked at Reg and looked at Starlight.

"You have a very smart cat."

"Yes, I know."

"Why didn't he enter?"

"I guess because Calliopia's allergic. Jessup said that the other day."

"I'm sure she was just being tactful. Fairies aren't allergic to cats, they are enemies."

"Is there anyone fairies are not enemies with?"

"Not many. So why didn't the cat come in?"

"Well, if they're enemies, maybe he doesn't feel like it. He brought us this far, but he doesn't want to have to deal with a fairy directly."

"When was the last time you saw a cat avoid someone because they didn't like cats? From what I've observed, they always show the most interest in the people who dislike them. And your tux has not been an exception."

Reg wondered why Corvin never called Starlight by his name.

"Why does it matter? He brought us here. We need to get Calliopia and get out of here."

Corvin walked back to the doorway and walked through. He looked relieved when he was able to walk back out without being stopped by some spell or forcefield.

"Satisfied?" Reg asked, exasperated. "Now let's get Callie out of here."

Corvin walked back in. Starlight and Jessup remained outside. Jessup looked down at Starlight.

"What's going on here?" she asked him. "Where did they go?"

Reg frowned at Corvin. "What?"

"I think we might have a problem," he said, voice grave.

Reg looked at him, then held her hands out in front of her and looked at them. "What? What are you talking about?"

"Marta?" Corvin spoke to Jessup. "What do you see?"

She didn't look at him. She bent down to pet Starlight, looking up and down the halls for trouble. "Pixie magic," she murmured as she stroked him. "I don't like this. Where are they? And where did all of the pixies go?"

Starlight looked into the room, but still didn't enter. Reg's stomach knotted.

"Can't she see and hear us?"

"It would appear not." Corvin looked at his hands, as Reg had done.

"But we can go back out. We're not trapped. Won't that reverse whatever spell they've put on us?"

Without waiting for an answer, Reg left the room, walking back out through the open doorway. But Jessup's manner didn't change. She didn't suddenly see Reg, but continued to look around her, alert for trouble, trying to sort it out.

Reg reached out to touch her. But the closer she got to Jessup, the thicker the air seemed to get. Before she could touch Jessup, the air was buzzing like she was standing next to a power transformer. She could feel the hair rising on her arms and scalp. She stopped, worried that if she were actually able to make contact with Jessup's skin, she would be zapped with an electrical shock like a bolt of lightning. She turned and looked back at Corvin, still in the room with Calliopia, nearly as pale as she was.

"Corvin? Do you know what's going on?"

He swallowed and didn't answer right away. He looked back at Calliopia. "I have an idea of what's going on," he admitted.

"What?"

"The pixies inhabit two worlds. Our world, and the world of shades."

Reg shuddered. "What's that? Do you mean the spirit world? Where the spirits go when they cross over?"

"No. It's not the same thing—at least, not as far as we understand. It's hard for humans to comprehend how the unseen worlds work and relate to each other. I don't know how much you know about pixies…?"

"Next to nothing."

"Well…" He considered what to tell her. "They have the ability to hide or disappear quickly. In some places, you can see them as shadows, if you are looking close enough."

Reg nodded. "Yes. I've seen that."

"Then you know more than you let on. That ability comes from the fact that they inhabit these two worlds, or two planes. They can be in the visible realm, or they can be in the shadow world. Much more difficult for us to see. Impossible for some. Easier for those who have the sight." He nodded at her.

Reg looked again at herself and then at Corvin. She looked out into the hall where Jessup was still looking lost and alone, but Starlight was gazing into the room watching them intently.

"So you think Detective Jessup can't see us because we are in the shadow world?"

Corvin nodded.

"How?"

"A jinx in that doorway. So that anyone who entered would be sent to the shadow world. Not a problem for pixies, but for someone like you or me, unable to travel voluntarily between the two worlds…"

"So how do we get out?"

"I don't know."

She waited for him to start postulating ideas, but he didn't. "As part of this world of shades, can we still interact with things in the real world?"

"I believe that we can, in most cases. If we want to badly enough."

"And Starlight can still see us."

Corvin looked at the cat. "So it would appear."

"But not Calliopia?"

Corvin studied the girl in the bed and pursed his lips. "I really have no idea. She looks pretty out of it."

"Did they drug her?"

"They might have used a potion or a spell on her. I don't imagine she's staying here of her own free choice."

Reg got close to Calliopia, again calling her name and trying to rouse her from her stupor. Callie sang a few notes, and then was silent again. The unfinished song gave Reg goosebumps. Or maybe it was just the chill of the underground cave.

"You have a psychic connection with Callie," Corvin reminded her. "Why don't you use that?"

"Oh." Reg flushed with embarrassment. "I guess I could try."

She closed her eyes and reached out to Calliopia. It seemed like she was far away, even though she was right there beside Reg. Callie stirred, and Reg was able to enter her thoughts, gently probing, trying to get some reaction out of her. But Calliopia seemed unaware that she was there, either in the room or in her mind. Reg focused, and looked around at the room through Calliopia's eyes, as she had done before.

The room seemed empty, just Calliopia lying on the bed alone. No one in the room; nothing but shadows.

"We're here," Reg told Callie firmly, trying to impress the thought on her mind. "We're here to help you."

Callie looked around the room more carefully. In the middle of the floor, she saw two large beetles.

Reg jumped and looked down, her own eyes flying open. She didn't see anything on the floor but her own feet and Corvin's.

"What is it?" Corvin asked, looking amused by her reaction.

"There are two beetles. Really big ones. A red one and a green one. Calliopia can see them, but… I can't."

"Maybe that's how we manifest to her when we're in the shadow world."

"But… what kind of sense does that make? We're not beetles. Why would we look like beetles? And how will we interact with the physical world if we're beetles and humans at the same time?"

"Try talking to her now that she knows we're here." Corvin said a few words in a language that must have been fairy, but Calliopia didn't react. "You try it. You have a connection with her. She's more likely to hear and understand you."

"Callie. We're here to help you. We came to rescue you."

Reg had no idea how two beetles were supposed to rescue Calliopia from the pixies, even if they were fairly large ones. It seemed like a ridiculous prospect.

Calliopia continued to look intently at the floor where she saw them.

"You want to go home," Reg said, trying to connect with Callie's emotions.

The fairy licked dry, chapped lips. Her mouth formed the word 'home.' Corvin nodded at Reg encouragingly.

"Yes," Reg said. "Home. Back to the castle. We're here to take you back to your family."

At these words, Callie's hopeful look faded. She closed her eyes for a moment, and a wave of despair and exhaustion washed over Reg.

"To the fairies," Reg said urgently, realizing that Callie was associating 'family' with pixies. "We want to take you home to the fairies."

Callie raised her eyes again.

"Yes. Yes, hang in there. We need you to tell us… what traps and spells are here. How are they keeping you here?"

Calliopia pushed herself up a little, leaning on her elbow and looking down at the beetles she saw on the dirt floor.

"What tricks be this?" she whispered.

"We are humans. Helping your parents. Trying to get you back to the fairies. Can you get up? Can we get you out of here?"

Calliopia moved slowly, getting into a sitting position and sliding her feet off of the bed. When her feet touched the floor, her head sagged, as if it had suddenly become very heavy. Corvin instinctively took a step forward to steady her, but he jerked his hand back when he got close to her as if he'd been shocked.

"Doesn't feel so good, does it?" Reg asked.

He nodded. "I've wondered why they don't attack us while in their shadow form. They always reveal themselves first." He stood near Calliopia, holding his hands out like he was warming them by a fire. She straightened up, gathering strength.

"That's a really handy talent," Reg observed.

"If you often find yourself rescuing ladies in distress," he said dryly.

He did seem to find himself in that position fairly regularly. Maybe Reg and Corvin needed to stop running into dangerous situations without first checking for traps. Assuming Corvin had the ability to check for magical traps. Reg didn't think she herself did.

Calliopia took a deeper breath and planted her feet more firmly in the dirt. She stood up. She looked around the little room.

"How do I get out?"

Reg gestured at the doorway. "I don't know what spells there might be around the door, but…"

Calliopia continued to gaze around vaguely. Reg reached out to Callie's mind carefully, looking out through her eyes again. She hadn't noticed before that there was no door. Just a room with four walls and beetles on the dirt floor. She directed Callie's mind to the wall she knew the door was in.

"Over there. I know you can't see it, but the door is there."

Calliopia walked over to the wall. She reached out her hand and touched it. She was a couple of steps to the side of the doorway, so when she reached out she did touch solid wall.

Jessup seemed to suddenly become aware of what was going on, turning her head to look at Calliopia, standing just a couple of feet away from her.

"Well, hello! You're up and around. Shall we see if we can get you out of here?"

Staring at a blank rock wall, Calliopia did not see or hear her. Reg tried to guide her down to the open doorway. Calliopia shuffled along, doubtful, not seeing any changes to the solidity of the wall in front of her.

"Right here. The door is right here."

Jessup watched Callie reach her hands out tentatively, feeling for the wall and finding only empty space. "That's right," she encouraged, even though as far as Calliopia was concerned, there was no one there.

Callie stood there for a minute, hesitant. They all waited to see if she would take the leap of faith and walk into what appeared to her to be solid rock. Eventually, Callie did. She stepped out of the prison cell into the hallway.

"There you go," Jessup cheered.

Calliopia startled at finding someone right in front of her, and threw her hands up in front of her face protectively.

"It's okay. It's okay, I'm sorry. I didn't mean to scare you. I'm sorry!"

Callie lowered her hands and looked at Jessup, frowning and shaking her head.

"Who are you?"

"Police," Jessup declared, pushing her jacket aside to show off her shield before remembering that she had lost it. She touched the bare place. "I'm with the police department. I've been looking for you, Calliopia."

"You were looking for me?"

"Your parents have been very upset. They'll be very glad to see you home safe." Jessup touched Callie's arm. "You'll come with me?"

Callie nodded hesitantly, looking around her. It was eerily quiet. Reg knew from her previous visit that there were plenty of pixies in the burrows, and it seemed beyond belief that they would leave Calliopia without guards, especially when they knew there were intruders in the tunnels.

Jessup looked back into the empty cell.

"What should we do?" Reg asked Corvin. "Just… walk out like this? Invisible? Will they be able to see us when we get out of here? Once we're above ground?"

"The shadow world doesn't just exist underground. I don't think it's going to make any difference whether we're down here or above ground. We're still going to have to figure out how to get back to the physical world."

Reg felt sick. Being stuck forever as a shadow was a worse fate than when they had been trapped in a locked room facing the possibility of dying of heatstroke. To be able to see and hear every-thing but never participate in it…

Corvin and Reg headed for the door to follow Jessup and Callie. Callie pointed to the ground.

"You see them?"

Jessup looked down at the dirt and gave a little jump. "Oh! Ugh. Yes. I see them. Yuck. They're not… your pets or something?"

Callie shook her head. "Helpers. Like you. Did they not come with you?"

Jessup stared at the beetles. She looked at Starlight. "Tell me that's not Reg and Corvin."

Starlight blinked at her. Jessup groaned. "No…! Well, we can't leave them here like that." Jessup wisely didn't go into the room to pick them up, still following Starlight's lead.

Reg and Corvin left the cell, joining the others in the hallway. Reg looked at herself, hoping that having left the cell, and Calliopia no longer being incarcerated there, she would suddenly rejoin the visible world. She and Corvin looked at each other hopefully, but of course neither of them could tell if the other had become visible. Seeing as there was no reaction from Jessup and Calliopia, and they were both still staring down at the ground, Reg had to assume that they were still not appearing in their usual forms.

"Should I pick them up?" Jessup asked, looking repulsed at the thought.

Calliopia shook her head. "They are not real bugs."

"Well, no. But if we need to run, and they get trampled…"

Callie nudged Corvin's foot with her bare toes, deflecting to the side and unable to move him or, Reg guessed, the beetle that the two of them saw.

"Not bugs," Callie repeated.

Starlight sniffed at Reg's shoe.

"What's the best way to get out of here, Starlight?" Jessup asked. "You brought us in, I assume you know the best way out."

Calliopia hadn't paid any attention to the cat until that point. She looked at him when Jessup addressed him, and her lips drew back in a snarl.

"None of that," Jessup warned, putting out her hand to caution Callie before she could try to kick Starlight or do something else to harm him. "He's the one who helped us to find you."

Callie dropped the snarl and folded her arms across her chest, looking the typical pouty teenager despite all that she had just been through.

Jessup had the fairy knife, still in the plastic evidence bag, in her hand. Calliopia frowned at it.

"My dagger."

"Yes. It's police evidence. We just thought it might come in handy here, and so far it has."

They started as a group down the tunnel, Starlight moving ahead to take the lead again. He sniffed at the air and moved slowly, much more cautious than he had been on the way in.

"This isn't right," Jessup said anxiously. "We shouldn't be able to just walk in and walk out." She looked down at the beetles. "Although… it's not like we haven't taken our losses."

"Where be the piskies?" Calliopia asked.

"Exactly."

They advanced through a few more passages, and then were face to face with what they had both feared and expected.

CHAPTER TWENTY-EIGHT

The mob of pixies faced Jessup, Calliopia, and the less-visible members of the party with sneers and shouts of anger. Ruan was at the front of the group and stared at Callie with an expression of pure hatred.

"Let us pass. Police business," Jessup said, acting as though she expected them to part and do as she said.

They didn't.

"Humans have no business here," one of the older pixie men said.

"We've been through all of that. I do have business here, it falls under the treaty. We have found what we were looking for, so we are ready to leave."

"Not acceptable. Leave the prisoner."

"Your prisoner is the subject of our investigation. So, no, you're not keeping her."

"She belongs here." It was Demelza, the pixie woman they believed to be Callie's biological mother.

Reg felt a twinge of guilt at the knowledge that they were taking Demelza's child away from her, in spite of the fact that Calliopia had been changed by her life with the fairies. It wasn't Demelza's fault that Callie had been kidnapped and she could do nothing about the fact that she had been turned into a fairy. They had done their best to take her and claim her back, but it was too late, the girl had already turned.

"I know she's a fairy now," Reg said quietly to Corvin, "but does that mean they have to be enemies? She used to be a pixie. If her parents still care about her, we can't take Calliopia away just because she's been changed to something else… they still have a claim on her."

"She can choose to come back. But she probably won't, because if she does, the pixies will kill her."

Reg's heart pounded. "Why?"

"Why do you think she was locked in that room with no food and no water and a spell that would steal her strength if she tried to step off the bed? Not all races have the same values as we do. Even amongst humanity, there are cultures and individuals who don't have the respect for life that we would consider to be normal. The pixies will gladly kill anyone who is not of pixie blood. And that includes a fairy child, even one of their own."

"That's horrible. How could they?"

"There are humans who kills their own children for no logical reason. And this kind of death, starving her, that's considered merciful. Pixies won't think twice about tearing you to pieces."

"She doesn't belong here," Jessup asserted, facing Demelza and the mob of pixies head-on, as if she didn't know what they could do to her. "I am taking her away. If you have a problem with that, you need to come to the police station and lodge a complaint there. Then those who are in charge will take a look at the accusations."

"If you try to take her away from here, you will be sorry," Ruan threatened.

Jessup looked down at him for a few long seconds, drawing out the silence before answering. Ruan shifted, his face dark with fury at her examination.

"You are the one who enticed her here. If the police decide to lay charges, who do you think they're going to be against?"

His expression didn't betray any guilt or shame, but Reg noticed he didn't look directly at Calliopia, either. Had he known that what he had done was wrong? Or had he just intended to get his sister back, thinking she would be part of his family again?

"We will leave," Calliopia asserted. "Or we will fight."

They seemed to be expecting this. The pixies who were looking for a fight surged forward. Reg grabbed at Corvin. "How can we do anything when we're not on the same plane?"

"We are," Corvin said calmly. "They live on both planes."

Reg wasn't so sure she wanted to be able to fight the pixies. But she wasn't going to get a choice. The pixies descended on Jessup and Callie. Reg grabbed the closest one and tried to pull him off. He struggled with her at first, and as Jessup had warned, he was incredibly strong; but then he started thrashing in Reg's hands, howling in pain. She remembered the blood seeping through her bandage.

No matter how many times they bandaged it, any time she used the psychic connection to Calliopia, the wound opened up again and started to bleed freely. She let the pixie go and reached for another. As soon as he started screaming and pulling away, she grabbed another. She didn't have to hit them. She didn't have to use a weapon. All she needed was her own blood, tainted with Calliopia's.

She ripped the bandage off and tossed it to Corvin. At first, his lip turned up in disgust, but then he realized what the unorthodox weapon was worth. He smeared both of his hands with blood and held it out in front of him, swiping at anyone he could get close to.

Jessup had attempted to hold the pixies off as she had to begin with, using her combat skills to hit and push and take the pixies down, but while they were smaller and lighter than she was, they were hardy and laughed at her attempts to hurt them. Jessup was forced to defend herself with the fairy dagger.

Calliopia was holding her own. Her blood might have turned to fairy blood, but she had the hardy body of a pixie. Fed by fairies, she was taller than any of her former family and had a longer reach. As with Reg, they had to be careful of cutting her, because her blood was another weapon against them.

For a few minutes, all Reg could think about was protecting her friends and herself from the pixie attack. There were a lot of pixies, but Reg and Corvin didn't have to do much to fend them off with the fairy blood, and the hall started to clear. Reg yelled and whooped.

"You'd better run! You'd better!"

Eventually, there were only a few attackers left. They held them at bay. Reg could see that the Rosdews were among the pixies still hanging on, and felt sorry both for them and for Callie. It wasn't fair that they had lost their daughter. It wasn't something that they could have done anything to prevent.

"It's over, Demelza. She's not yours anymore. Let us take her out of here where you don't have to think about her anymore. You can go on to other things, spoil Ruan and get him married and have baby pixies. Callie is never going to bring you anything."

Demelza moved forward, her face flushed and furious. "Callie? There is no *Calliopia*. They stole my baby girl! You have no idea how that hurts a mother. And now you take her away again?"

"I have to. She doesn't belong here and you will kill her. I can't stand by and let that happen."

"Better I kill her than she is raised by other kin!"

For the first time, Reg thought she understood what her social workers went through, taking children away from their parents, shopping them back and forth from one family to another trying to find the home that would work the best. Forever hurting either the bio family, the foster family, or the child. Always the bad guy, no matter how hard they tried to protect the children.

"I can't let you kill her. Her fairy family loves her. They will be happy to have her back. Wouldn't you rather know that she was happy and well?"

"No!"

Until then, she'd just been trying to hold Demelza off to

reason with her. Reg gave up on that and managed to get ahold of Demelza's arm, closing her hand tightly around it. Her blood was flowing freely, and Demelza shrieked, trying to shake loose. Reg held on as long as she was able, squeezing the blood out until Demelza's arm began to smoke. Horrified, Reg released her.

Demelza stepped back, still screaming. Her arm was blackened and a tight coil of smoke rose from it, the smell acrid and nauseating. Demelza began to chant in her pixie tongue, and her husband and son and the remaining fighters started to circle, gathering closer and closer together. Reg watched them with fascination. As she and Corvin were in the shadow world, the pixies couldn't hide from them. They circled and quieted, and then eventually slunk off, sticking to the shadowy walls of the tunnels.

"We did it!" Reg cheered. "We fought them off."

"That might not be all," Corvin warned. "They may be falling back to a new position and have other, fresh fighters ready."

Starlight gave a yowl. Reg looked down at him. She'd completely forgotten him in the fight, but it didn't look like the pixies had forgotten him. His fur was ruffled and he had a torn ear. But his fangs were bloody and he looked remarkably smug.

"What is it, cat?" Corvin demanded.

Starlight looked this way and that, sniffing the air, his ears rotating like little radar dishes. Then he started out again, leading them once more.

"Can you get us out of here without another fight?" Corvin asked.

Starlight looked back at him. While Reg hoped that the answer was yes, Starlight didn't look confident that he'd be able to avoid another pixie attack. They were, after all, on the pixies' home ground.

"Are you okay?" Jessup asked Calliopia, as they gathered their wits and followed Starlight's lead. The knife in Jessup's hand was bloody, and was no longer neatly encased in a sealed evidence bag. Jessup was going to be in trouble with the police department.

"I shall fight more," Callie declared, marching forward.

In spite of having fought barehanded, she seemed to be in remarkably good shape. Luckily for them, the pixies tended to eschew blades and rely instead on their hands, pikes, or staves. Perhaps there was less danger of injury from fairy blood if they used bludgeons rather than sharpened weapons.

CHAPTER TWENTY-NINE

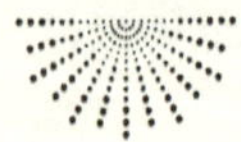

They wound their way through the tunnels. In a couple of places, Reg was sure they weren't going to be able to get through the cracks and crevices Starlight found, but they squeezed and forced their way through, and in the end, none of them got stuck. At least not permanently.

They stumbled out into the light. The sun streamed down on them, blinding after the darkness of the underground. Reg looked around for their car, but it was nowhere to be seen. She didn't recognize any landmarks.

Jessup appeared to have the same dilemma. She looked this way and that, but her car was not there. She'd said before that she only knew one way in, and they'd now found two other routes. The trouble was, she didn't know the way home.

Reg sat on a curb, breathing and getting used to the light of the aboveground. Calliopia was going through some kind of ritualistic greeting of the sun, and after so many days underground, Reg couldn't blame her. Having been inside Callie's mind, she knew how the girl had despaired of ever seeing the aboveground again.

"Which way is home?" Calliopia asked Jessup. "I must get home."

"I don't know. I have no idea where I am."

Starlight wandered in circles, sniffing at bits of grass that had forced their way up through the cracks in the sidewalks. But he didn't seem to have any immediate ideas of how to get Callie home. Jessup reached into her pocket to retrieve her cell phone, but it wouldn't work. Not just no signal, but the screen was smashed and she couldn't wake it up.

Jessup sat down on the curb next to Reg, and stared at Reg's feet in the gutter. "Well, we got you out. Now how do we turn you back into human beings? I assume you don't want to go through the remainder of your lives as beetles."

Reg reached out to touch Jessup. The air got thicker and began to buzz and vibrate as she got closer. Reg touched Jessup with the very tips of her fingertips, just the lightest brushing contact she could manage. Jessup jumped and looked to her side. She squinted her eyes.

"You're there," she said, frowning. Her eyes followed Reg's shape from head to toe. She could see her! "Barely," Jessup said. "Like a shadow."

Reg nodded her head. "Yes, yes. We're here. Just in the shadow world."

Jessup looked at the other beetle and followed Corvin's shape up. "Corvin too? But you're very hard to see." Jessup held her hand out tentatively to touch the shadows, but didn't reach far enough. Maybe, like Reg and Corvin, she could feel that boundary around them.

"So what do I do to get you back…?" Jessup pondered. She looked at Calliopia. "Do you know? You must know something about pixie magic."

Callie rolled her eyes. "I am not a pixie. I know nothing about their magic."

"You're not a pixie now, but you were born one, and you've just spent a week with them. And since fairies and pixies are enemies, you must know something about each other's magic. How can you fight an enemy you don't know?"

The corners of Callie's lips curled up slightly. "You are not as stupid as you look."

Reg winced. "Ouch!"

Corvin chuckled beside her. "From a fairy, that's actually a sincere compliment. They consider us ugly, stupid, and clumsy. Not a surprise, since they are gifted in so many ways. Some of the social niceties don't translate…"

Calliopia considered Jessup. "The pixies have to appear to fight us," she suggested.

"They can choose to appear. But Reg and Corvin can't choose, or they would appear now. There must be a way to make them visible."

Calliopia tugged on her ear, thinking about it. "If we can make them appear, then I can go home?"

"Sure," Jessup said. "If I could talk to them, we could figure out where we are and how to get out of here."

Reg was sure Jessup could figure out on her own how to get out of the broken-down slum they had surfaced in and back to her car or some other form of transportation. She certainly knew the area better than Reg. But if Calliopia saw the exchange of information as reciprocal, she seemed more inclined to help. Fairies weren't well-known for helping humans—at least not in the fairy tales Reg was familiar with.

"This one talks in my head," Callie gestured toward Reg.

"That would be Reg. She's been helping me to find you. She was cu—she has a strong psychic gift. Can they tell us what to do to help them?"

Reg looked at Corvin, but he shook his head. "I would need to do some research. If we could get back to my library…"

Reg touched Callie's mind. Unlike Ruan, Calliopia didn't seem to mind Reg's presence there. She listened to Reg for a moment, her head cocked slightly.

"The warlock does not know what to do," Callie reported with amusement. "He wants to read."

"We don't have time for that," Jessup said impatiently. "Tell me what you know, Calliopia. There must be something we can do."

"You are not going to like it."

"No doubt. Would pixie blood do the trick? We've got plenty of that."

Calliopia considered this seriously for a minute, chewing on a strand of hair, then shook her head. "They vanish their wounded. Blood does not keep them visible."

"Too bad. So? Teach me what you know. How can I get them back?"

"You must hold on to her and not look away."

Reg and Corvin exchanged glances. That didn't sound too awful. Reg had been bracing herself for some complicated and lengthy spell, having to drink horrible tasting potions, or to lie naked in the Florida sun for a full day.

"But I get a shock when I touch them," Jessup pointed out.

Calliopia shrugged her shoulders. "I said you would not like it."

"Well, I'm not going to like it any better if I wait." Jessup reached toward Reg. Reg braced herself for the jolt of electricity.

"Wait," Corvin said.

Reg pulled away from Jessup. "What?"

"She should do me first. If it's too hard on either of us, I can do the research to see if there's another way, before putting you through the same thing. I can help Marta get out of here safely, you can't."

"How can you help her?"

He looked around covertly, as if afraid he might be overhead. "I know this place. I have contacts here. I can get us out."

Reg looked at him, suspicious. Corvin Hunter, she had discovered, was all about Corvin Hunter. If he wanted to go first, it was a fair bet that his reasons were selfish and it wasn't her welfare he was concerned about.

"Why really?"

"What do you mean, really? Because I want to get out of this shadow world and back where I belong. And to get all of us out of this place. It isn't the best place for a couple of women to be hanging around by themselves, even if one of them is a cop."

"They're not alone."

"Must you argue with me about it? We're both going to get changed, but one of us has to go first. Logically, that should be me."

She didn't like his logic, but she couldn't dispute it. She wasn't going to be of any help to Detective Jessup. If only one of them could be changed at first, then it should be the person who could help her.

"Fine," she said grudgingly. "You go first."

They moved around each other, swapping places. Jessup couldn't see them clearly, and squinted at the movements of the shadows. "What's going on? Is something wrong?"

"They changed the order," Calliopia stated. "They want you to change the warlock first."

"Well, the warlock it is, then." Jessup reached for Corvin, paused, then pushed through the resistance. Corvin tried to guide his hand into her grip, but his body resisted the joining of their hands just as much as Jessup's. It was like trying to push together the north ends of two magnets. The two of them continued to push against the force, until their hands connected. There was a visible jolt, but Corvin tightened his grip on Jessup, refusing to let her go.

"Look at me," he commanded, when her eyes rolled back and her body tried to pull away. He stared at her fiercely. "Look at me, Marta!"

Calliopia watched Jessup, smiling smugly. "You have to look at him."

Jessup resisted, looking like she was walking into the wind. "How long?" she demanded through gritted teeth.

"Until he is fully visible."

Jessup tightened her grip on Corvin and forced her eyes to him. The grip and the gaze were obviously both painful. Jessup moaned, trying to push through it. Her knuckles were white as she held on to Corvin's hand.

Her eyes got wider, and Reg knew that Corvin was starting to become visible to her.

"Now?" she asked Calliopia breathlessly.

"Not yet."

"I can't…"

"You can," Corvin and Calliopia both said at the same time.

Jessup's head started to bow and her eyelids started to shut.

"You have to look at him. The whole time."

Jessup blinked and forced herself to look at Corvin as he slowly appeared before her. It was several long minutes before her muscles started to slacken and her body slowly relaxed. She looked at Corvin, breathing heavily.

"Now?"

"Now you can let go," Callie agreed.

Jessup did so, sighing.

"Thank you," Corvin said politely.

"Why do you insist on running into rooms without checking for traps first?"

He ducked his head, acknowledging his guilt. "A shortcoming of mine."

"I need someone who is going to follow orders instead of barreling straight into dangerous situations." Jessup coughed and let her chin drop down, lowering her head and rubbing the back of her neck. "That was brutal."

No one pointed out that they still needed to bring Reg back as well. As Corvin had anticipated, it was too demanding a task for Jessup to do twice without a break. Jessup cupped her hands over her eyes for a few minutes. Then she rubbed her eyes and looked at Corvin.

"Why did you switch places?"

"We decided that I was the one who could be of the most help to you under present circumstances."

Jessup looked around her. "I suppose. So what is your advice?

We can't go far without wheels. For all I know, my car could be just on the other side of that hill, and I'm so turned around, I'd walk away from it."

"No. We're a good distance from where we started out. And I'm afraid that overground travel is going to be even more arduous than underground."

"Other than the fact that we wouldn't have to fight pixies on the way back."

Corvin rolled one shoulder. "Don't be so sure. There are bound to be plenty of sentries and tripwires overground that would tip them off to our presence."

"I suppose."

"I have contacts," Corvin said, looking around. "A well-placed word or two should have us out of here. Then we can get Reg back..." His eyes searched for her shadowy shape. "You can get Calliopia back to her parents and we can take care of other incidentals."

"Like payment," Jessup said dryly.

"I don't do this for my own entertainment. And obviously this time..." he looked down at his hand, which was red and inflamed. "There's going to be a surcharge for danger to life and limb."

"It's your own fault. I just did what I had to to get you back."

Reg sat watching them, wondering if they had already completely forgotten her. Starlight sniffed his way over and breathed on her foot, where he saw the beetle.

"Yes, it's me," Reg told him. "I'm still here. Being invisible. Or a beetle. Or a shadow. Depending on how cats see denizens of the shadow kingdom."

Corvin's eyes fell on Starlight. "Why did we even bring that blasted cat? A lot of good he's done us!"

Starlight rose to his feet, hissing and puffing out his fur indignantly.

"He's the reason that we got out of there in one piece," Jessup argued.

"He's the reason we're here instead of at the car."

"He's helped. Even with the fighting. So leave him alone. We needed to find another way out of that rabbit's warren, and he found it. Who else could have done that?"

It was a rhetorical question, so Corvin didn't try to answer.

"Reg is... somewhat disabled this time, so no using birds as messengers. There isn't anything you could send as a messenger, is there? No new ability that you've developed?"

Jessup's lips pressed tightly together, signaling that she did not appreciate his jibe. "Look, Hunter. My talents are more... ordinary than yours. But that doesn't make them any less serviceable. If we all had the same gifts, not only would it be a boring world, but the criminals would get away with everything. I'm a good investigator and I'm working this case. You should show me some respect."

"You're right," he admitted. "And I know your lack of magical gifts is a sore spot, so I should be more of a gentleman. I've been... a little off my game."

Jessup nodded. "Did something happen between you and Reg? I got the feeling she's... a little more..." Jessup searched for the word, "...cautious than she was before?"

"Yeah, I screwed things up," Corvin growled, "and I'm not going to say anything more about it than that."

"Okay." Jessup shrugged. "It's too bad. She seems like someone who could really *get* you... as a friend."

Corvin just shook his head and didn't say anything.

"*Now* can we go home?" Calliopia asked, exasperated.

"Let's get the show on the road," Corvin agreed. He stood up and looked around. "The only viable solution I can think of is a private club I know of near here. They can provide us what we need to be out of here."

"Nothing shady, Hunter. We want this to be all aboveboard."

"What you want is for it to work. Without endangering your job or pitting us against the pixies again."

Jessup didn't argue. Reg suspected the "aboveboard" comment was just to cover her butt in case anybody ever asked what her instructions had been. Surely she didn't actually expect Corvin to operate in the light. Reg had a feeling he didn't usually solve his problems through official channels. That was why he was a consultant and not a policeman. If Corvin had been a cop, he probably would have brought the entire organization crashing down in a day.

"This way," Corvin directed. "Let's all stick together. I don't want anyone saying or doing the wrong thing. Don't look at anyone funny. Keep your eyes down and to yourself. There are some not-so-nice characters around here who wouldn't think twice about slitting your throat."

He and Jessup walked with Callie between them, forming a protective phalanx. Reg and Starlight followed behind. Reg wished she could pick Starlight up, but didn't think the cat would appreciate it, particularly not in the shadow state Reg was in. She didn't want to zap him or light his fur on fire.

"What kind of club is this?" Jessup asked.

Corvin looked over at her.

"You said this was a club we're going to. It's not exactly the right time of day for dinner and dancing, so I'm wondering what kind of a club it is."

"It's…" Corvin's eyebrows went up as he considered the question. No doubt trying to look enigmatic. He rubbed his short beard. "An *exclusive* club," he said. "They're open all hours; no need to worry about that."

"An exclusive club for what? Golf? Billiards? Exotic girls?"

Corvin licked his lips. "A little bit of this, a little bit of that. It all depends what the members are looking for."

Reg's stomach was tight. She was suddenly glad she was still invisible. She was glad if they were going into some sort of den of iniquity that no one would be able to say they had seen her there.

There is no right or wrong, she'd heard from a number of the practitioners in Black Sands. Reg herself didn't have the same values as the stricter members of society. But she still held to some of humanity's taboos and didn't think that a club that was a free-for-all for members to satisfy their every desire was a good idea. There should still be limits. Especially on people like Corvin, who had so much power. If he were allowed to do whatever he pleased… Reg gave a shudder. Someone had to put limits on him.

Corvin turned and looked toward Reg, and even though she knew he couldn't see anything more than a faint shadow where she stood, if anything at all, she could have sworn that he read her expression and met her eyes. She looked away. He could have his exclusive club, as long as it kept him away from her.

He had said that the club was nearby, and perhaps it was when driving a car, but on foot it was a good deal farther away than Reg felt like walking. They were all footsore and weary when they reached Corvin's little piece of paradise.

The building that he turned in at gave no clue as to what lay within its walls. There was no club name on the outside. There were no lineups outside, no gaudy neon lights to draw the eye. To know what went on there, visitors would have to have been told ahead of time.

"Here?" Jessup asked, looking surprised.

Corvin gave her a smile. "Not somewhere that was on your radar?"

"No. Not at all, in fact. So what kind of delicacies does your little gentleman's club offer?"

"Whatever the clientele desires. You'd have to talk to the management to get any details. I'm sure I couldn't tell you anything."

Jessup snorted. "Right."

Corvin tapped on the door. No electric doorbell. They stood there for a few minutes. Reg was anxious for him to knock louder or to have Jessup pound on it like the cops always did, but then the handle turned and the door opened.

"Mr. Hunter," a tall woman in a red dress greeted him, "how nice to see you again. And you brought company…" Her eyes flicked over Jessup and Callie. "Welcome. No car to be parked today, Mr. Hunter?"

"No, that's part of my problem."

She ushered them in without demanding any more details or to see anyone's identification. They went through a few rooms draped in velvet and other expensive ornamentation. The pile of the carpet felt about an inch deep, each step Reg took sank down into it. They were led to a room that might have been called a parlor, with several chairs and couches in close proximity for chatting as a group in comfort. The woman motioned to the furniture.

"Please have a seat. Your hostess will be with you in a few moments."

CHAPTER THIRTY

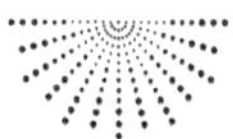

Reg watched the tall woman walk away. Her red dress was cut so low behind that it was practically backless. Corvin was also watching her retreat, but with a different expression from Reg's.

"Your *hostess?*" Jessup repeated. "Is that what you're calling her?"

"What would you call her?" Corvin asked innocently. But he had a wicked twinkle in his eye.

Reg didn't sit down. She watched the others sit, getting comfortable in the thickly padded upholstery. Starlight sat back on his haunches directly in front of Reg, as if he were a palace guard protecting the queen.

It was only a few minutes before a younger woman entered. She didn't look much older than Calliopia.

"Corvin," she greeted with a smile of pleasure that seemed genuine. "It has been too long! What can I get you today?" She looked around at the other visitors. "Drinks? Entertainment? What can I do for you?"

"We need a car," Jessup said flatly. "Preferably one with gas in the tank and that hasn't had the ignition punched. I think that should be about all that we really need you for today."

If the young woman was surprised, she didn't let it show.

"I'm sure that can be arranged. Are you sure there isn't anything else?" She gave Corvin a playful pout. "You must let me do something for you. I get paid by the service, and just the provision of a vehicle… you'll make me a pauper, Corvin."

Jessup scowled about the woman ignoring her and speaking to Corvin when Jessup was the one who had taken charge of their order.

Corvin responded to the young woman's flirtatious manner, smiling at her, his cheeks flushing. "Perhaps we could come to an arrangement."

"Good. I'm glad to hear it. Maybe you and I could retire to another room…?"

Corvin stood up.

"You're not leaving us all here," Jessup snapped, "while you go off on some assignation with this—"

"You're perfectly safe here," Corvin said, cutting her off as he took the young hostess by the hand. "As long as you stay here while arrangements are being made for transportation. I promise I won't be long."

With that, he left them to themselves in the luxuriant room.

"You care for him?" Callie asked Jessup.

"Care for Corvin Hunter?" Jessup snapped. "No, of course not! He's an occasional police consultant, and not, I'm coming to think, a very reliable one! There is nothing personal between us."

"Oh." Calliopia nodded at this slowly. "Humans are so hard to read."

"It's alright," Jessup brushed it off. "You're not doing so badly." She looked at her watch. "Once we get out of here safely, we can take you home."

"My parents will be tired of waiting for me."

"I don't think so. They'll be so happy to see you. So happy that you got away from the pixies and are safe."

Callie nodded, her eyes distant. Reg wanted to talk to her to ask her about the life that would be waiting for her when she got home. She hoped that she wouldn't be hidden away and smothered by overprotective parents who felt guilty for allowing her to be stolen away in the first place. They wouldn't want her to see any boys, not without thoroughly vetting them first, fearful that another Ruan might be lurking beneath an otherwise pleasant exterior. They wouldn't want her to go out anywhere alone, or be late, maybe even to go to school.

It wouldn't be an easy life for her. And if fairies were emotionally affected like humans were by trauma, it could be that much harder. Fear, guilt, anger… Callie had been through a lot while she'd been held by the pixies.

She'd fought back the best she could, but in the end it hadn't been enough. She had needed the police to step in and rescue her. And could the pixies even be charged for what they had done? For taking back a child that was theirs by birth?

Reg rubbed her head. Shadow world or no, she had a real headache.

Her hand was, of course, bleeding. Reg assumed that her blood would also be invisible and would not stain the carpet or the furniture in the room, but she still didn't like to leave it bleeding and uncovered. With no one to watch her, she tore a strip from her shirt and wadded it up over the wound, pressing tightly to staunch the bleeding. Starlight stared at her and yowled.

Everyone in the room looked at him. "What's wrong?" Callie asked.

"I don't know. Maybe he can see Reg. Is everything okay, Star?"

Starlight looked around the room, most notable in the absence of Corvin, and made a snorting sound as if to say it was all his fault.

"I know," Jessup agreed. "I don't like it either. He brings us here to help… and then he takes off with the first pretty face…"

"Second," Callie corrected.

"What?"

"Second pretty face."

"Well, yes, I guess so. The point is, he's supposed to be here, helping us, and he's off pursuing his own… appetites. It's disgusting."

Calliopia got up from the couch and wandered around the room, looking over the fine decorations with a scowl.

"She said there were drinks. Where do you think they are?"

"There probably isn't anything in here. We have to order what we want."

Callie pulled on a cord that Reg had assumed was a curtain cord, but no curtain opened. There was no effect that Reg could discern. But in a few moments, the door opened again, and the woman in the red dress entered. She raised her eyebrows. "How may I serve you?"

"Drinks," Calliopia said imperiously.

The woman bowed her head. "Of course. What can I get you?"

"Milk." Calliopia considered for a moment. "And mead."

"Certainly. And the others…?" The woman looked at Jessup, then at Starlight, then considered the space that Reg currently occupied.

"Milk for the cat," Callie said. She looked at Jessup.

"I'm on duty, so… a Coke?" Jessup suggested.

The woman gave another nod, and retreated.

"Sorry," Jessup said in Reg's direction. "I don't even know if you can eat in your… beetle form."

Reg considered herself. She didn't have any idea whether she could eat or drink in her current situation. She wasn't hungry or thirsty, so maybe she didn't need to. Maybe she was in a sort of limbo and wouldn't need anything until she was visible again.

Starlight began washing.

CHAPTER THIRTY-ONE

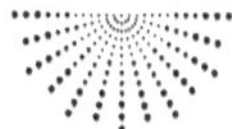

She watched the others with their drinks, waiting for Corvin's return. It seemed like it was taking forever. All they needed was to borrow a car for a few minutes.

Callie was apparently very thirsty, gulping down both her milk and her mead and ringing for another round. If Reg was right and she hadn't had anything to eat or drink since she had been kidnapped, then fairy or not, she badly needed fluids, especially after their long walk.

"How long will the warlock be?" Callie asked, setting her second milk glass aside.

"I don't know. I thought he would be back by now. Guess maybe he's having too much fun."

"We could get the car and go without him."

"Yes... or I could get a phone and call for a police unit to back us up, but then I'd have to explain where my car is and how I managed to end up all the way over here without any way of getting back... I'd rather they thought I had something in my head besides rocks."

"Then we shall get a car."

Callie got up again and pulled the bell cord. In a few minutes, the door opened, and this time it was a man, dressed in a well-tailored black suit with red tie and pocket square. He smiled at Calliopia, who was standing with her arms folded, looking cross.

"What can I do for you ladies?"

"We would like a car."

He studied Callie for a moment. "I suspect you are not even old enough to drive one. At any rate, we do have a car ready for your group, once Mr. Hunter has finished his business."

"How about you get us two cars, and we'll take one and Hunter can take one," Jessup suggested. "We can get to where we're going and he can take whatever time he needs. We both win."

The man's smile did not dim, but he pursed his lips and made a calming gesture with his hands. "I am not authorized to arrange for another car for your group. I'm sure Mr. Hunter won't be much longer."

"I thought the idea was that we could have whatever we want," Jessup challenged.

"You are not the member. Mr. Hunter is."

Jessup rolled her eyes at Callie and slumped back in her seat. She could identify herself as a police detective and insist that they help her or she could call her colleagues for an assist, but she still didn't appear to be ready to expose herself to the attention of her superiors.

The man gave a little bow. "Would there be anything else?"

"More milk," Callie gestured to her empty glass.

"Of course."

He took the empty glasses and left to get refills.

"We will go," Callie said. "The car is waiting. We will just take it. Go to my home, and then you can come back here and pick up the warlock."

"I don't know if they'll—"

Calliopia was already headed for the door, her movements swift and graceful. She seemed to be growing in front of their eyes. Reg was sure that either Callie was taller, or she herself was shorter. Did things become smaller in the world of shades?

Calliopia wasn't about to wait around any longer. She opened the door and headed out the way they had been escorted in. Jessup hurried after her, not about to let her missing person disappear again. Reg and Starlight followed the two of them.

Calliopia was faced with three men coming the other direction without any staff escort in evidence. She stepped impatiently to the side to allow them to pass her so she could get outside. But the men didn't pass, they continued to block her way.

"Here's a pretty little fairy," an obese man said, eyes on Callie.

Reg swallowed. She could see the whole scene play out in front of her. She had seen it so many times before; different times and places, different men, but the same scene. She closed in on them, not sure what she was going to do, but determined to stop them before they could do anything to harm Calliopia.

But his words made Reg look back at Callie. *A pretty little fairy?* Even Jessup had admitted that for a fairy, Calliopia was particularly plain. But that had changed. Reg couldn't identify any one thing that had changed in Callie's appearance, but she had transformed from plain and unattractive to a simple beauty. Despite a week's incarceration in a pixie's cell, her brown hair shone with health. Her paleness was the bluish cast of her fairy parents' rather than the pastiness of the pixies, living for generations underground. Her pale blue eyes were lively.

"Keep going," Jessup told Callie. "Let us through, gentlemen."

"Human, but not a bad-looking one," the tallest of the men observed, looking down at Jessup. "I think I'm up for a little entertainment, how about you?" he said to his cohorts.

"I am a police detective," Jessup said tightly. "If you think you can get away with harassing me, you'd better think again."

"You really can get anything you want at a club like this," the fat man chuckled. "Even police detectives. You want to show me your handcuffs, sweetheart? Maybe even your gun?"

He reached out and grabbed Calliopia by the arm rather than Jessup, pulling her close to him. "Young fairies… you don't see a lot of these around. They're a rare breed, you know."

"Leave her alone!" Jessup warned, but the two other men were ready and were able to grab her before she could reach her handcuffs, gun, or any other deterrent.

"Release me," Calliopia commanded, giving an imperious little shake that was intended to demonstrate to the man what she wanted. "I am going home."

"I don't think so, actually."

Callie pulled her arm back. When he didn't release her, she looked at Jessup.

"Where is my dagger?"

"It's in my—"

"Do you actually think we would let one of you put your hands on a blade?" one of the men holding Jessup laughed. "Even a little thing like you could do damage with cold steel. But unarmed..." he gave her arm a squeeze and bumped her with his hip. "Unarmed, I think I can manage."

Reg forced her hand closer, until she was able to reach through the buzzing magical field to touch the man's arm, which she did. She had seen that even just skin-to-skin contact between someone on the physical world and someone in the shadow world caused pain, and the fairy-tainted blood still leaking from Reg's wound wasn't likely to improve things. She was braced for the electrical shock she would receive, but it still took her breath away, and every cell in her body told her to let go immediately.

The tall man had no warning what was going to happen. He howled in pain, letting go of Jessup to grab at his arm. Jessup pulled her sidearm and pointed it at one of the men who had been holding her. Both of them had let go and were staring in horror at their companion, who had released Calliopia and was writhing in pain.

Holding on to him hurt Reg too, so once her friends were out of immediate danger, she let go of the man.

He collapsed, leaning against the wall. He gasped for breath, holding on to his arm and looking down to it. The fairy blood meant that the man's arm was not just red like Jessup's and Corvin's hands, but blistered and obviously very painful.

"Serves you right," Reg told him, though she knew he probably couldn't hear her.

"Thank you, Reg!" Jessup declared. "Enough is enough. We have a job to do. We're taking Calliopia home. No more waiting. No more roadblocks."

They had attracted attention. Other patrons were looking in through the doorways, a couple of the hostesses of the club drew close, and Corvin appeared, the young hostess on his arm looking star struck.

"We're leaving," Jessup repeated.

"What are you doing?" Corvin demanded. "Why didn't you stay in the room and wait for me?"

"You take off and we have no idea how long you're going to be. My job is to get Calliopia home. I'm not sitting around some club waiting for you to… satisfy yourself. It's time to go. Are you with us or not?"

One of the hostesses surged forward. "Please, I don't know what's going on here, but everyone needs to get back to their rooms. We don't want any trouble. If you're going to be disruptive, we must insist that you leave. All of you."

"That's just what we're doing," Jessup asserted. "What I was doing when these three *gentlemen* decided to detain us. I don't know what's usually on the menu here, but I can assure you that *we* are not!"

The woman shook her head. "Who are you? And who are you here with?"

Corvin stepped forward, raising his hand and giving an apologetic shake of his head. "I'm afraid that would be me. Some people… you just can't take them anywhere. I'm sorry for the disruption. I believe arrangements were being made for a vehicle, and then we will be on our way…"

The woman with the backless dress who had first let them into the club arrived as Corvin was giving this explanation.

"Your car is ready, we have just been waiting until you were done. It would seem that your friends are… impatient to be on their way." The woman looked around at the other people watching the scene. "Everything is fine. I would ask everyone to return to their activities. It's all taken care of…"

The man with Reg's handprint impressed on his arm in red groaned, holding it against himself. "These people attacked us!"

The woman's eyes were quick as she took in the flushed faces of the man and his companions. "That is unfortunate. If you would go with Marnie, we will have someone look at that for you…"

The hostesses moved smoothly and efficiently to separate the two groups and restore the curious onlookers to their rooms. Corvin was reunited with Jessup and Calliopia, the young escort excused to deal with the next patron.

"You couldn't wait for me?" Corvin asked. "This isn't the kind of place you want to be wandering around without an escort. I was only gone for a few minutes. I haven't held you up."

Jessup scowled. "I think it was longer than you realize."

Corvin looked at his watch and frowned. "Regardless, you should have waited. Taking off on your own is just asking for trouble."

"I'm capable of taking care of myself."

"You didn't have just yourself to take care of. And by the looks of his arm," Corvin nodded in the direction the tall man had been taken. "You weren't the one who took care of it. Regina was."

"Reg helped," Jessup admitted. "But even without her, I would have managed."

Corvin raised his hands palm-up. "I'm glad it all worked out for you."

Without him arguing the point, Jessup decided to let it go. "So are you finished… whatever it is you've been up to?" she asked, looking him up and down.

He had the look, Reg thought, of the cat that got the cream. Her stomach twisted when she thought of how Corvin had looked the morning after he had tricked her out of her powers. He wasn't glowing quite as much as he had then, but the shadows of fatigue she had previously noticed under his eyes had vanished and he looked thoroughly pleased with himself.

What did the club offer him that satisfied his hunger? Did they offer magical objects like Jessup did, which retained the power they had been imbued with? Or did they offer him living subjects, who he could glamour like he had Reg, charming them into giving him their gifts?

The thought of vulnerable girls being offered to sate Corvin's hunger made her feel nauseated. Her heart raced and she wanted nothing more than to punch him right in the middle of his smug face. And the face of anyone who enabled him, too.

Corvin looked in her direction like he could hear what she was thinking, looking amused. He looked back at Jessup, suppressing the smile. "Yes, I've had my injured hand looked after and have had a chance to refresh myself. I think we're ready to go on."

"About time," Jessup growled.

The woman in the red dress took Corvin's arm. "This way, then."

Reg followed, watching the woman curiously. She was the first woman she had met who didn't appear to be affected by Corvin's charms. Even those like Sarah and Jessup, who knew the danger Corvin presented and fought back against his charms were still affected by him. Watching them, Reg could still see how they were affected, but fought their attraction to him. With the woman in the red dress, Reg could see no sign that she was affected by him. Was it because she knew him so well? Maybe she had been around him for long enough that she had become immune to his charms? Or was there something else that protected her?

They were led to an underground parking structure, which started Reg's heart racing and sweat trickling down her back. She wasn't prepared to spend any more time underground. She looked at Calliopia, who was also looking uneasy about having to go below the surface. Corvin and the woman in red seemed to be oblivious to this and Jessup's attention was more on them than it was on Calliopia.

Their shoes echoed in the emptiness of the parking structure. Reg just hoped they would all move quickly and not make any extended goodbyes or inspection of the vehicle.

They reached a black luxury vehicle. Maybe a Cadillac; Reg wasn't much of a car person. The woman handed Corvin the key fob and gave him a peck on the cheek. "Just bring it back when you are done, Mr. Hunter. I look forward to seeing you again."

Corvin watched her retreat before turning his attention to the car and clicking the remote to unlock the doors. They got in. Jessup watched Reg's feet and didn't close her door until after she was in. Corvin started the car. Reg could barely hear the engine purr to life.

"Now, where were we going?" he asked, faking uncertainty. "Chick-a-Fil? Did you want to go get something to eat?"

"To my home," Calliopia insisted.

Corvin laughed. "Oh, yeah."

Calliopia turned her eyes back to Jessup, frowning. "He's kidding," Jessup advised. "It's juvenile. Just go with it."

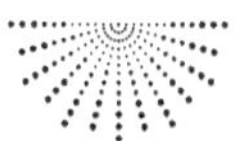

CHAPTER THIRTY-TWO

Corvin definitely knew his way around the neighborhood, as he claimed. He took the twists and turns out of the dismal neighborhood with confidence. Then they were finally out of the slums and Reg felt buoyed up. As long as they had remained close to the pixies' domain, she had not been able to shake the worry that they were going to be attacked again. That it couldn't possibly be over.

But they were finally on their way to getting Callie home. All smooth sailing. Starlight stood on the seat to watch out one of the windows. Calliopia took a few deep breaths.

"Soon," she told them. "I can smell it."

"Not far now," Corvin agreed.

Reg tried to relax. Soon they would have finished the job of returning Calliopia to her parents. They could take Reg home, make her visible, and she could go to sleep and recover from all that had happened. Her bed was calling her.

Starlight paced restlessly across the seat. If Reg had been in the visible world, she would have patted or held him to calm him down. But being in the shadow world, any time she reached toward him, his fur stood up in a crackling, staticky puffball and he looked at her crossly.

Reg recognized the bend in the road and knew that when they went around it, the Papillon castle would be visible.

Callie gave a happy sigh.

Corvin drove the big car up the winding drive, until he finally reached the house. Calliopia jumped out of the car. She didn't wait for the butler, but threw open her door and ran into the house. Reg followed with Corvin and Jessup, but Jessup insisted that Starlight remain in the car.

"It will only be a few minutes and he would just cause trouble inside."

Reg was unable to protest. She would have to set Jessup straight once she was part of the real world again. Starlight was a good cat; he wouldn't have caused them any problems with the fairies.

At the door, the butler shook his head when he looked at them.

"You may go in for a moment," he told Jessup, "so that the family can express their appreciation. Then you must go. They need this time to be alone with their daughter."

"Where does that leave you?" Corvin teased.

The butler looked at him with icy eyes. "You, however, may not enter. You are banned from fairy households."

Jessup looked at Corvin, raising her eyebrows. "You didn't tell me that."

"I… wasn't exactly aware of it."

"What have you been up to?"

"We'll discuss it another time."

"Sounds like you'd better go back and keep Starlight company for now."

"I'm not sitting in the car with a cat."

"You rode with him on the way over."

"Yeah, but that's not the same."

Jessup shrugged. "Suck it up."

"I brought you here. And Calliopia. I think I deserve a little of that appreciation."

"You did the job you're being paid for. Sorry you don't get the warm fuzzies."

He glared at her, but Jessup didn't back down. Corvin turned around, shaking his head, and walked back toward the car.

The butler was looking in Reg's direction. "And you brought… a pixie?"

"No. No, she's a human. One of our consultants. But we had an unfortunate run-in with a pixie spell. Do you think your masters would have the spell to countermand it?"

He considered for a few moments, then finally nodded, and stood back to allow them in. Reg trailed behind Jessup.

They followed Calliopia's excited voice to the atrium-like seating area they'd been brought to before. But no one was sitting down. Calliopia hugged both of her parents, something Reg hadn't expected with how reserved the fairies normally were.

"Oh, I'm home," Calliopia declared. "I'm home, I'm home, I'm home."

"Yes," her mother agreed with a reserved smile. "You are home once again. We are most grateful." Her arms were empty, but her face still showed the weariness from having carried the changeling for so long. Reg wondered what had happened to it. Had the baby vanished in a puff of smoke? Mrs. Papillon aimed a smile in Jessup's direction. "Thank you for all that you have done."

"I do have some questions for you," Jessup said, guarded.

"Calliopia is back. I think the time for questions is over."

"No, there are still some blanks that need to be filled in. For instance, how you came to have Calliopia in the first place?"

"She is our daughter."

"Your kidnapped daughter."

"Yes. She was kidnapped."

"I mean *you* kidnapped her. As a baby. You kidnapped her from the pixies."

Mrs. Papillon just looked at Jessup. "She was our daughter."

"But you kidnapped her from the pixies."

The woman spread her hands wide. "How Calliopia became part of our family is no one's business."

"It is when you break the law."

"It does not break fairy law."

"But it breaks human law, and you asked the state to step in and intervene when the pixies took her back."

"She is not a pixie."

"Not anymore."

Calliopia leaned in and kissed her mother on the cheek. "I am full fairy now," she declared.

"Yes, you are," her mother agreed. "You have come into your own." She turned to Detective Jessup. "Thank you for all that you have done. If you would go… Calliopia needs to get some rest. This has been a long ordeal."

Jessup recognized that she had been dismissed. She searched for something to say. Calliopia turned around to face her.

"Where is my dagger?"

"The dagger is evidence," Jessup said.

"But it is mine!" Calliopia argued.

"If you have something that belongs to Calliopia, you must return it," Mr. Papillon interposed. "You cannot be allowed to leave here with something that belongs to her."

"It isn't here," Jessup said, which was only a partial truth. She had left the dagger in the car, perhaps anticipating the situation. "How did Hawthorne-Rose get it in the first place?"

Mr. Papillon's eyes went to his daughter. "Children are not always careful with their possessions."

"She didn't drop it or give it to a friend. Tell me how a police officer got it. And not just any policeman, but a dirty one, one involved in dark magic in this community."

"There is no dark magic," Calliopia said. "Only magic."

It sounded like a catechism. Something that had been repeated to her many times.

"How did you learn the blood spell?" Reg asked Calliopia in her head. "Who taught that to you, Calliopia?"

Calliopia and her parents all looked in Reg's direction at the question. Jessup caught the looks.

"What just happened? Did something happen? Reg?"

Reg had no way to talk to Jessup, except through Callie, and she wasn't sure Calliopia was going to want to be a translator for her. There was silence as they all looked at each other, though Jessup couldn't find a place to focus on for Reg.

"Well…" she covered a yawn. "I guess I should be getting out of here. Only… I can't go until Reg has been restored. I thought that you might be able to help me with that…"

The fairies looked at Reg. Whether they could see her clearly or not, Reg didn't know. But they at least knew where to focus their eyes.

"If you bring me back from the land of the shadows, Detective Jessup won't have any more reason to stay," Reg coaxed Calliopia.

Callie looked at her parents to see what they wanted her to do.

"You know how to restore her," Mr. Papillon said. "But it is not a very pleasant process."

"Maybe there is another way?" Callie suggested. "A potion or incantation?"

"It is ancient magic," her father told her. "This is the way it is done."

"This is the way it is done," Calliopia repeated. She walked across the room to where Reg stood and reached out both of her hands. Reg had already seen it done, and she wasn't in any great hurry to go through the pain; only she wanted everything to be back to normal so she could go home and relax and get some rest.

"This is the way it is done," Calliopia said in song-song, forcing her hands and Reg's closer together. Reg gritted her teeth and did her best to push toward Calliopia, until finally the opposing forces gave way and they could touch, skin to skin. Even prepared for the shock and the pain, Reg wasn't prepared. She still jumped and screamed and tried to pull away from Calliopia

"Look into my eyes," Calliopia said. She was blinding white. Reg had never known anything solid could be so bright before. It was like staring directly into the sun. Reg did her best, squinting, trying to see Calliopia's face in the middle of the halo of white light.

The burning continued to grow in intensity, as if Reg had put her hand on a hot stove and left it there. She tried desperately to writhe away. How had Jessup and Corvin managed to hold on for so long?

"Keep looking," Callie urged, when the burning started to slacken and Reg figured it was okay for her to let go and look away.

Then finally, the pain had disappeared and Calliopia dropped Reg's hands. Reg looked down at them, astounded that her fingers were not blistered to the bone. They were red, but not as bad as the man Reg had touched at the club. Maybe not even as bad as the hand Corvin had been complaining about.

"Wow," Jessup said. "Corvin and I didn't light up like that, did we?"

"No," Reg agreed hoarsely. "You didn't light up at all."

"Must be a fairy thing."

"Now you can return to your homes," Mr. Papillon urged.

"I just want to know who taught Callie the bloodline magic," Reg repeated. "That's not the kind of thing you learn in fairy school, is it? Somebody wanted her to know how to find out what her heritage was."

"There are many ways to learn these things."

"So you taught her?"

He blinked at Reg's leap in logic. "I did not say that."

"You didn't say she learned it at school, or at the library, or from your wife or some other relative or teacher. You could have said any of those things. That tells me that *you* were the one who taught it to her."

"That does not make logical sense."

"Not to you, maybe, but then, I have other gifts. I can see things that no one tells me."

"Callie will need a rest now. And so, I think, will you. You have worked very hard today. You are getting very tired."

She tried not to respond to his suggestion, but couldn't help yawning. This provoked the tiniest hint of a smile in the corner of his mouth.

"We could always ask Hawthorne-Rose," she told Jessup. "If we offered him the right deal, he'd tell us how it was that he was able to leave this house with a possession that wasn't his. Or how the pixies managed to kidnap Calliopia without anyone else in the household hearing anything."

"Magic," Mr. Papillon hissed. "You simply don't understand magic."

"You're right. I don't. But I am very good at detecting lies. Or the truth, when it occasionally peeks its head."

Everyone just looked at her.

"Calliopia... did you give Detective Hawthorne-Rose your dagger?" Reg asked.

Callie stared at Reg. Her shining expression dimmed.

"Why did you?" Reg demanded. "What was the plan?"

No one answered. Reg looked around the room and tried to sort it out in her own head. She knew Hawthorne-Rose was a smuggler of poached animals and magical artifacts. He hadn't confessed, but they hadn't needed a confession from him. He'd attacked Reg in her own home, and not a lot of evidence was needed to prove that charge. Reg didn't see a lot of artifacts around the Papillon house, but she imagined they must be there. Fairies collected treasure, didn't they? Or was that dragons? Leprechauns?

"Something rare," she mused. "The dagger itself was rare. Blades are unmade after they shed fairy blood. That would make it very rare. Dangerous and valuable. Wouldn't it?" she asked Jessup.

"It would."

"Did Hawthorne-Rose steal it? Or did he pay you for it? Maybe he even paid you to get your blood on it in the first place.

Maybe there was no magic, just a girl cutting herself for the money."

"Such a thing would never even be considered in a fairy household," Mr. Papillon insisted.

"I thought there was no right and wrong."

He closed his mouth and stared at her morosely.

"We can always ask Hawthorne-Rose," Jessup said. "We know where to find him."

CHAPTER THIRTY-THREE

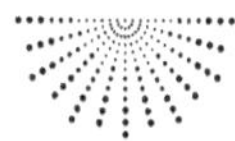

Starlight was pleased to see Reg when she returned to the car with Detective Jessup. He jumped into her lap and rubbed against her, with only the usual amount of static electricity.

"I'm glad to see you too, Star." Reg rubbed the fur on his nose and his white spot. "You've been very helpful to us today, haven't you?"

She looked at Corvin. "Cats don't like pixies or fairies," she said, remembering something he had said earlier. "Why not?"

"They can't exactly tell us why, can they?" He chuckled at his own intelligence. "Maybe it goes back to when fairies were described as little creatures, like bugs and butterflies and cats would be their natural predators. I don't know."

"But the fairy tales came from the truth," Reg protested. "Not the other way around. Fairy tales didn't make cats and fairies into enemies."

"No. But history doesn't tell us why."

"Maybe it's because pixies and fairies both lie so easily. And cats don't like lies."

He raised his brows. As he drove them back to Reg's cottage,

Jessup told him about Reg's suspicions. He considered them from various angles.

"You may be right," he admitted. "There aren't a lot of ways that a fairy blade could come into a cop's hands through legitimate means. It isn't like he was breaking up fights in the playground or performing weapons searches of their lockers. There would be little need for a police detective to be present at a fairy school. Even less so at a fairy's home. Unless, for example, their daughter has been kidnapped and they report it to the police to get help getting her back."

"And they didn't report it until after Hawthorne-Rose was in jail."

"It's still worth thinking about. But... there's not much we can do about any of this. Selling an artifact isn't illegal." Corvin glanced over at Jessup. "At least, not usually. Even if Calliopia did sell it to Hawthorne-Rose, that's not against the law."

"I just think... there's more to this than meets the eye. A lot more."

"As someone who spent much of the day invisible... I concur."

"But does it mean anything to us?" Jessup asked. "We found Calliopia. We returned her to her family. We've done our job. The police can't interfere with the lives of other races. We can only be involved when we are asked to be, or when it turns out to be part of a case we're already working."

"Isn't it, though...?" Reg asked.

"No. There's nothing for us to pursue. Not yet."

* * *

When they got to Sarah's house, they saw that Letticia was there, looking around impatiently for them. She looked disapprovingly at the big black car.

"Is this something new? I thought I said Regina was supposed to be taking it easy, not gallivanting all over town taking in the sights. Come on. Let me in so I can take a look at that hand."

Reg picked up Starlight and led the way. Letticia and Jessup followed her into the cottage, but Corvin didn't cross the threshold. Reg pointedly ignored his reasonable requests to be allowed into the cottage and his promises to behave himself.

"You don't invite a wolf into the fold on the promise that he won't eat the sheep," Letticia contributed. She and Jessup were clearly on Reg's side of the matter and didn't let Corvin's arguments gain any footholds.

Letticia unwrapped the makeshift bandage around Reg's injured hand.

"I can't believe you would go off and fight with an injury like this. You knew it would just make it worse."

Reg sighed. "We had to get Calliopia out of there. We knew she was in danger. A full fairy being held by the pixies? We couldn't just leave her there and let them... do whatever they do to fairies..."

"Humans interfering with the magical races... never turns out well."

"Well, in this case it did. It all turned out just fine."

Letticia studied Reg's cut hand closely. Reg was quiet and still, then bent down to get a better look herself. "It's not looking so bad!"

"This is most unexpected," Letticia said, not sounding pleased.

But Reg was delighted to see that the wound was finally starting to knit together, instead of the split getting wider and more ugly.

"What did you do to it?" Letticia demanded.

"Uh... nothing. It started to bleed again, and Jessup put more yarrow on it and dressed it again. Then... there was a fight with the pixies."

"And you protected your injured hand."

"Well, no... not actually... and then we were turned invisible—"

"Sent to the world of shades," Corvin clarified from somewhere outside, his voice coming in through the window.

"Whatever. That." Reg flapped a hand in Corvin's direction. "Then… not much else. Took Calliopia back to the fairies. She brought me back to the visible world…" Reg looked at her hand. "Maybe that was what made it better. Her holding my hand."

"More fairy magic," Letticia muttered darkly. "I have brought some rowan berries. They should help to reverse the injury caused by the fairy blood. And you need to rest it. No more fighting and chasing all over town. Lie down and relax for a few days."

"Okay," Reg agreed, smiling. "You've got a deal."

* * *

It was some time before Jessup headed home. Reg watched her go from the doorstep and then walked toward her bedroom, yawning. A nice long sleep was just what she needed. But a few moments later, she could hear shouting. She listened for a minute, not sure of the source, then thought that it was Jessup. Pausing only to slide her tired feet into a pair of flip flops, Reg cut through Sarah's yard and hurried to the front of the house to see what was going on. Jessup was in a full-on shouting match with Corvin, waving her hands and yelling loud enough for the whole neighborhood to hear.

"What happened? What's wrong?"

Jessup turned to face Reg. Her usual calm demeanor was gone.

"*That* is what's wrong!" she pointed to her car, parked at the curb.

It took a few moments for Reg to realize that Jessup's car should not have been parked at the curb. That was where they had left the big black car, which would need to be returned to the club, and Jessup's car retrieved from where she'd left it before entering the pixie tunnels.

"Oh. Who brought it back? That was nice of them."

"Nice? Sure it was nice. And they drove off the car from the club."

"They must have sent someone to retrieve it, then."

"My things were still in that car."

"Oh. Didn't they put them in yours?" Then Reg saw that Jessup had her soft-sided briefcase in her hand. She blinked, trying to figure out what Jessup was so upset about.

"Yes. They put my bag into my car. Everything except the dagger!"

"Calliopia's dagger?" Reg echoed faintly.

"Yes!"

"Oh… but I'm sure if you called them and explained about it being missing, they would make sure it got back to you."

"You're sure of that, are you?" Jessup's voice was shrill. "That was *evidence!* It wasn't even supposed to be out of the bag. I did you a favor by bringing it over here, and then what a fiasco it all turned out to be!"

Reg gulped. It wasn't her fault that the knife was gone. A lot of things tended to disappear when Reg was around, but she hadn't had anything to do with the loss of Calliopia's dagger.

"I'm sorry, Detective Jessup. It… it wasn't me."

Jessup was brought up short. "You? I don't think *you're* the one who took it, Reg." She cast a look over at Corvin, who was still hanging around, his own car parked behind Jessup's.

"Oh. You think Corvin had something to do with it?"

"Of course. Who else? It's his club. He called them to get the car. He's the one who made all of the arrangements. And then a rare weapon imbued with fairy blood disappears all by itself? Either he did it alone, or he did it with the assistance of that exclusive club of his!" She turned toward Corvin and started yelling again. "So help me, Corvin, I'll make sure you never have anything to do with any other police investigation again for the rest of your life! You can forget about asking me for favors or advances or access to magical objects that I just happen to come across in the course of my investigations. You will never have anything to do with another police case in Black Sands!"

Corvin was attempting to remain calm, but his face was red. Reg had seen him angry before and didn't really want to experience it again. He was dangerous enough when he was in a good mood.

"I didn't have anything to do with the disappearance of your evidence," he said through clenched teeth. "I will, of course, place a call to the club to ask them to please check the car, but if the dagger was that important, maybe you should not have left it in the car."

Reg could see immediately that this was part of the reason that Jessup was so angry. She felt guilty, because she was the one who had left the dagger in the car instead of keeping it on her person. She was the one who had allowed it to be stolen.

"I'm sure it will turn up," Reg assured her. "If you left it in the car, then that's where it will be. Someone at the club will find it and bring it back." She forced a smile in Corvin's direction. "They aim to please, right?"

"I'm sure it will turn up," Corvin agreed, his smile just as stretched.

Reg wished she could be sure. It was only too obvious to her that Corvin was hiding something.

* * *

Reg tossed and turned restlessly. She told herself it was just because she was too tired. It had been a long, eventful day, and she was just too tired at the end of it to settle in for sleep. Her body ached. She couldn't stop thinking about the knife, Jessup, and Corvin. The knife had not been returned by the club and Jessup knew she would be facing discipline, maybe even dismissal. Reg hated to see how upset Jessup was about it. Even though Reg was just a consultant that the police department had hired, she had started to feel like she and Marta Jessup could be friends.

Reg knew that if she had been the one responsible for the loss of something so important, she probably would have run rather than to stay and face the music. But Detective Jessup was determined to report the theft and take whatever discipline they felt appropriate.

So Reg was overtired, and she was worried about Jessup. She couldn't complain that her throbbing hand was keeping her up, because for once it was feeling better. Still sore, as one would expect from a knife wound, but not like it had been.

She didn't dream about Calliopia. That was no doubt because Callie was home with her family, back where she was supposed to be. Back in her own home, and her own room, with her own parents—or the fairyland version of her own parents. Jessup had reported the infant kidnapping of Callie from her original pixie parents to the authorities, but she didn't think anyone was going to pursue it.

"Calliopia's parents are right… it isn't any kind of crime under fairy law. It's sort of their method of adoption, perfectly normal and acceptable. And since no one reported it to human authorities back when it happened… there's really no way for us to get involved now unless they ask. Under the treaty… fairies are allowed self-governance, with a few exceptions. The pixies won't pursue it, even if they are the injured party."

Since Callie was a full fairy now, she belonged there with the fairies. There was no question in Reg's mind that Callie should not be returned to her pixie parents.

But there *was* something that kept niggling at the back of her brain, and no matter how much she tried to push it out and get the sleep that she needed, Reg couldn't let it go.

At first light Starlight jumped up on the bed meowing for his breakfast, so Reg decided there was no point in trying to sleep anymore and got out of bed. She was still in her pajamas when Sarah came to the cottage to check up on her and make sure she had everything she needed.

"You look like you should still be in bed," Sarah observed.

"I know… but I couldn't sleep, so I thought I might as well get up."

Starlight yowled plaintively at Sarah as she looked in the cupboard and fridge, telling Sarah—quite untruthfully—that he was hungry and being neglected by his owner. But Sarah wasn't fooled.

"Sarah, what's an ordeal?" Reg asked.

Sarah shrugged. "Something hard. A difficult time in your life. Is that what you mean?"

"So it's not something specific, like those ten trials of Hercules?"

Sarah turned to look at Reg, leaning on the counter as she thought about it. "You mean the twelve labors of Hercules," she corrected. "And… not exactly, but an ordeal can also be a sort of a test of loyalty. That's not the way it's usually used today, but in centuries gone by… people were put through terrible tortures, and if they survived, that was taken as proof of their innocence or loyalty. If they died, then obviously that meant that they were guilty and deserved to die. Witchcraft was one thing they tested for that way."

Reg's heart beat harder. Mrs. Papillon had said that Calliopia had been through an ordeal. Had she just meant it in the generic, modern sense of the word? Or had she meant something more? Had she been put through what she had been on purpose, to see if she would remain true to the fairies? She'd been taken from her home, imprisoned, and had to go without food or water. In the end, she had survived the ordeal and her parents had accepted her back home. On one hand, it was difficult to believe they could put their own child through something like that, but on the other… Reg knew they had lied to her, and that they were almost as good at lying as she was. Almost as good as the pixies.

But the case was closed, and chances are she would never know the full truth of the matter.

EPILOGUE

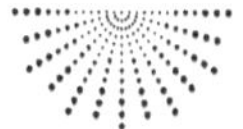

*S*arah had still been there, having a protracted cup of tea and gossiping about people that Reg didn't actually know, when a loud cawing outside caused her to turn her head.

Reg sipped her tea. "Might be a cat in the yard. I've noticed that they tend to get really loud when there's a predator around. Must do it to warn the rest of the flock."

"No," Sarah said, "this is different."

She was the bird person, so Reg didn't argue. She just watched Sarah go to the door and look out. Sarah was out of sight for a moment, and Reg heard her say 'thank you,' and then she returned. She held up a piece of paper rolled into a scroll.

"Delivery."

Reg took it from her when it was offered. "Was this delivered by a crow?"

Sarah nodded as if that was perfectly normal. Maybe in her world, it was.

Reg broke the seal on the scroll and pulled it open. The swooping calligraphy gave Reg an immediate headache and was impossible for her to sort out. She turned it toward Sarah for help. "I can't read this old-fashioned writing."

Sarah put her glasses on her nose and peered down at the page.

She only had to take a brief glance to see what it was about. She made a face.

"Corvin."

"He sent me an invitation to something?"

"No. It's from his coven. Asking you to attend at his upcoming examination for his violations of coven rules."

* * *

Reg stared into the crystal ball, anxious and unsettled, trying to focus her mind. As she gazed at it, a picture formed in her mind.

She saw Calliopia walking down the long, winding drive from her house to the highway, wearing a long dress similar to those her mother wore, topped with a black cloak Reg recognized. When she saw it, she could still feel the soft fabric between her fingers and the way it had helped her to see Calliopia and sense who she was.

Reg thought at first that Callie might be walking out to the highway to meet the school bus. But Ruan had laughed at the idea of them taking the school bus. Instead, as Calliopia reached the end of the private drive, an old beaten-up station wagon pulled over to pick her up. Callie walked up to it without hesitation and opened the door. She gathered the folds of her dress and cloak around her and slid into the seat.

There, she greeted a familiar, curly-haired boy with a kiss that was not fraternal. He gave her a wide smile and drove the station wagon back onto the highway.

Did you enjoy this book? Reviews and recommendations are vital to making a book successful.

Please leave a review at your favorite book store or review site and share it with your friends.

Don't miss the following bonus material:
Sign up for mailing list to get a free ebook
Read a sneak preview chapter
Other books by P.D. Workman
Learn more about the author

Sign up for my mailing list at pdworkman.com and get Gluten-Free Murder for free!

PREVIEW OF A CATASTROPHIC THEFT

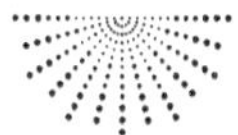

*R*eg had been trying to sleep through a cacophony of bird calls in the garden outside her window, sheet pulled tightly over her head. Unfortunately, the sheet did not provide a sufficient barrier to block out their noise. All hope of sleep fled when Starlight decided it was breakfast time. He jumped down from the window where he'd been perched watching the avian activity and onto Reg's bed, yowling impatiently to tell her how hungry he was.

"Not yet, Star," Reg protested. "I'm not getting up for a couple more hours yet."

Starlight had other ideas. He pawed at her head through the sheet, not giving in.

"I didn't get enough sleep!"

He wasn't persuaded.

Reg groaned. She knew she wasn't going to be able to get any more rest once the cat decided it was time for her to get up. It was one of the joys of cat ownership that no one had bothered to tell her about. She pulled the sheet off of her face and Starlight touched his nose to hers, then rubbed the length of his cheek down hers, purring loudly. Reg pushed him away a little and scratched his ears.

"It wouldn't be so bad if I hadn't been up half the night."

Being nocturnal, Starlight already knew that Reg had been up late to hold a midnight seance for a client, which meant she had only been in bed for a few hours before the birds had started making their racket. Keyed up and overtired, the little bit of sleep that Reg had been able to get had been restless and filled with wild, unsettling dreams.

Reg yawned noisily. Starlight put his ears back, looking at her like she'd belched at a fancy dinner party.

"I'm tired," Reg reiterated.

There was no point in staying in bed any longer, so she forced herself to get up and wandered into the bathroom for her morning ablutions. Starlight didn't follow her into the bathroom as he sometimes did, wary of being flicked with water so Reg could have her privacy. He was waiting by his bowl when she made it out to the kitchen. Reg frowned, looking down at his bowl. She could swear that he'd actually eaten some of his dry kibble. Maybe he would actually eat the new brand that she'd paid an arm and a leg for at the specialty pet store. The clerk who had helped her had extolled the health benefits of the dry food, showing her the ingredients to verify that it was actually made from premium meat rather than the combination of grains and byproducts Reg had found on the label of the cheap grocery store box she had previously bought.

"Do you like that? Did you have some of it?"

Starlight just stared at her, waiting for her to hurry up and give him his morning meal.

Reg saw that her appointment book was on the island counter, which meant that Sarah had been by at some point and written someone into her calendar. Tired of surprise visits, Reg had decided to put a system in place to help her keep on top of the appointments that Sarah set up.

Sarah was not Reg's secretary, but her landlord, a senior witch whose connections in Black Sands often put her in contact with people who were looking for psychic services. She had taken it upon herself to provide Reg with the clientele she needed, as well as keep the fridge stocked and maintain everything else in the furnished cottage in her backyard in top condition.

While Reg sometimes wished for the peace and privacy she should have been able to enjoy as a paying tenant, she couldn't deny that Sarah's intrusions were an unexpected benefit and had resulted in her being able to build up her psychic services business in Black Sands much more quickly than she had anticipated.

In the past, things had always gone the opposite way. She had aged out of the foster care system without any significant skills and hadn't had any opportunities for further education. She would come up with brilliant ideas of ways to make money, but they never worked out the way she expected them to. Money just didn't come in or people caught on to her scams too quickly, and before she'd managed to raise more than a comfortable living, she was forced to move on to avoid trouble and would again be looking for a way to get rich.

She paged through the calendar to make sure she was aware of her schedule for the next few days. Starlight rubbed against her legs, encouraging her to put something more interesting into his bowl.

"Okay, okay. Let's see what we've got."

Reg opened the fridge and surveyed the contents. There was a round plastic container that was unfamiliar. She popped the lid to have a peek at the contents. Some kind of stew that Sarah had probably made too much of and was trying to pawn off on her; or else she had deliberately made enough for Reg because she was concerned about Reg's less-than-healthy eating habits—though Sarah's weren't much better.

"Let's try some of this."

Reg spooned a generous helping of the stew into Starlight's bowl and put it down on the floor. He sniffed at it for a minute, then apparently deemed it safe for feline consumption and started in on it. Reg put the container back into the fridge and looked for something better suited for her own breakfast.

* * *

Having a written calendar and Sarah acting as her scheduling secretary apparently didn't keep Reg from having unexpected guests. She had eaten her non-Sarah-approved breakfast and was just having a cup of tea and deciding how to approach her day when there was a knock at the door. If it had been Sarah, she would just have walked in, but the door didn't open.

Reg went over to look out the peephole, much more careful about letting just anyone into the house than she had been in the past. But the diminutive figure she saw through the peephole was not Corvin or some other threat. Reg opened the door, smiling.

"What can I do for you, Detective Jessup?"

Marta Jessup gave a little shrug, her Asian complexion taking on a slightly pink hue. "I hope I didn't get you up." She nodded to the tea, "but it looks like you already have the kettle on?"

"I've been up for ages." Reg stifled a yawn, wishing she were back in bed. But maybe she'd be able to sneak in an afternoon nap between consultations. "Come in and have a cup with me."

Jessup accepted her invitation and in a few minutes they were in Reg's living room, as snug in the upholstered wicker chairs as one could be. Jessup sipped at her tea, which Reg noted she had added quite a bit of sugar and milk to.

"I wonder if you would consult for me on another case," Jessup suggested.

"Sure." Reg nodded. Her consultation on the previous case, that of a missing adolescent fairy, Calliopia Papillon, had been both successful and profitable. "What can I do for you?"

"We haven't had any success in finding the missing knife."

"Hawthorne-Rose's knife?" Reg automatically ran her thumb over the healing cut in her hand. The knife was, she knew, a rare artifact. Fairy steel rarely fell into the hands of anyone outside of the kin, and especially not one that had been polluted with fairy blood. It should have been unmade before it could fall into the hands of a human like Hawthorne-Rose.

"I've talked to everyone I could in any position of authority at Corvin's club. They all maintain that when they picked up the car, there was nothing in it. No knife. They suggest that someone must have taken it out of my bag before the car was retrieved."

"Well, they would, wouldn't they?" Reg gave a shrug. If possession of such a rare and valuable object had fallen into Reg's hands, she certainly wouldn't have been eager to return it to its rightful owner. Not without significant compensation. The police couldn't prove that anyone at the club had it, so they couldn't make threats to get it back.

"I can't prove whether they have it," Jessup echoed Reg's thoughts, "or whether Corvin or someone else took it before the car was picked back up by the club."

"My money is on Corvin. It wasn't me."

"I suspect the warlock too," Jessup admitted. "Even after all the times he's assisted with investigations in the past… I'm not sure he could resist the pull of a powerful object like the knife."

"He'd be risking never being able to do any other work for you. Would he take that chance? When you've provided him with other artifacts as compensation before?"

"Could he delay immediate gratification for something he might get in the future? I don't know. He doesn't have the best record for demonstrating willpower."

There was a knot in Reg's stomach. She tried to breathe through it. Jessup didn't know of Reg's latest conflict with Corvin, but she knew that Corvin had previously stolen Reg's powers. He had returned them to her, something unheard of, in order to save Reg and himself from Hawthorne-Rose, but that didn't mean he didn't want them back again. In fact, he seemed quite determined to possess them once more.

"No," Reg agreed, "willpower is not high on Corvin's list of virtues."

"At the moment I have no way of proving that Corvin has the knife, or that his club does, or whether I'm just chasing my tail here and it's someone else altogether. So I wondered… if you could put me on the right track."

Reg nodded. "Yeah, I'd be happy to help."

She stared for a minute into her cup, at the tea leaves swirling in the bottom. It wouldn't be hard for her to locate the knife. She had located lost objects that she had no connection to in the past. The knife had drawn her blood, so she had a strong physical connection with it. She closed her eyes to focus, which didn't give her a headache like rolling her eyes back in her head. Jessup didn't need a show like less sophisticated clients. No need for over-dramatization.

She reached out with her mind, feeling for the knife. She was surprised not to get an immediate hit. She frowned, squeezing her eyes shut more tightly and drawing her brows down, focusing intently. Jessup sat quietly, waiting, and didn't distract her from the process with questions.

Reg kept her eyes closed and made a noise to call Starlight to her. She shouldn't need a psychic boost to find the knife, yet obviously she did. She heard the patter of Starlight's feet and he jumped up into her lap. The only time the cat actually came when he was called—other than for meals, which she never had to call him for—was when she needed him for a psychic reason.

Reg scratched his ears and pressed her face into the velvety fur on top of his head. Starlight was still, but it was an active, focused stillness, not like when he was sleeping or cuddling. Reg imagined the knife. She tried to conjure up a detailed picture of it in her mind. She had seen it several times. She had been injured with it. It had been joined with her.

But it was like there was a wall around the knife. She couldn't locate it. She tried to see the wall itself or the area around the wall. If it were in a box or protected by some kind of enchantment, then maybe she couldn't see the knife itself but would be able to see its location. Still, nothing came to her. Starlight dug his claws into Reg's leg. She tried to harness all of his energy and hers and to focus it on the task, but she still failed to find the knife.

Reg breathed out in a long sigh and opened her eyes. "I can't see it," she said, shaking her head. "I should be able to, I don't know why I can't."

Jessup nodded, not looking surprised. "I wasn't betting on you being able to, but I figured it was worth a try."

"I don't understand why I can't reach it. It shouldn't be that hard, when I've seen it and… err, had it in my hand… before."

Jessup's eyes flashed amusement. "Yes. Well, in my experience, these paranormal phenomena never quite work out the way you expect them to. And you can never be sure what the other person is up to… what kind of magic or other power they might have on their side."

"But if it's Corvin…" Reg wanted to say that she had a connection with him and she should have been able to use that, but she couldn't figure out how to say it in a way that wouldn't make it sound like they had a relationship.

"If it's Corvin," Jessup picked up the thread, "he's had your powers. He knows better than anyone what you're capable of and what he'd need to do to block you. It wouldn't be hard for him to guess that I'd come to you to help find it."

"I suppose." Reg still didn't think Corvin should be able to block her. They'd been so intimately connected in the past.

Starlight fluffed out his fur and looked at her contemptuously, which told her that he knew exactly who she was talking about. There was no love lost between Corvin and Starlight.

"I'm not going to see him," Reg told the cat. "We're just talking about whether he has the fairy steel."

Starlight made a little burping meow, jumped down, and walked away. Reg shook her head. "I'll never understand cats."

"It actually seems like you understand him pretty well."

"Then maybe I understand him too well."

Jessup laughed and nodded. "I'm not sure any of us wants to know what cats are thinking about us."

"Mostly, I'm just the provider of fish."

"I'm sure there's more to it than that…"

"Not a lot. If you want to know what cats think about… mostly it's about food."

"Well…" Jessup shifted, preparing to stand, "I appreciate you trying, Reg. If something comes to you later… let me know."

"Sure."

There was a hurried knock on the door that made Reg jump, and the door opened. It was, of course, Sarah. She popped into the room and looked around, her eyes wide, looking disheveled. Sarah, a grandmotherly type, always looked neat and tidy and was the master of quick changes, so Reg was surprised to see her in such a state.

"Sarah? Is something wrong?"

"My emerald!" Sarah's breathing was quick and labored. "I can't find it. I don't know where it is. My emerald!"

CHAPTER TWO

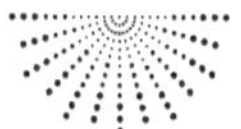

"Come sit down." Reg was already halfway across the room to her, concerned about her condition. "Tell us what happened."

She reached Sarah and took her by the arm to escort her to the seating area. She didn't want Sarah to have a heart attack or faint from exertion.

"You remember my emerald necklace," Sarah said, falling heavily into the chair. "The one that I wore to the dance."

"Yes, of course. It was beautiful." Reg had never seen such a large stone. It had glowed with a life of its own and hung from a thick chain of braided gold.

"But it's gone. I don't know where it could have gone! Someone must have taken it."

"I don't think anyone could have gotten into your house without you knowing about it," Reg soothed. "You haven't been out anywhere. I'm sure it's just misplaced."

"Misplaced? You think I could misplace an item like that? I'm very careful with all of my possessions, but that one most of all. I wouldn't ever *misplace* it."

Reg held up her hands in a motion that was both a shrug and an attempt to stop Sarah's protest.

"I'm sorry. I didn't mean to insult you. I only meant…"

Sarah's eyes riveted on Jessup. "Marta, you have to help me. You can find it for me. Someone has stolen it!"

Jessup looked first at Reg, eyebrows raised, and then at Sarah. "The first thing we'll need to do is to conduct a thorough search of the house, in case it did fall back behind something or get moved somehow." She looked at her watch. "I don't know if I have the time to help out with that right now. I'll have to come back later and take a look around and take your report, if it hasn't shown up."

Sarah glared at her. "We're not talking about a trinket here," she said icily. "This is grand theft. My emerald is priceless."

There was an awkward silence, during which Reg wanted to point out that if Sarah's necklace was worth so much money, she should have been keeping it in a secure safety deposit box or safe, not just in a jewelry box or drawer in her house. She was sure that Jessup was thinking exactly the same thing, but neither of them was willing to incur Sarah's wrath by saying it.

Jessup looked at her watch again. "I really do have to go, but I'll have the department send someone over to take your report and open a file. Then I'll touch base with you again later. Okay?"

Sarah nodded, her lips pressed together in a thin pink line.

Jessup stood. "I'm sorry. I will get someone right onto it. But… the officer they send over to take your statement will likely not be a practitioner, so watch what you say. If you make them think you're a crazy old lady claiming to have lost a magical necklace, they're not going to take you seriously. Focus on the intrinsic value of the emerald itself."

"I'm not stupid."

"I would never suggest that you are. But you're used to dealing with others in the community, and the person they send over will likely not be open to the idea of… paranormal phenomena."

* * *

After Detective Jessup left, Reg did what she could to calm Sarah down, putting the kettle back on to boil and assuring her that the police department was bound to find out who it was that had stolen Sarah's emerald.

"Who are we kidding?" Sarah wailed, her normally neat blond hair askew. "The police department has no chance of finding my necklace! How are they going to figure out who it was that took it? And where it is being kept now? This is a job for a clairvoyant, not the police."

She turned her gaze to Reg, who was too drained from looking for the knife to even consider trying to locate Sarah's emerald. Reg explained the reason for Jessup's visit.

"I can't look for your emerald right now, but I'll do it later, when I have a little strength back. Right now… I just can't."

Sarah's lips pressed together again, and Reg knew she was thinking about how she was always the first one to help others, yet both Jessup and Reg had given excuses and put her off.

"I'm sorry. Really, I am. If I had known about your necklace a little earlier, I would have told Jessup that the knife would have to wait. I know this emerald means a lot to you. I'll help you all I can. I just don't have the energy right now to find anything."

"Of course," Sarah agreed, but she didn't sound at all convinced.

"I'll come over to the house and help you to look physically," Reg offered. "I can't use my powers right now but I could have a look around."

"I've already looked. It isn't in the house. Someone came into the house and stole it."

It sounded just as unlikely as it had the first time Sarah had asserted that an intruder had taken the necklace.

"Did they take anything else? Electronics? Other jewelry? Cash?"

"They took the most valuable thing in the house. Why would they need to take anything else? They knew what they were looking for. They knew exactly what they were doing."

"But you have a lot of other jewels. They weren't interested in anything else?"

Sarah studied Reg suspiciously and Reg couldn't help the flush that rose to her cheeks. She hadn't stolen anything of value from Sarah. If she had, she'd have been able to keep it from her face. She was good at lying, but she didn't have the same ability to cover her embarrassment at being suspected when she had done nothing.

Of course she had taken note of Sarah's vast array of jewelry. Of course she knew how valuable Sarah's trinkets were. Sarah hadn't exactly tried to hide them from her. But Reg hadn't taken them. If she'd taken them, she would have done it in a way that would have diverted suspicion from her, or she would have immediately left town. And no matter how valuable the emerald was, she wouldn't have been satisfied to have left everything else and taken only the one piece of jewelry.

"If it was me, would I still be here?" Reg asked.

"Maybe you thought I wouldn't believe it was you."

Reg shook her head. "If I had something like that in my pocket, I wouldn't be waiting around to see whether you suspected me or not. I'd be putting as many miles between you and me as possible."

Sarah studied her. Reg didn't know whether Sarah would believe her because Reg was being honest with her about it, or whether she wouldn't believe her because Reg was as much as admitting that she might have considered stealing such a valuable object.

"I didn't steal it," Reg said, looking her in the eye. Maybe Sarah just needed to hear it from her, straight out. "I didn't take your emerald or any of your jewelry."

"Can I trust you, though?"

Reg swallowed, looking at her. Would she have been able to resist the emerald any more than Corvin would have been able to resist the knife, if the opportunity arose? Could she have decided, in the face of such a temptation, that her life in Black Sands was more important and valuable to her than the cold, hard cash that such a prize would bring in?

"I wouldn't trust me."

Sarah nodded her agreement. "No."

* * *

A Catastrophic Theft, Book #3 of the Reg Rawlins, Psychic Investigator series by P.D. Workman can be purchased at pdworkman.com

ABOUT THE AUTHOR

Award-winning and USA Today bestselling author P.D. (Pamela) Workman writes riveting mystery/suspense and young adult books dealing with mental illness, addiction, abuse, and other real-life issues. For as long as she can remember, the blank page has held an incredible allure and from a very young age she was trying to write her own books.

Workman wrote her first complete novel at the age of twelve and continued to write as a hobby for many years. She started publishing in 2013. She has won several literary awards from Library Services for Youth in Custody for her young adult fiction. She currently has over 60 published titles and can be found at pdworkman.com.

Born and raised in Alberta, Workman has been married for over 25 years and has one son.

* * *

Please visit P.D. Workman at pdworkman.com to see what else she is working on, to join her mailing list, and to link to her social networks.

* * *

If you enjoyed this book, please take the time to recommend it to other purchasers with a review or star rating and share it with your friends!

facebook.com/pdworkmanauthor

twitter.com/pdworkmanauthor

instagram.com/pdworkmanauthor

amazon.com/author/pdworkman

bookbub.com/authors/p-d-workman

goodreads.com/pdworkman

linkedin.com/in/pdworkman

pinterest.com/pdworkmanauthor

youtube.com/pdworkman